Trouble
at
Red Wall

Trouble
at
Red Wall

Joe Bryceland

iUniverse, Inc.
New York   Bloomington

Trouble at Red Wall

iUniverse books may be ordered through booksellers or by contacting:

iUniverse
1663 Liberty Drive
Bloomington, IN 47403
www.iuniverse.com
1-800-Authors (1-800-288-4677)

*Because of the dynamic nature of the Internet, any Web addresses or links
contained in this book may have changed since publication and may no
longer be valid. This is a work of fiction. All of the characters, names,
incidents, organizations, and dialogue in this novel are either the products
of the author's imagination or are used fictitiously.*

ISBN: 978-1-4502-0088-2 (pbk)
ISBN: 978-1-4502-0089-9 (ebk)
ISBN: 978-1-4502-0090-5 (hbk)

Printed in the United States of America

iUniverse rev. date: 1/12/10

Thank you to my wife Geri and our children Joe, Dawn and Jon for their support and to my special niece Kristen who taught me to "show the story" and for all her help getting me started.

A LESSON WELL EARNED IS A LESSON WELL LEARNED.

1 Heading Home

THE COLD, piercing rain flew out of the darkening skies, biting the rider's hands. His body was covered with soaking wet clothes; his head was barely protected by a weathered Stetson hat. The strong, calloused hands worked hard to keep his big black horse from turning its back to the, late spring, storm. Matt Benton knew that the town of Red Wall was ahead of them, but he also knew that the big stallion he was riding wanted nothing more than to put the storm to his hindquarters and protect his eyes from being stung by the whipping rain pellets he had been enduring for the last few hours.

Matt had made a poor decision earlier in the day when he'd left Walt Bauer's ranch, hoping to make the thirty-mile ride to Red Wall before the storm hit. Now he was in the grip of a fierce plains storm. The rain was falling as a sodden sheet of grey as far as his eyes could see. The booming thunder surrounded them, while the crackling lightning momentarily lit the dark prairie in front of them with each strike. Every thunderclap shook the ground they rode on, and, every time the lightning struck, the hair on the back of Matt's head stood up. He wondered if anyone had ever drowned on the open prairie.

Matt had met Walt Bauer the day before while he was in Fort Wilson to sell his herd of wild mustangs. Roundup had been very successful this year, and he had driven almost two hundred head of "nasty-minded broncs," as his *segundo*, Orville Piker, liked to call them, from his ranch on the Colorado Flats to the army post at Darby.

At the post, the commanding officer, Captain Alpern, had introduced Matt to Bauer, a local rancher interested in buying some horses for his *remuda*—the herd he kept and used for all his ranch work. Matt planned on riding to the nearest train depot at Red Wall the next morning, so he agreed to meet with the rancher that afternoon after paying off his men.

Matt left Bauer on the captain's porch and set off for the harness shop where his foreman, Orville, was getting his saddle straps repaired. The shop was set at the end of a dusty commercial street called Merchants' Row. A small bell tinkled when Matt opened the door. The interior smelled of old wood, oiled leather, and dust. Near the back of the store, Matt saw Orville sitting on a barrel. He was tying a hitch in a leather cord while watching a man in a tattered apron working on his straps. Orville looked up at the sound of the door opening and watched his boss approach him. "Well, it looks like we part company here, Matt," Orville spoke out in his soft voice.

Orville was a tall, lanky sort with streaks of grey in his mostly black hair. His face was the color of the brown leather straps he was having repaired. Deep lines ran down his cheeks, like gullies.

Wintry blue eyes looked out from under full brows. He spoke quietly most times, but, as Matt's second in command on the Cross River Ranch, he was heard by everyone when it counted. "I'm not ready to ride them steam trains again just yet," he told his boss, "and it will only take a few days of hard riding to get back to the ranch without those two hundred ponies to push. I'll meet you back at the ranch when we get there," Orville said.

Matt had already thanked his crew for their good work when he'd bought them drinks at the Post Tavern, the local watering hole. He'd told them he would leave their pay, along with their bonuses, with Orville—and that he hoped to see them all for the next roundup. Matt reached into his shirt and took out a thick envelope. He'd been paid in cash, and his crew's money, along with Orville's, was in the envelope.

"Try to keep them civilized tonight; we've got a contract for another two hundred head next spring—and maybe more. I don't want anyone here getting sore at us," Matt said with a smile, as he gave his top hand the payroll for the crew. "That's the deal then; I'll be waiting for you and the boys when you get back. Good Luck," Matt said.

Orville stuck the envelope in his shirt and grinned a question. "Any idea how I keep these yahoos civilized after two weeks on the trail?"

Matt shook his head back and forth, still smiling. The two men shook hands, and Matt went looking for the rancher he had met earlier.

He saw Bauer standing in front of the fort trading post.

"Mr. Bauer, are you ready to talk horses?" he asked, as he walked up to the stout, grey-headed man who owned the nearby Double Bar Ranch.

Bauer pushed away from the wall he was leaning against. He squinted into the late afternoon sun and put his hand on Matt's shoulder. "Sure are, young feller. Why don't you spend the night at my ranch? We'll talk there. I'm sure you wouldn't mind a home-cooked meal, and you can get an early start in the morning. You have to go right by my spread to get to Red Wall anyway."

"Well, that's very neighborly of you, sir; I sure would appreciate a good meal after eating trail grub for two weeks," Matt answered. A home-cooked meal was a blessing to any cowboy, and Matt sure wasn't going to pass one up.

The two men rode into the large, well-kept ranch yard an hour later. A lane lined with whitewashed rocks led the way to the large, blue-painted house. Mrs. Bauer watched through her kitchen window as her husband rode in with the young stranger. She was a sturdy-looking woman with a pretty face that looked younger than her years, and she was always happy to have company. Mrs. Bauer walked outside to greet her husband and their company. Walt introduced Matt to his wife as they dismounted. Mrs. Bauer took an instant liking to Matt, and told him and her husband dinner would be ready as soon as they washed up. A ranch hand walked up from the barn and took their mounts. Walt hugged his wife and then led Matt to a small shed behind his house. As he began working the well-worn handle on a water pump, cold water splashed into a cut-down wooden barrel sitting on a three-legged stool. A bar of soap sat on a shelf under a cracked mirror, and a towel hung on a wall peg. After washing, Matt and Walt Bauer walked through the back door into the Bauer's large kitchen and sat down at the table. A cast iron cook stove with a large pot sitting on it caught Matt's eye. The steam wafting from the pot sent a delicious aroma throughout the room. The table was already set for three. Mrs. Bauer served the two men and herself and sat down. As soon as she offered a short grace, they tucked into her hearty stew and fluffy biscuits.

The conversation was friendly, and Matt quickly felt comfortable with the Bauers. A half hour later and finally full, Matt pushed away from the table. "Food like this sure makes a man yearn to settle down with a good woman, ma'am," the visiting wrangler said to his hostess after he had finished the last of his apple pie.

"Then, what are you waiting for?" Nancy Bauer couldn't help kidding the handsome young man sitting in her kitchen. Matt favored his half-Cherokee, half-Scottish mother—with dark brown eyes, high cheekbones, and black hair, which he wore full to his shirt collar. His sturdy frame stood about six feet tall with only bones and muscles making up his one hundred and eighty pounds. He had a quick, natural smile that answered her question for him. She smiled back at him.

After dinner, Nancy Bauer retired, and the two men talked well into the night exchanging stories of the battles they'd fought and the rivers they'd crossed. Despite his young age, Matt fairly held his own, matching Walt Bauer story for story. They also made a deal that Matt would deliver as many as fifty mustangs to the Double Bar the following spring when he made his next delivery to the army post. Long after sunset, Matt set his dry whiskey glass down on the kitchen table and stood up. He said goodnight to Walt and went to sleep in a spare bunk in the bunkhouse.

Tired as he was, sleep came easily, and the grey, stormy morning came quickly. After a hearty breakfast of ham, eggs, griddlecakes, and coffee, Walt asked Matt to stay a while and let the coming storm pass over. "That sky don't look too friendly, son," Walt told the young mustanger, as he looked up at the roiling grey clouds in the distant sky. "Why don't you stay here 'til that storm passes?"

"No thank you, sir. That storm looks pretty far off, and, if it's only thirty miles to Red Wall from here, I should be able to beat it and make the night train. Thanks for everything."

As he rode out of the ranch yard at a fast gallop, Matt waved and called back to the Bauers,

"I'll see you next spring with your horses."

The Bauers returned Matt's wave as they watched him leave.

2 Shelter

Matt figured he had traveled a little less than halfway to the train station at Red Wall when he realized he should have listened to Walt's warning about the storm. Travel was slow and difficult, and the night would soon be on them. He was caught "between the devil and the deep" as Orville would say. The trail he was riding offered no place for him to get out of the storm that had arrived much sooner than he'd thought it would. The mountains he saw over his left shoulder might contain a cave or two, but they were very far away. They weren't much more than barely visible grey outlines way off in the distance. He could only press on and try to find shelter ahead.

Matt lifted his head and looked as far as he could in all directions as the wind-whipped rain slapped his face like a cold hand. He knew the stallion was having a hard time staying afoot and not giving in to the soft, muddy earth that wanted horse and rider to fall into it. The black had always been an independent animal, just barely broke to the saddle, and he was in a very mean mood now. For the last few miles, whenever Matt had relaxed and let the big horse turn his head, the horse had nipped at his rider's legs. Matt knew he had better find some shelter soon or his horse would throw him and turn his back to the storm, leaving Matt to walk to the train station at Red Wall. They had been traveling on flat terrain since leaving the Double Bar, but up ahead a few small hills appeared on his right, and Matt steered the complaining horse toward them. He hoped he might find some trees or boulders that they could use as shelter from the wind and rain.

Matt rode to the top of the closest hill. He saw the small barn first, and then the cabin on the far side. "Yippee!" Matt couldn't help yelling, as he urged the black forward. But, on the other side of the hill, the wind was quieter and Matt heard a yowling that wasn't his own. In the field that fronted the house, someone was struggling with a cow. Screams of anguish were coming from the cow, and more yowls were coming from the cowhand who was trying to get the cow to do what it didn't want to do. Matt shifted his weight forward and kneed his horse in the direction of the commotion. He stopped a short distance away, not wanting his horse to spook the angry cow any further. Matt shouted into the chaos and asked what the problem was.

"She's due to birth any minute, but she won't go into the barn," a hoarse, tired voice cried out.

Kneeing the stallion again, this time toward the barn, the wet drover raced to the reddish-brown building. He dismounted near the big door and pulled it open as a welcoming target for the cow. "Now—get her moving," he shouted through the rain, which was falling harder now.

"She won't budge," came back a desperate reply.

Matt ran across the muddy farmyard to the stubborn cow and the small cowhand who was trying to move her.

"Here, let me have that rope," Matt shouted over the howling wind. "She needs to know the door is open and smell the hay," he said, as he pulled with all his might.

The large black-and-white cow took a few timid steps at Matt's urging and then suddenly had a change of heart and ran into the barn at a slow, awkward trot. The cowhand walked over to Matt and shouted over the wind, "Thanks, mister, I should have known. I always open the door when I want to milk her, and she comes right on in," the breathless voice said. "Mighty wet out here; come on in and put your horse up in a stall, if you like."

Matt led his horse into the barn and put him in a back stall near two large draft mules. Each mule stared at the intruders and greeted them with unfriendly-sounding snorts. The big black seemed unconcerned; he began chewing at bits of hay he found at his feet. Matt walked back to the barn entrance and closed the door, just as a white goose waddled in.

As soon as the cow lay down in her familiar spot, the birth process began. The cow's owner stayed with her as the new calf quickly arrived and was cleaned by her mama. Matt watched the scene as he loosened the cinch on his saddle and took care of his horse.

Several minutes later, the calf stood on wobbly legs near its mother. "You should name it Storm," Matt said, as he shook the rain off his hat and approached the cowhand. "I'm Matt Benton out of the Cross River Ranch in Colorado, and I sure would appreciate it if me and my animal could wait out this storm here in your barn. We won't be no trouble, and I'll pay for some grain for my horse if you can spare any."

"That won't be necessary; we've plenty of grain," the cowhand said. "You're welcome to stay—and thank you for your help." The cowhand stepped back away from the cow, stood up, and looked into Matt's face. Matt was astonished to be looking into the face of a pretty young woman. She reached a strong hand out for Matt to shake. She was still wearing a rain hat that reminded Matt of the ones he'd seen sailors wearing in an adventure book he'd read about the open seas. When she took it off, soft brown hair fell to her shoulders. Her smoky grey eyes looked troubled as she spoke. "My husband's in bed feeling poorly, but he'd want to thank you too. I'll bring you some hot coffee and food in a little while. Meanwhile, there are some old lengths of cloth in the chest by the rear door. You can use them to dry your horse and yourself."

She patted the tired cow and left the barn, followed by the honking goose that had followed them in.

The day was near done, and the light in the barn was a grey shadow. Matt unsaddled his stallion and then found the cloths in a finely carved wooden chest in the rear corner near the small back door. He started rubbing down his now-calm horse.

"It feels awful good to be out of that storm don't it, pardner?" Matt said, trying to get back on the good side of the horse he favored to ride over all the horses he kept in his remuda.

The big black stallion wasn't his fastest horse, though fast enough, but he was the strongest and most sure-footed of all his horses, and Matt felt good riding him. He was sure the horse had some Arabian or Tennessee Walking Horse in him. He could travel from sunup to sundown and be ready to ride the next morning.

Matt checked the horse's hooves for stones, which were easily picked up in mud and soft dirt. The young wrangler found a small stone stuck in the shoe on the black's right forefoot. "Maybe this is what's had you all mean today," he said as he picked the stone out with his pocketknife. He walked the horse around the barn and was pleased to see the horse didn't favor the leg.

"There, you're good as new," Matt said, grateful that the horse didn't seem to be hurting. Matt looked around and found a pitchfork hanging on the front wall near some other barn tools. "Someone sure keeps a neat barn," he said aloud to the stallion he called Raven because of his coloring. Raven's coat was the color of a midnight sky, and the sheen from the rain made it even shinier now.

"Thank you," the woman's voice answered.

She stepped back into the barn while Matt was looking for the pitchfork.

"I'm going to give my horse some of this hay if it's all right with you," Matt said, as he stuck the tines into the stack of hay in front of him.

"A horse needs a good meal after the kind of traveling you two have done, please give him as much as he'll eat. I brought you some dinner and coffee," she said, putting a cloth-covered tray down on the milking stool near the first stall.

"It's a small place but it's all we can do to keep it going," the woman sighed, looking around the barn.

"My husband Jacob said you're welcome to stay the night, if you like."

Matt nodded his head, with a small grin of relief on his face. "That sure would be kind of you Mrs...." he answered.

"Langer, Emily Langer." Mrs. Langer smiled at him. "I hope you enjoy the meal, I'll stop back in a while."

The young farmer's wife walked over to the newborn calf and stroked its still shiny head. The soft glow from the lantern cast a golden hue in the barn.

"You have a beautiful baby. Doesn't she Anna?"

Emily spoke to the sleeping mother cow as the newborn took her first feeding in the damp barn. The goose Matt had seen earlier was honking its reply as they left the barn.

Matt could still hear the woman talking to the goose as they hurried away from the barn.

It must be lonely this far from town, even with a husband, he thought.

It didn't take Matt long to finish the food the woman left. It was hot and very tasty.

This Jacob Langer was a lucky man to have such a fit looking wife who could cook so well and do the chores needed doing on a farm, like taking care of that cow, Matt thought.

"Some men are luckier than others," he said to himself, as he checked on his horse before finding a spot to bed down for the night.

As Matt listened to the wind and rain crash into the well-kept barn he realized there were a few leaky spots in the roof.

Strange, a barn this well built would have a leaky roof, he thought.

"Still, it is a right fine building," he said aloud, again talking to Raven.

"Thank you again," said Mrs. Langer, appearing around the corner of the stall.

"My father built this barn and the house six years ago. He was a carpenter back east before we moved out here."

Emily Langer returned holding some clothes over her arm, with the goose at her side.

"I found some things my husband's grown out of," she said. "You'll catch your death in those wet ones you have on. You're welcome to try these on and keep them, if they fit."

"Well thanks ma'am, if you're sure he won't need them. I sure would like to pay for them though. I'm not a drifter, ma'am, I have my own ranch over by Colorado Flats and I was heading to Red Wall to meet the night train. I'm anxious to get home and I thought I could save a few days of travel by taking the train part-way."

The young woman busied herself collecting the dinner ware and coffee pot. She put them on the tray and started out of the barn.

"Might I help you carry something to the house ma'am? It don't seem right you doing all this work on my account," Matt asked.

"I can handle it, thank you; I'm most appreciative of your help earlier with Molly. I never would have gotten her in the barn and her and her calf would be laying out in the storm right now if it weren't for your help. Sleep well."

Emily closed the door with her foot, her arms laden down with the food tray. Matt thought he heard giggling and honking as the woman ran through the rain to her house. Matt checked on Raven again and then set up his bedding. Later he changed into the dry clothes Mrs. Langer had given him and lay down to sleep.

3 Gunfire

Morning woke Matt's sleepy mind with the sound of thunder.

Strange, he thought, as he lay on the bed of hay he had formed the night before,

I was sure that storm would be gone by now. It should be long gone.

As the sleep cleared from his mind, Matt realized the thunderclaps he heard were rifle shots. He could hear the bullets pluck into the roof of the barn. He crawled over to the small window by the first stall, where the cow and her newborn lay. Matt peered out to see the flash of rifle fire from a stand of trees, a short distance from the front of the house. It was difficult to see much more than the flash of each shot as the night had not fully given in to daybreak. *Well that explains the leaky roof,* Matt thought. *But those fellas sure can't shoot too good.*

Matt strapped on his gun-belt and drew his rifle from its saddle scabbard. He moved quickly to the back of the barn. The cowboy slowly opened the back door and looked out into the dull shadows of the new day and searched them for more attackers. Satisfied that the gunmen shooting at the front of the barn were the only bushwhackers, Matt started for the back of the house. His first concern was that his hostess was safe. A small alley not much wider than a pair of mules separated the house and barn. Blackness was the only inhabitant of the space. Matt bent low and crept past the opening.

Behind the house, he tapped on the back window and called for Mrs. Langer. He could see her sitting on the floor by the front wall. She felt safe there. The thick logs the cabin was made of would prevent any bullets from coming through. And she knew they always shot at the roof, anyway. Hearing Matt's call she ran to the back window and opened it slightly.

"Please, Mr. Benton, stay hidden 'til they leave. They'll be gone soon and you will be able to leave safely then," she said.

Matt was worried about the woman who had offered him shelter the night before, but looking at her now she didn't seem to be afraid.

Matt held up his rifle. "Ma'am, let me chase them away."

Emily spoke firmly. "No, Mr. Benton, I don't want you shooting back at them. Please, I'll explain later."

Emily Langer begged him with her eyes and then she closed the window and crawled back to the front wall. She turned back, her eyes troubled; she didn't see her guest by the window. She hoped he would do as she asked and stay out of sight.

Not satisfied to do nothing, Matt left the window and ran bent over past the house and headed for the stream he saw as he was riding down the hill the day before. The stream came out of the woods and ran past the side of the house away from the barn, about twenty yards away. Matt continued bent over along a stone wall that guarded the path down to the water. The water was rushing with full fury up onto the tall banks of the wide stream, about thirty feet wide at this point but there was room for him to move unseen along the side of the near bank up to the woods where the gunfire was coming from. He treaded carefully on the slippery rocks, some green with moss.

Matt reached a spot past the place the gunmen were firing from, he left the stream and ran into the woods behind the attackers. He moved cautiously and found their horses picketed on some tree branches. The four horses moved nervously each time a shot cracked into the air, their hooves stomping the muddy earth into a sloppy puddle. The nervous horses gave Matt an idea. He crouched low and made his way to the horses and spoke to them as he did to his wild broncos when he was trying to put a saddle on them for the first time. When he was satisfied of their cooperation Matt untied the reins of each horse and led them down the trail. The trail, not much more than a deer path, moved away from the gunmen and across the stream Matt had walked in earlier. On the other side of the stream the trail ran down a long, grassy hillside and then onto the open prairie that made up most of the area. Matt took his hat off and slapped their rumps, sending the four horses racing down the hill and away from the gunfire. *They won't stop till they're back in their own corral,* Matt thought, as he watched the horses race into the distance.

Matt crossed the stream again and made his way back to the spot behind the men firing on the farmhouse. He lay down behind a thick bush as one by one the rifles stopped firing until a welcomed silence was in the air. Matt stayed down behind the wild growing chokeberry bush where he would be unseen from the trail. He wanted to learn what he could about the shooters.

"Hey, Patch, where the hell are them horses?" the first man to appear shouted. He was a large, rough-looking man with a gruff voice.

"Right up on the trail, Lucky," a voice from the ambush spot yelled back.

"Well, you better get up here and find them," Lucky called back.

The second man came into sight and whined, "I tied them to this tree, boss." An average-sized man with long sideburns on a thin, freckled face patted the tree Matt had released their horses from.

"You sure didn't tie them tight enough then," said one of the last two gunmen as they reached the trail next to their partners. "You're lucky I don't send you back to the ranch alone to get us some new mounts," barked the man named Lucky. "But I ain't sure you could find your rear end much less the Box T. Let's get going. We got a long walk ahead of us."

One of the other men, an older, seedy looking poke, asked, "Why don't we go down there and git us some rides?"

"No!" The big man said the word like a gunshot. "We do this my way... 'til it don't work."

When Matt was sure the gunmen were well on their way, he went down to the ambush site. Although a lot of bullets had just been fired, the number of shell casings he found in the area convinced Matt that this hadn't been the first attack from this spot. Matt retraced his steps, carefully walking on the slippery, green, moss-covered rocks that formed the bed of the stream, and returned to the barn.

4 Emily's Enemies

"Easy, boy," he said to Raven as he looked him over for any wounds. "You seem to be fine."

"He hasn't been hurt, mister, I checked on him too. They never hurt anybody; they just shoot into the roofs to scare me," Emily Langer spoke as she knelt beside the newborn calf, stroking its back. The calf was standing next to its mother on legs much stronger than they had been the night before.

"What's this all about, Mrs. Langer?" Matt asked, as he walked over to the woman.

She stood up and smoothed her dress. It was a simple, grayish blue cotton dress, similar to ones Matt had seen on many women, but it looked different on her, he thought.

"I'm sorry you were woken up like this, but there really was no danger. They usually don't come two days in a row, and, since they were here yesterday, I thought you would be safe enough until you left this morning." Emily looked around as if trying to find a way to end the conversation. Finally she looked at Matt, who was studying her with a furrowed brow. "There's coffee ready in the house, and I'll make you some breakfast while you get ready to leave," she said.

Matt took his hat off and walked over to the newborn calf and patted its hindquarter. He looked at the strong young woman with the worried eyes. "But why don't you fight back?" the bewildered cowboy asked her.

Emily shook her head and sighed. "As long as I don't shoot back, they'll just try to annoy me by making holes in my roof. Pretty soon they'll learn I don't scare so easy and leave me alone."

"Pardon me, ma'am, for saying, but I seen a lot of shooting, and eventually one of those bullets is going to find a living target,… meant to or not," Matt said.

Emily looked at Matt and pursed her lips together. A dimple on her cheek deepened, and she nodded her head slightly. "Well, thanks for your concern, mister, but we'll be all right. Come in the house for breakfast when you're ready." Emily spoke as if to end the conversation.

"Come on, Anna," she called to the goose, standing in back of the cow, out of sight. The honking bird waddled behind the woman as she left the barn. Once again it seemed to Matt that the two were having a conversation as they walked to the cabin.

"This whole situation don't sit right with me, boy," Matt said to Raven as he started saddling him. "Her husband must be mighty sick. She didn't mention him one time just now. There's more to this than I can see right now, but I can't just ride off and leave a woman being attacked, with no one to help her. Besides, I want to send all bushwhackers back to the devil where they come from." Matt's face turned into an angry snarl whenever he thought of ambushers. His father had been shot from ambush while he was driving the stage from Triple Forks to Matson, in the Colorado Territories. The story would remain with Matt forever.

♣

A posse had been sent to check on the overdue stage. When they found Billy Ackman, the shotgun rider, he was mortally wounded, but still alive. "We never had a chance," he said, his face contorted in pain. "We was just rounding Six Boulders when they opened fire on us—two rifles, kept firing 'til we both hit the ground. Tom Benton's behind those trees. I'm pretty sure he's dead."

Billy had lain still on the ground with four bullets in him as he listened to the highwaymen talking: "They're both dead Silky," the one leaning over the shotgun rider said. "Let's get the money from the boot and get gone before someone comes along."

Later, the dying man pleaded with the posse to find the two robbers and send them to hell. He then closed his eyes for the last time. Although Matt was only fifteen, he started looking for his father's killers right after the burial of the two stagecoach employees. His mother had died four years earlier after a long illness, and the youngster had no other family. Matt sold what belongings his father and he had, keeping only his father's Colt .44 pistol and Winchester rifle. The stage company sold him one of their riding horses at a cheap price and gave him his father's pay. He outfitted his horse and set out to find the bushwhackers.

Four years later, while he was working on a cattle drive in Montana, two men rode into camp near evening looking for work or a free meal. They said their names were Luke and Wayne. "But," said the man named Luke, "I call him Silky 'cause he's so smooth with the ladies."

Matt and several other drovers were sitting by the fire eating their dinner. When Matt heard what the man said, he stood up and walked to his bedroll. He took a hard look back at the two men and strapped his father's Colt .44 onto his hip. He walked slowly back to the two riders and stood before the one called Silky, a tall, reed-thin man with no chin and rotted teeth. Matt said, "I never knew anyone with that name before."

"No, sir," said the other one named Luke, "He's the only one in the world with that name, and I give it to him. Ha, ha, don't it fit him though?"

Matt drew his gun and put it to the head of the man named Luke. "I'll ask you one time for an honest answer, mister. If you tell the truth, I'll holster my pistol and let you draw your gun against me. If you lie to me, I'll shoot your head off and ask your friend the question." Matt cocked the hammer back on his pistol. The click echoed throughout the silent camp.

"Did you two rob the stage from Triple Forks four years ago?"

The crew of the cattle drive were all looking on, many with their mouths open. Only the low moaning of the cattle could be heard. Will Stomer took the makings for a cigarette out of his vest pocket and moved to stand beside Matt. Stomer, the boss of the drive, a barrel-chested man an inch or two shorter than Matt, spoke up. "Are you sure of yourself, son?" He continued to roll his smoke. Stomer was a good leader, and all his men respected his ways. He looked at Matt with eyes that always demanded an honest answer. He lit his cigarette, and the smoke drifted past those eyes.

"Yes, sir, I am," said Tom Benton's son.

Matt pressed his gun against the man's head. "Start talking. You don't have much time left on this earth."

The killer in front of him waved his hands frantically and pleaded. "Wait! Wait! Mister, yeah, we did rob that stage. If you lost something on it, we'll pay you back—right, Silky?" He looked over at his partner who stared back sullenly at him.

Matt stepped back and holstered his father's Colt. "Mr. Stomer, count to three," he said.

The longhaired, unshaven man named Luke moved his hand toward his holster, and Matt drew his gun and shot the killer through the heart. The man was dead before he closed his eyes.

The camp cook, called Viejo, held a shotgun firmly against the back of the other bushwhacker. Matt put his gun away and looked at the cook.

"He's mine, Viejo. You can put that scatter-gun up now."

Walking closer Matt looked through hooded eyes at the other killer. "Draw your gun or die with it in your holster, you coward." Matt sneered at the man. Later, one of the men who had been watching said he saw Hell through Matt's eyes. The man called Silky drew his gun. Although he was much faster than his friend, he was no match for the son of the man he had killed four years earlier. Matt had practiced every day with his father's gun, waiting for this one duel. He shot this one in the belly—two shots in the center of his shirt.

"It took poor Billy hours to die. You're going to suffer too," he said to the dying murderer, knowing a gut wound was a long, painful way to die.

The trail boss had some of his drovers carry the two bodies away from camp, "We'll bury them later," he told his crew.

As the outlaws were being carried off, Stomer spoke up. "This was a fair fight, and Matt killed two murders, as I seen it, and that's the way the story leaves this camp." No one disagreed. Stomer turned to Matt. "Matt, take Santos and check on the herd. The shooting might have them a little jumpy."

"Yes, sir, boss," Matt said as he nodded toward the young Mexican cowboy who had joined the crew at roundup. "C'mon, amigo, let's go sing to them steers."

Matt knew his boss just wanted to give him some time to sort the recent events out in his head. He appreciated everything Will Stomer had done for him since he was hired for his first cattle drive two years earlier. Matt had spent the first two years after his father's death searching daily for the killers. He would take work only long enough to get a stake, and then he would ride off looking for the man named Silky and his partner. After hiring on with Stomer's crew, he confided in the cattleman about his search for his father's killers.

"They'll likely be looking to their back-trail every day, son, best let them find you," the older man had advised the young avenger.

It took four years in all, but the boss sure was right, Matt thought as he rode out to the grazing cattle. He looked over the lounging herd and felt the weight of the long search lift from his shoulders. A soothing relief settled in his mind. The knot in Matt's stomach eased, but, for some reason, there was no joy.

The pistol shots hadn't bothered the cattle. Tired from a day's hard walking, they milled about lazily cropping the grass at their feet. Matt and Santos finished their watch singing quietly to the cattle.

The next morning, as the crew moved about finishing breakfast and saddling their mounts, Matt stopped by the fire and filled two cups with coffee. He brought them over to Stomer who was stomping into his boots. Matt handed a cup to the drive leader and sat on the tailgate of the chuck wagon next to him. Matt told his friend and boss Will Stomer that he would be leaving the crew at the end of the drive.

"I've saved most of my pay, Mr. Stomer, and as you know I've been wanting to get my own spread. I'm going to sell mustangs to the army; they're always looking for fresh horses."

Stomer sipped the hot coffee and looked soberly at Matt. "Be sorry to see you go, Matt. You're one of the best men ever rode for me, but I wish you the best of luck. If you ever need help, just send word," said the trail boss using Matt's shoulder to push off the wagon.

Four days later, after the herd had been signed over to the new owner, Matt collected his pay and thanked Stomer again and said good-bye. "Mr. Stomer, I can't thank you enough for all you taught me. It was a real pleasure working for you. As soon as I get my ranch, I'll write you."

The young rider and his boss shook hands and wished each other good luck.

Matt walked his horse down the main street of the noisy cattle town at trail's end, heading for the railway station to buy a ticket on the next train heading south. He had never ridden a train before, but he knew it could cover ground much faster than his tired horse. He was anxious to get back to Colorado and find a suitable piece of land for his horse ranch. When the train pulled into the station, he loaded his horse in the next-to-last car, which was reserved for the animals of the passengers. The floor was covered with fresh hay and seemed clean. Satisfied his horse would be safe and comfortable, Matt found a seat in the passenger compartment. Sitting with his back against the forward wall, as he had been advised by Will Stomer, Matt tried to relax. "And keep the windows closed so the soot and sparks don't get you," Stomer had also suggested.

The train filled up with business folks and other assorted men and women. A lean, leather-skinned cowboy, several years senior to Matt, sat down next to him and said, "Howdy, name's Orville Piker. I'm heading south to get away from the cold winter a'comin."

"Name's Matt Benton. Howdy," said Matt as he shook the rawhide-tough hand extended to him by Orville.

The conductor made some hollering noises, and the train lurched forward. Not long after the train started moving, two drunken cowboys Matt had noticed in town earlier started a ruckus with a young couple across the aisle from Matt.

"I just want to know the young lady's name," insisted the taller of the two drunks.

"It's none of your business," said the smallish, town-dressed man sitting next to the lady.

"It is now," the bothersome cowboy said as he pulled out a pistol.

"He's not armed," pleaded the young woman. "Please leave us alone."

"Annie, I'll handle this," said the man sitting next to her. As he started to get up, the drunk cracked the barrel of his six-gun on the man's head.

"Hold it!" Matt yelled and leapt to his feet.

The cowboy with the gun in his hand turned toward Matt.

"Stand still mister—" He started to say more, but Matt grabbed his gun hand and bent it up toward the ceiling of the car.

The two men wrestled for the gun, and Matt won, taking the weapon away from the drunk.

"Don't do it, partner." Matt heard a menacing voice say behind him. When he turned around, Matt saw the other drunken cowboy with his hand raised over his head and his gun butt ready to crack Matt's skull.

But Orville Piker had his Navy Colt pointed at the man's back. "Now you two boys walk to the door and jump off this train or I'll throw you off," Orville said.

After a few words of back talk, Matt and Orville Piker escorted the two drunks to the back of the car and watched as they jumped into some weeds along the track. Luckily for the two troublemakers, the train was just reaching the top of a long up-hill grade and was moving slowly. A heavy plume of thick, black smoke accompanied the two into the distance.

"Thank you, gentlemen," the lady's companion said, rubbing the back of his head. "I'm a preacher, and I don't carry any weapons on me. Will those men be all right?"

"Sure, the train was going slow. They'll just have a long walk back to town," Orville assured him.

"Thank you, sirs. My husband might have been hurt more if you hadn't helped," the young woman said. She was a thin girl with ivory-white skin; thin veins showed through it.

"No trouble, ma'am, they were annoying me too," spoke the cowboy who had saved Matt from a terrible headache.

"My first train ride will be memorable, that's for sure," Matt said, as he shook Orville Piker's hand. "Thanks for watching my back, mister."

"You'da done the same for me, fella." Orville grinned and sat down.

The two cowboys talked together for the rest of the trip, and, before they reached their destination, Orville agreed to ride for Matt, catching wild mustangs.

That had been three years ago, Matt realized, as his thinking came back to the present and the fight he would soon be in. *I have to help these people. Only a coward would ride off and leave this woman to stand up to these vermin alone,* he thought.

"She's just plain wrong to think these bullies will stop harassing her unless she fights back," he said to the big black horse, as he led him out of the barn.

The sun was burning away the early morning mist, and the air was warming, giving a hint of the coming summer season. Matt saw the young woman hitching up the mules he had shared the barn with the night just past.

"Hello, Mr. Benton, I'll be with you in a few minutes, as soon as I get Samule and Youmule hitched up," she said.

Watching her work, Matt was reminded why he didn't like mules or cattle. *Too ornery*, he thought. After struggling with the animals for a few more minutes, Emily completed the job and walked over to Matt. "Please come in the house and have some breakfast before you leave," she said.

"Thank you, ma'am." Matt tied his horse to the hitching rail in front of the cabin.

5 Emily's Husband

Matt opened the heavy, thick door for his hostess and was once again reminded of the solidness of the buildings on this farm. He sat down at the table and looked around the small, well-cared-for room. "This is a mighty nice little house, ma'am. You and your man must work awfully hard to keep this spread running so well."

"Thank you, Mr. Benton," Emily said.

While Emily Langer busied herself with the food, Matt couldn't help looking at the door across from him. *That must be the bedroom*, he thought. *Why doesn't her husband come out and check on this stranger in their house?* Matt couldn't help thinking how strange it was that Emily's husband hadn't even stirred when the shooting was going on. *He must be sicker than she wants to let on*, figured the curious cowboy. *All the more reason to stay and help.*

After putting the food and coffee on the table, the hard-working farm woman excused herself to go start her chores. "Help yourself and take your time. I have some work to do in the field. Please stop by before you leave," she said as she closed the door. Matt heard her calling, "Anna Goose, where are you?"

Once again, the hungry horse wrangler quickly ate the food prepared by Mrs. Langer. He picked up his steaming cup of coffee and walked over to the door he had been looking at since he'd come into the cabin. A small table with a Bible and a lamp on it stood next to the door. *I know this ain't right, but I have to find out if he's in any condition to help his wife,* Matt thought as he slowly opened the door. He looked around the room. A bed covered neatly with a knitted blanket, a chair, and a dresser with a mirror and a lamp were all that occupied the room.

"Hello?" Matt said to the empty room. *I'll be darned! She doesn't have a husband. She just wanted to make sure I behaved myself. That woman is too brave for her own good, living out here by herself. Now I'm sure I have to help her. No man would respect me if I didn't, especially myself.*

"What are you doing?" An enraged Emily Langer opened the cabin door and saw Matt looking into her bedroom.

Matt turned to look at his hostess, a guilty look on his face. "I'm… I'm sorry, ma'am, I just wanted to thank your husband," Matt lied.

"You had no right to go into that room," Emily complained, her voice still angry. Even her eyes were angry.

"You're right, ma'am. I didn't. And I lied to you just now—I'm worried about you and wanted to know if you really did have someone to help you. I mean you no harm, ma'am, but I've dealt with bullies before, and they won't quit 'til they get what they want. Why don't you tell me what it's all about? Maybe I can help you."

Emily's face was red—more from embarrassment at hollering at the man who was trying to help her than from anger. She smoothed her dress with work-worn hands and spoke softly. "It's not your concern, Mr. Benton. Thank you, but I can take care of myself." Her face was set in a stern reprimand, but her eyes didn't agree.

"Where is the Box T?" Matt asked.

"How do you know about the Box T, Mr. Benton?" Emily shot back, a surprised look on her face.

Caught again, Matt decided he wouldn't lie to this lady another time, so he told her about his excursion up the stream and how he'd let the horses of the bushwhackers go. "I heard one of the men—called Lucky—mention it," he told her. "Do you know him?"

Emily took her hands off her hips and looked at Matt. "Yes. He's the new gunman on the Box T. The owner, Mr. Tanner, hired him to run me off my land. I wish you would leave now, Mr. Benton. I will handle this my way."

"Can't the law help you, ma'am?" Matt asked.

"There is no law here. Sheriff Brock's jurisdiction ends at the town line, and no marshal patrols in this area. I don't want any gun fighting over this land, and I don't want you to get hurt, so please leave, Mister Benton," she pleaded.

"Miss Langer, please believe me—men like these won't stop even at hurting a woman. If you won't fight back, at least go into town 'til a lawman can get here and settle this legally."

Emily walked to the window, pushed back a pale blue curtain, and looked out. "If I leave my property, they'll come in and take it over, and say I abandoned it."

Matt put his now-cold coffee on the table. "Why is your land so important to them, Miss Langer?" he asked.

Emily turned to him. "Because they want to control the water in the stream. It comes out of the ground on my property and splits into two sections. The largest stream stays on my land and runs on down to feed the Muller's farm below mine. A smaller stream runs over to the Box T Ranch, which is my neighbor to the west. George Tanner, the owner, says he needs more water for his cattle in the dry weather, because the other stream on his land isn't big enough to handle all his cows. But he still keeps increasing his herd."

A knocking at the door accompanied by a loud honking noise interrupted their conversation. Emily opened the door and scolded the honking goose. "Stop banging on my door or you'll get splinters in your beak again, Anna Goose." Still honking, the goose walked over to Matt and pecked at his boot. "Don't worry, she likes you. If she didn't, she would be biting your leg," Emily said with a small, forced smile. "I'm not crazy, Mr. Benton. I know Anna is just a bird, but we seem to understand each other, and she's good company for me."

"I can see that," said Matt reaching out to pet the neck of the goose pecking at his boots. "Well, I'll leave now, if that's what you want, but I wish you'd let me help you, ma'am."

"No thank you, Mr. Benton, we'll be fine." Emily held the door open.

Matt rode away from the farm at a normal pace until he was out of the sight of his hostess. Then, urging Raven with his knees, he pushed the stallion to a fast run and headed toward the town of Red Wall. Emily had given him directions the night before. Matt had known since the shooting that he couldn't leave without helping this brave woman. His plan was still growing in his mind when he reached the town a little more than an hour later.

"I must have been closer than I thought yesterday," Matt told his horse, as he realized he spoke to animals too. *Must be the loneliness*, he thought.

6 Red Wall

The town was easy to spot; it sat at the bottom of a tall cliff of startlingly red clay. Rocks the color of red roses dotted the land nearby. It was said by the Cherokee Indians, who had been forcefully moved to these plains, some forty years earlier, and put on reservations, that the rocks bore the blood of their fallen braves. The cliff towered over the town and was the highest point for hundreds of miles. On a bright, clear day it could be seen for miles. And, when the sun reflected off the cliff, every building in town was washed in red hues. Even the bridge that led into the town glowed red. The bridge crossed Little Creek, a runoff from the creek that came out of the ground on Emily's land. Only one wagon with an outrider could cross at a time. Red Wall was a town that had been around for many years, but was just now growing because of the recent train station added at the end of Main Street. The railroad always brought lots of new people to a town—some good and some bad—and this town was no different than most.

Although it was still early in the day, the two saloons in town were doing a brisk business. Matt rode down the main street until he found the general store he knew must be there— every town had one. He pulled up to the rail that guarded the boardwalk and tied Raven to it. He stepped out of the saddle and walked into the store, then strode to the counter where a tall young man with wire-rimmed glasses was counting out candy to a small boy. Matt looked around at the full shelves and the clothing hanging on the pegs along the wall while he waited for the clerk to be free. A glass case with pistols and revolvers of all types stood under a rack full of rifles. There was very little empty space in the large store. Hats and pots and pans filled another wall. When he finished with the youngster, the clerk said hello to Matt and asked if he could be of help.

"Sure thing," Matt told him. "I need some supplies. If you'll give me some paper and a pencil, I'll list them for you and pick them up after I run some other errands."

The clerk reached under the counter and produced the writing materials and handed them to Matt. Matt set the paper on a barrel top and began writing. When he was finished, he handed the list to the clerk and set out to find the sheriff.

The sheriff was sitting on a chair, feet up on a post, in front of one of the saloons Matt had ridden past on his way into town. "You the sheriff?" Matt asked the man.

"Yeah, I'm Sheriff Brock, what can I do for you?" The slim man with slicked-back, dirty-blond hair and a sore-looking scar across his nose looked Matt up and down. There was no friendliness in his stare. The star on his dirty grey shirt hung on a torn pocket.

"Do you know what's happening out at the Langer spread?" Matt asked him.

"I heard there was some problem out there, but I can't get involved in any trouble outside of the town line. Wish I could help her, but my hands are tied. What's your interest in it, mister?" the skinny lawman asked.

Matt rubbed the back of his neck and looked down at the sheriff. "I figure it's any man's business to help a lady who's being shot at."

The sheriff took Matt in, looking at him more carefully. He took his feet off the post and rocked his chair forward. He stood up and put his face inches from Matt's. "I don't know that's a fact, mister, but this town is as far as I'm legal." The two men stared into each other's eyes and sized each other up. Matt smiled and turned to walk away. Seeing he wasn't going to get any help from the sheriff, Matt waved good day and returned to the general store.

"Are my goods ready?" he asked the clerk as he entered the store again.

"Almost, mister. That was quite a list you gave me," the clerk said as he finished putting some of Matt's supplies in the second of two sacks.

Matt paid his bill and left the town the same way he'd come in. The sheriff and another man watched him ride out. Matt turned to look at them and received a gnarly stare back from the husky man who stood next to the sheriff. *Not a very friendly town,* he thought as he set off to start his plan.

Matt spent a good part of the rest of the day exploring the nearby country and what appeared to be the Box T headquarters.

Then he headed back toward the farm he had stayed at the previous night. Matt skirted the house at a safe distance. He reached a spot close to the ambush site and set up camp. *This should be close enough to hear them coming,* he thought. *Maybe I can discourage these dry gulchers without any bloodshed, if my plan works. Now I just have time to look around here a little and have some supper.* Matt remained a wary horse wrangler as he finished taking care of his stallion. He built a small fire and made his evening meal. Darkness fell before long, and the young rancher settled into the bed he'd made in the tent he'd purchased in town earlier. The weather had warmed since the rainstorm, and getting comfortable wasn't hard for the tired cowboy.

7 Bushwhackers

The hoofbeats of the four horses brought Matt fully awake before the false dawn of the next day. "They're so sure of themselves they don't even try to hide their coming," Matt whispered to his big stallion as he calmed the animal by holding his muzzle close to him. Satisfied that the horse would remain quiet, Matt moved to his hiding place of the previous day. He had just enough time to get out of sight when the four riders appeared and dismounted their horses.

"Damn it, Patch, you better tie these horses good this time or you'll be lucky I don't shoot *your* roof off." The apparent leader, named Lucky, spoke with a menacing glare at his cowering cohort.

"I will, boss, but them lunkheads just git too scared of all the noise we make shootin' at that fool woman down there," Patch complained as he found a solid branch and tied all four horses to it. He turned to address the animals. "You damn lunkheaded horses better stay put or else we'll all be in bad trouble with Lucky." He took his rifle from its saddle holster and left to join the others.

Once in place, all four riflemen started firing at the farmhouse again. Hoping Emily had taken her own advice and stayed under cover, Matt moved toward the four tied-up animals. Speaking quietly once more, he calmed the nervous horses and released them. This time, he broke the branch loose from the tree so the gunmen would think the frightened horses just weren't going to stay around with all that gunfire ringing in their ears. *No sense letting them know I'm around just yet,* Matt thought. Matt led the horses through the stream and once again sent them on their way with a wave of his hat and some quiet shooing.

Matt returned to the thick brush and lay down and waited for the firing to stop. In a short time, the welcome silence returned, and, once again, the man named Lucky was first to appear.

"Patch! Patch! You damn jackass, you picked the weakest limb to tie them horses to and now they've run off again. I oughta make you carry me back to the ranch on your scrawny back!" he screamed.

The two other bushwhackers soon appeared and started inspecting the broken tree limb.

"He warned you, Lucky," one of the men said.

Lucky took his hat off and slapped it hard against his leg. "Shut up! I know he warned me, that's why he's lucky I'm not cutting his ears off right now." The big man was in no mood to be lectured.

The leader of the gunmen realized this wasn't a good time to be hard on his men as they had another long walk back to their ranch in front of them. "Let's get started," he snarled as he started his men on their second long walk in two days. As soon as they were out of sight, Matt left his hiding place to return to his camp. He saddled Raven and headed down to Emily Langer's cabin.

Matt could hear the braying of the mules as soon as he got near the small homestead. He stepped down out of the saddle and looked around. *That's strange,* he thought, *yesterday the shooting didn't seem to bother those mules much. I thought they had gotten used to the noise.* A sudden fear overcame him as Matt realized Emily Langer wasn't yet in sight.

"Miss Langer! Miss Langer!" he shouted toward the closed door of the farmhouse. *She should be out checking the animals,* he thought, *and she must have seen me riding in. Why isn't she out to greet me and ask what I'm doing back on her farm?* Worry hurrying his steps, Matt ran to the barn where the sound of the mules bawling hadn't quieted yet.

Matt ran to the barn door and swung it open. His eyes strained to see in the darkened quarters. "Miss Langer," he cried out again, fear accenting his voice. When no answer came back, he started toward the two screeching mules. "You boys have got to quiet down," he said, his voice sending a calming tone to the mules. "What's got you so—," he stopped short as he saw Emily Langer sitting in the stall across from the two noisy mules. She was rocking from side to side with the still body of Anna Goose in her lap. He could see a small black hole in the bird's chest, and bloody feathers lay around Emily in the hay. Tears streaked Emily's pained face as Matt looked into her anguished eyes. Realizing the goose must have been shot by a ricocheting bullet, Matt set out to calm the mules and restore some order in the barn so he would be able to concentrate on helping the heartbroken woman. He used the same techniques he used on the wild mustangs he tamed, and soon managed to get the two agitated mules settled down.

"Let me look at her, Miss Langer," he said, as he knelt down by the distraught woman.

"She's gone. Those cruel cowards have finally killed someone, just like you said, Mr. Benton." The broken-hearted woman sobbed.

"Let me have her, Miss Langer," Matt whispered. "Take the mules out and let them graze. I'll take care of Anna Goose," he said. *Maybe it's best for her to get busy with her work around here and take her mind off things for a while,* Matt thought. He reached down and took the goose from her lap, and then helped the grieving woman to her feet. Emily looked bewildered and angry as she stood. Slowly, she opened the mules' stall, grabbed them by their halters, and left the barn, guiding them to their pasture outside. The mules seemed eager to leave the barn.

Matt took a shovel off the wall and carried the dead pet to a spot overlooking the farmyard. "This is a good spot, Anna. Emily will be able to look up and see you from most of the yard, and you can keep an eye on her too," he said as he laid the bird in the small grave he had just dug.

After covering the fresh grave with large stones to mark the site and to keep scavengers away, Matt went looking for the farm owner. He found her hooking up the mules to their harnesses, behind the plow. The spring planting still had to be finished. "Miss Langer, why don't you say good-bye to your friend. I'll finish that for you."

Emily, head down, handed Matt the reins and walked to her pet's grave. Matt led the mules to the hitching rack in front of the cabin and tied them there. He took Raven into the barn and unsaddled him. After seeing to his horse, he finished harnessing the two mules and then started busying himself with chores he had noticed needed to be done. He looked over later to see the grief-stricken woman walking behind the mules in the section near the new grave. She had sat by her lost pet for a short time and then had gone over to the mules and started them working. When the sun was directly overhead, Emily called Matt and asked him to come in to the house.

"Mr. Benton, I want to thank you for all your kindness. Will you share lunch with me?"

"Sure will, Miss Langer," Matt answered.

"Please call me Emily," she said.

"I will. And please call me Matt."

The kitchen was quiet and cool when Matt sat at the table after washing up. "You've had a real bad morning, ma'am. Is there anything I can do?" Matt was concerned, and he studied Emily's every move as she went about putting their lunch on the table. Her eyes were red, but a determined look had hardened them.

"No, I just have to keep busy doing my chores and running the farm the same way I did after Pa died," she replied.

"What happened to your pa, ma'am? And why do you stay here by yourself, if you don't mind me asking?"

Emily tilted her head to the side and closed her eyes momentarily. When she opened them, she continued to serve the noon meal while she explained. "My mother died on the way out here from Pennsylvania. She took sick a few weeks after we left home. Pa offered to turn back, but Ma said she wanted to keep going and have a nice farm away from the cities back East.

We were on our way to California, but Ma died during the night when we camped by the stream that runs through this property. We buried her the next morning, and then we went into town to find the owner of the land. Pa figured it was just as nice here as it would be in California, and he could stay near Ma. Luckily, the land was owned by two sisters who were willing to sell. Dad made his offer, and they accepted. It wasn't until after we started building that we found out that Mr. Tanner, our neighbor, had been trying to buy the land. But the sisters didn't like him and had refused to sell to him. He offered Pa a little more than we paid for the land, but, when Pa refused, Mr. Tanner got mad.

"They tried to scare Pa by bullying him when he went into town, but one day Pa grabbed the biggest of them and beat him to within an inch of his life. Things seemed to settle down for a while, and Pa got the buildings up and crops planted. Then one day, near a year ago, Pa went into town for supplies, and the wagon turned over on him. I found him late that afternoon when I got worried and went looking for him. I managed to get him home, but his insides must have been crushed. He died the next morning without regaining consciousness, and I buried him near my mother. A few weeks before he died, he told me that, if anything happened to him, I should sell the ranch to anybody but Tanner and then go on to California. But I've grown to love it here, and I want to stay near my folks. I don't shoot very well, although Pa tried his best to teach me, so I figured, if I showed Tanner I wasn't afraid of him, he would get tired of wasting his time and leave me alone. Now I see my choice is to leave or to fight. Well, I won't give Tanner the satisfaction. He'll have to kill me now to get this land."

8 The Plan

Emily stood up and dabbed at her eyes with her apron. A thoughtful quiet settled over the cabin, and Matt took the opportunity to think through his plan again. Satisfied that it was the best way to fight back, he confided to Emily. "Emily, bushwhackers killed my father several years ago. Every time I think of someone being shot at from ambush, I get angry. Besides, I can't leave you here to fight these men by yourself. So, with your permission or not, I'm going give Tanner and his men a fight."

Emily began clearing the table and looked down at Matt. "Very well, Mr. Benton. I guess if I'd have listened to you earlier, poor Anna would still be alive."

"You can't bet on that, but, once you start fighting back, they'll try even harder to hurt you. And no animals or buildings or people will be safe." Emily sat back down across from Matt and looked directly into his eyes, paying close attention to every word he was saying. Matt continued, "The only way I know to stop a bully is to make it cost him more than he's willing to pay." Matt tapped the table and spoke again. "Emily, I've been in some nasty disputes before and I know how to take care of myself, so I need you to stay out of sight. If you could stay in town or with your neighbors—the Mullers—for a while, I'll only have myself to watch out for, and I'll be able to move around much easier."

When he finished, Emily put her apron on the table and leaned forward, her arms folded on the table in front of her. "No, Mr. Benton, this is my land and I'm not afraid to fight for it. I was just hoping to build the peaceful farm Ma and Pa wanted without any bloodshed. But you're right about Tanner being a bully, and I have always suspected that he might have had something to do with Pa's death. Now I can see that murder isn't more than he would do to get this land."

Matt looked at Emily, admiration and worry clouding his face. "It's going to be very dangerous once we start fighting him, and you will have to leave your house for a while."

Emily leaned back, her hands resting on the chair arms, her face hard. She had made her decision. She lowered her eyelids, and her beautiful grey eyes seemed to turn black. "I'll do whatever it takes to beat him and keep my land. What is your plan, Mr. Benton?" Her words were firm; there was no compromise in them.

Matt stood and looked around. "I want to check whatever guns you have. And, if we're going into a fight together, you'll have to call me Matt," he said with an easy look on his face.

"I will, Matt, but I really don't like putting you in danger like this."

Matt's smile disarmed her. "My old trail boss Will Stomer once told me, if a man don't face up to danger once in a while, he gets old without living."

Matt was hoping that his plan to annoy the gunmen would be enough to let the Box T know the harassment of this woman had to stop. But the death of the beloved goose made the feeling of danger much more imminent. He was sure that, sooner or later, a stray shot or a ricochet bullet could kill Emily too.

♣

"… well that's most of my plan," Matt said, as he finished explaining his idea to Emily. "And, for now, I think you'd better plan on staying away from the cabin for a while. Maybe you could stay with the Mullers in the evening and tend the farm after the morning commotion?"

"No, that would only put the Mullers in danger as well. Mr. Muller offered me help earlier, but he's an old man. If he were harmed, I'd feel terrible. I can camp out too, if that's what's needed," Emily answered.

Things were getting more complicated than Matt had intended. He wanted Emily to be farther away from the trouble. *But if it will keep her out of the line of fire, I will just have to make the best of it*, he thought.

"While I was in town yesterday, I picked up some provisions for myself, but I wasn't counting on having any company. If you're sure you won't go into town or stay with your neighbors, I guess camping out with me will be the next best thing. But out there I'm in charge, and you have to obey my orders. Will you agree to that?"

Emily reached above the door, her back to Matt. She brought down a rifle that had hung there for who knew how long. She turned to look at Matt and spoke firmly. "Yes, but I want to do my part, Matt. I can't let you fight my battles for me all by yourself."

Matt nodded. "Very well, you can start preparing now. You'll need some extra clothes and food. We may have to stay hidden for a spell. I'm going to do some scouting around. I'll stop by later and take you to my camp. Can you be ready to leave in two hours?"

Emily stood the Sharps rifle against the wall. "I'll be ready. Be careful, Matt."

9 The Enemies' Lair

Matt looked down on the Box T homestead from his hiding place. *It must be a large ranch*, he thought, as he considered the large buildings. He had found this spot the day before on his way back from town. Two large trees had fallen over onto each other. The resulting tangle of branches and drying foliage formed the perfect covering for an ambush. The site was approximately two hundred feet from the compound, set up on a small ridge. Matt watched several cowhands move around by the large corral where at least twenty horses milled about. The corral was directly between Matt and the two ranch buildings, and led into a large barn on the right side across from the bunkhouse. *This will be a good spot to start giving them a taste of their own medicine*, thought Matt as he knelt behind the two fallen trees. He studied the buildings for a while and considered how they would fit into his plans.

On the ride back to the Langer farm, Matt had to duck into some woods so he wouldn't be seen by the four riders coming from the direction of the town of Red Wall. He couldn't be sure, but Matt thought they looked like the same men who had been shooting at the farm earlier in the day. *I guess they don't have any honest work to do on the Box T, so they must go into town to celebrate after shooting at a woman,* Matt thought as he resumed his journey back to the Langer farm.

Matt arrived back at the farm to find Emily loading a large wagon with some of her belongings. The mules had already been put in their braces and were calmly chewing the grass at their feet. Matt stepped out of the saddle and looked at Emily. "Emily, we can't take that wagon with us. We're going to have to move fast and be hard to find once we start to fight back. This Tanner isn't likely to quit so easy after throwing his weight around here for so long."

Pushing back some fallen hair from her face Emily said, "I realize that, Matt, but, after we drop the supplies at your camp, I'm going to take the wagon down to the Mullers'. I want to leave some of Ma and Pa's belongings with them for safekeeping. I'm sure they won't mind."

Matt wasn't surprised by her answer. He knew she was tough and she understood how bad things could get. It could be that her house and barn would be destroyed before the fight was over. But Matt promised himself, if that happened, there wouldn't be a Box T building standing either. And Box T cattle would be stampeded all over the country.

Matt helped Emily load the last of her household goods on the wagon. He threw a rope across the wagon and tied the load down tight.

"Okay, Emily, we'd better get started before we lose the light."

"I'm ready to leave now, Matt."

"Good, We'll leave the wagon and the mules there too."

"I can't do that. The mules have to protect Molly and her calf. They're not strong enough to travel yet. They need at least another day to gain strength."

"Very well, but let's get started." Matt looked up to the sky as he spoke.

It was very near dark when Matt and Emily returned to the barn after dropping off the camp supplies and then stopping at the Mullers' place. Emily had ridden Youmule back to the farm and Samule followed them into the barn.

"You two have to protect Molly and her calf 'til I get back," Emily instructed the two large mules as she went about setting food and water out for all the animals.

When she was finished, she closed the barn doors and walked over to the horse and rider waiting for her. She stepped into the stirrup Matt had left open for her. She took Matt's hand and climbed up onto the back of the big horse.

Emily said, "Okay, Matt, my animals should be all right until tomorrow. We can go to the camp now." She put her arms around Matt and held on.

The camp was situated in a stand of trees behind a small hill not far from the spot the Box T men had been shooting from. Matt had cleared a place for his tent and a small campfire. The smoke from their fire should be lost in the leaves of the trees that surrounded them. *We should be safe here for a while,* Matt thought.

The camp was well hidden, and, if they kept lookout from the hill, they would see anyone coming even from far away. Matt moved about easily getting the camp ready for the night. "We'll make a small fire tonight, but, from then on, we'll do our cooking while it's still light out so we don't give away our position. The extra blankets should keep us warm enough, and the tent will keep us dry," Matt said.

"I'm sure we'll be fine. Now, while you care for your horse, I'll start the fire and make us some dinner."

"Good idea. And then we'll hit the blankets early. We're going to have to sleep light once we start fighting back. Remember, after tomorrow, we're going to have to stay alert at all times."

Emily assured Matt once again that she understood the danger they would soon be in. She busied herself starting a small fire and preparing a meal as the daylight faded away. The campfire allowed for only glimpses of each other as they talked through their dinner. After supper, Matt and Emily spoke quietly across the campfire for a while longer and then went to their bedrolls. The night was dark and still; only the stirring of small animals disturbed the quiet. Tired from a long day, they both slept through the night.

Raven was first to hear the approaching horses. He had been tethered on a long rope, and his wet muzzle pressed against Matt's shoulder.

"Quit shoving, I heard them too," Matt lied to his horse as he quietly slipped out of his blanket. Matt quietly gathered up his hat and guns and saddled Raven. He moved stealthily out of camp without waking Emily. If the plan went as he hoped, she would be back in her home soon and out of danger. Matt walked Raven into the woods and hid near the spot where the gunmen had tied their horses the day before. He had arrived just in time to see the first rider cross the stream followed closely by his three partners.

Matt peeked out from behind a tree and watched as the man named Lucky warned his man. "Patch, if them horse ain't here when we get back, I'm going to skin you alive."

Lucky signaled the other two men and they went down to their shooting spots. Matt had expected them to leave someone to watch the horses this time, and his plan allowed for it. He waited for the shooting to start, and, as he figured, the man left to watch the horses got nosey and kept looking down toward the cabin.

10 Fighting Back

Matt moved quietly over the leaf-covered ground. He drew his pistol and hit the guard on the head with the butt of his gun. The groan of the falling man couldn't be heard over the sound of the gunfire. Matt checked on the three shooters and saw them busy at work firing on the empty house.

"Come on, feller, you're going for a ride," Matt said, as he lifted the unconscious man and laid him across the saddle of one of the horses. Matt took out his knife and cut a short piece of rope from a lariat hanging on the saddle horn. Soon he had the gunman's hands and feet tied together and lashed to the stirrups. He untied the four horses, gathered up their reins, and led them to a spot behind some trees where they couldn't be seen from the trail. Once again he hid himself and waited for the three gunmen to return to their horses.

A few minutes later, the firing stopped and the three shooters appeared in the clearing where they had left their horses. "Dammit,

Patch, this ain't funny. Where the hell are them horses?" Lucky shouted into the trees. "Spread out and look for that fool. He probably took the horses to water," he commanded.

When the two men went looking for the horses, their leader sat down on a stump to wait.

"Let that rifle down easy, mister, and sit still." Matt's voice had a meanness to it he hadn't used in a long time. He'd sneaked up behind the big man and now had his pistol in the man's back. "Call your men back here and don't give me away," he growled at his captive as he lifted Lucky's handgun out of its holster.

"Hey, you two get back here," Lucky hollered, as he'd been told.

"Well, you're not stupid, I'll give you that much," Matt told the leader of the four troublemakers.

"Did you find him?" the first returning gunman asked as he neared his sitting leader.

"Shut up and stand still," Matt ordered. He was kneeling, concealed behind the big man named Lucky. Only his arm and gun could be seen.

"What's going on?" the second man out of the woods asked.

"Don't move," Matt ordered again. "Both of you—let those rifles down easy and then undo those gun belts."

"What should we do, Lucky?" the younger of the two—a scrawny, red headed man—asked.

"Do as he says, Red, he's got the better hand right now."

"What's your interest in this, mister. You her man?" Lucky tried to talk to the man behind him without turning his head.

"No, I just don't like cowards who shoot at a woman from an ambush. Walk away from them guns." Matt gave the order as he pointed the two standing men toward the creek. "Now start walking and don't look back."

"I got a bad leg, mister," the older member of the trio complained as he reached down to feel his boot.

"Shut up and do as he says," the big man said, as he stood up in front of Matt. "We'll deal with him later when our hands are full. We're leaving, mister, but you'll regret mixing in on this."

The three Box T hands started off toward the creek and away from Emily's farm. Matt's soft whistle brought his big horse to him and he mounted up. He gathered the other four horses and crossed the stream headed for the Box T. Looking back at the rider bound to his horse, Matt could see he was tied securely and wasn't going to fall off.

"Lets' cover some ground," he said, as he gave his big horse a nudge with his knees. The five horses and two riders soon passed the walking trio of men and rode off into the distance.

Matt arrived at his hiding spot by the fallen trees overlooking the Box T before full light and released the three empty horses. With a slap of his hat, he sent them down a narrow road toward the corral next to the barn. Matt tied Raven next to the horse carrying the Box T rider named Patch, looked around, and then grabbed his own rifle and the one belonging to Patch. He looked down at the ranch buildings and centered on the smoke coming from the chimneys on top of the bunkhouse and the main house. Matt knelt down behind a thick branch and rested his rifle on it.

Let's see how they like it, he thought, as he levered a shell into the chamber. He fired four quick shots from his own rifle. All four bullets thunked into the chimney pipe on the bunkhouse roof. He knew that, inside the small building, the pipe from the roof connected to a potbelly stove the men used to warm their sleeping quarters. The impact of the bullets would shake the pipe violently causing soot and sparks to erupt out into the still, dark room. The sleeping hands would be waking to a nightmare of smoke and a loud banging noise all around them.

"What the hell's going on?" several scared voices screamed in the confusion. Some old newspapers left near the stove for kindling caught fire from the sparks and added to the panic.

"Get out, get out!" a hoarse voice coughed from the darkness as the men scrambled to the only door.

The first man to grab the door suddenly jumped back as bullets crashed through the bottom panel of the door. Matt had switched his target to the door and pumped four more quick blasts into the bottom panel, not wanting to hurt anyone just yet.

This is your warning, he thought as he re-sighted on the chimney of the bigger house, which was larger because it was for the main cook stove. The cook was busy rustling pots and pans for the morning breakfast and didn't hear the gunfire. But the owner of the Box T heard them and was running into the kitchen when the cook stove seemed to disappear in a cloud of billowing black dust. Again, the expert rifleman behind the fallen trees had hit his mark as four shots shook the tin pipe on top of the roof. Sparks once again found dry kindling and set it on fire. The soot and sparks continued to cover the room, coating everything in it with oily black dust.

"Get your damn gun and get outside! We're under attack!" the angry voice of George Tanner barked. George found his wife

Liz coming down the stairs. Although she was, as ever, ready to fight beside her husband in defense of their property, he bundled her to the safety of the root cellar before returning to the fray.

The cook finished stamping out the fire and ran to get his gun.

Outside, some of the men had run into the ranch yard firing their guns wildly up into the tree line. "Where are they?" a soot-covered cowboy demanded as he emptied his six-gun at no particular target.

Matt had stopped shooting at the bunkhouse and was concentrating on the main house. Firing into the windows, he shattered all the glass he could see from his vantage point high above the ranch buildings. After unloading his own Winchester, he used the rifle belonging to Patch. It didn't shoot as true as Matt's gun, but the skilled rifleman corrected to the left and hit most of his targets. Matt reloaded his own weapon, and watched as the owner of the Box T ran out into the yard and hid behind a water trough. Matt placed three bullets in the water in the trough. Although the water slowed the slugs down, they still had enough power to punch holes in the wood. Three geysers of water splashed on the ranch owner causing him to jump up and start firing into the woods above him.

Matt held his fire and hollered a warning. "Don't bother that woman anymore, Tanner!"

He slapped the horse Patch was tied to and sent him down into the yard.

"There he is!" shouted a blackened ranch hand as gunshots rang out again. The men were shooting in the direction of the trail Patch's horse was taking to his corral.

"Stop firing—that's not him," another man shouted as the horse with the bound rider rode closer.

Matt used that diversion to mount his horse and ride away from the Box T. Raven's long stride covered the ground quickly, and Matt soon caught sight of two of the men he had sent off on foot earlier. Not wanting to be seen clearly just yet, he rode past them at a far distance.

"Where's the third gunman?" he spoke out loud as he stood up in the stirrups trying to see farther off in the distance. The third man, named Wallace, had stopped shortly after Matt passed them earlier that morning. "I ain't walking back to the ranch again, no sir. I'm going down to that farm and find something to ride. Who's going with me?" he'd asked.

"You ain't going to find nothing to ride down there but two ornery mules, but go ahead and satisfy yourself," Lucky told him.

"I can ride anything with four legs, and, if them mules give me any trouble, I'll just take a board to 'em," he replied as he left his two partners and set off toward Emily Langer's farm.

Out of sight of the others, he reached down into his right boot and took out a small handgun. "Never show all your cards to nobody," he whispered to the gun as he checked that it was loaded.

Emily woke with the first shots that morning, and, true to her word to Matt, she stayed in the camp until the firing stopped. After waiting a while for the gunmen to leave, she picked up her father's rifle and headed down to her barn to check on the animals. She opened the barn door and was greeted by the low mooing of Molly nursing her young one. Otherwise, the barn was quiet and seemed unchanged from yesterday. She closed the door and went into her cabin to see what damage had been done by this latest assault.

Just as Matt had warned her, she noticed many more bullets had found their marks much lower in the living area. The kerosene lamp on her sewing table had been shattered, spilling its liquid on the floor near her bedroom door. Two ricocheting pieces of lead had found the large cooking pot that hung over her fireplace. One shot had gone right through—a dented piece of lead rested on the bottom of the empty black pot. The other shot had left its mark—a deep scratch on the side—and then veered off to rest in the chimney wall.

Matt was absolutely right, she thought, as she opened the back door to head back to the barn, *the attacks have gotten more aggressive.*

Wallace was passing behind the house on his way to the barn when the back door swung open. Emily, caught by surprise at the sight of the intruder, called out, "Stop where you are! This is my property!"

The gunman saw the woman in the doorway with the rifle in her hand and snapped off a quick shot in her direction. The young farm owner fell back away from the door, and the Box T hand hurried to the small door at the rear of the barn. He pulled it open and hurried inside. He was soon engulfed in the dark interior of the unlit barn. "That damn woman better not cause a ruckus if she knows what's good for her," he grumbled to himself. He stepped forward still talking. "I'm mad enough about walking back to the ranch two mornings in a row, and I'm damned tired of getting up early every morning while the rest of the crew warms their bunks. She better stay low 'til I get out of here." He continued to grouse to himself as he stumbled his way forward in the dark barn. He felt the floor shuddering and heard the snorting of Samule two seconds before the mule's large head crashed into his chest. The man's body flew back and smacked into the rear barn wall, separating him from his revolver. Samule had heard the gunman enter the barn and, acting on instinct, had rushed in to the attack. Turning his hindquarters to the fallen intruder, Samule sent his deadly hooves flying, only to miss the terrified bully by inches. The small back door flew open and the gunman tumbled through it seconds before the head and shoulders of the angry mule appeared in the doorway. Frustrated that he couldn't get his massive shoulders through the small opening, the mule bared his huge teeth and sent a screeching roar at the fleeing coward.

"Someone's gonna pay for this," the gunman grumbled aloud as he raced for the safety of the woods on the other side of the creek.

Matt reached the camp just as the sun was turning the grass a bright green. A slight breeze was exciting the campfire back to life.

"Emily, it's Matt... don't shoot," he called out as he entered the camp area.

When he didn't get a response, he looked into the tent and called out into the woods. He searched the deserted site and realized Emily must have returned to her farm to see to her animals. A frown creased his face and a shiver ran up his back. He felt as he had felt as he rode in the cold rain a few days earlier.

Matt mounted Raven and rode at a gallop down to the farm buildings.

"Emily! Emily Langer!" he shouted over the sound of the braying mules. He heard the animals as soon as he reached the farmyard and raced to the barn. "Where are you, Emily?" he yelled. Matt lifted the metal latch and started to open the big barn door. The door crashed open knocking Matt back ten feet. He landed on his back, his senses not understanding where the explosion had come from. When he looked up he saw the large mule Emily called Samule charging at him. Matt had no chance to run, so he rolled his body into a ball and covered his head. The earth under him shook just as he'd felt it shake during the stampedes he'd helped stop while he was riding for Will Stomer. The hot, smelly breath of the enraged mule assaulted his face, but no teeth had sunk into his body as yet. Matt cautiously looked up into the big angry mule's face and started talking gently to the large animal. "You know me, Samule. I'm here to help Miss Emily. Now be a good boy and back off and let me get up."

Samule pawed the ground, each stomp pounding the earth inches from Matt's ear. The mule studied Matt for a few more seconds then moved over toward the cabin.

Matt stood up and holstered his pistol. He'd pulled it out just before covering up. The last thing he wanted to do was kill one of Emily's mules.

I'm sure glad I had faith in you, Samule, he thought as he strode through the cabin door.

♣

"Emily! Emily!" Emily's body was lying in a pool of blood. Matt knelt down and picked up her head. He felt sticky, blood-splattered hair above her right ear. A small wheezing sound came from her partly opened lips. *She's still alive! I've got to get her to a doctor right away*, Matt's instincts told him. Matt tore some cloth from undergarments he found in her bedroom and tied the hasty bandage around Emily's head. Sorrow and anger crushed Matt like two mountains falling on him, reminding the young rancher of his father's death at the hands of the two outlaws he'd taken revenge on only a few years ago.

There's nothing more I can do for her here, Matt thought as he raced out the cabin door and into the barn. The mules turned their heads and looked at Matt. They were still agitated. The stomping of their hooves on the dirt floor reverberated throughout the barn interior and sent up a cloud of dust.

"Calm down, boys, we got important work to do. Emily needs our help," Matt pleaded. Moving slowly and constantly talking in soft soothing tones, Matt gathered up the mules and headed for the Mullers' farm. A small trail next to the creek led Matt through some woods and out to Emily's neighbors' farm about a mile away.

The Mullers were angered by the news Matt brought them and offered to help him as much as they could. "I'm just grateful you unloaded the wagon and put all her things in your shed, Mr. Muller. I'll need the wagon to get her to town."

Burge Muller and Matt went about hurrying to get the two mules hitched up to the Langer wagon. "This is the Devil's doing, and them Box T people have got to pay for this. I'm sorry

I wasn't more help to that poor girl. I just hope it ain't too late," Burge Muller said in an agitated voice.

"They'll pay more than they can afford to, Mr. Muller, I'll make sure of that."

"Be careful, son, those Tanners are a rotten lot. They'll shoot you in the back if it suits 'em."

Matt nodded agreement. "I have to go now. I'll come back later with the animals. Thanks for everything."

The mules cooperated more than Matt could believe possible, and they were back at the Langer farm within a half hour. Matt ran inside and checked on Emily as she lay on the floor. She was still breathing, although her breaths were much more ragged and shallow than they had been before. He rushed into her bedroom and pulled the mattress off her bed, leaving all the covers intact. Working quickly, he carried the bundle outside and arranged them in the back of the wagon. Then he ran back into the cabin and picked up the unconscious Emily and carried her outside.

Matt placed Emily gently in her wagon on top of the mattress and covered her with the blankets. He took some rope from the barn and tied it around her body and the mattress. "That should keep her from moving too much," he said aloud as he tied Raven to the back of the wagon. Matt climbed into the wagon seat and called to the two mules, "Come on, gid yap, we have to get her to town and quick." The team of mules responded to the needs of their fallen friend as though they knew exactly what had happened, Matt was sure.

They rolled into Red Wall in late morning, and no one in the streets seemed to notice the cargo in the back of Matt's wagon. Matt was sure he had seen a doctor's shingle when he was in town getting his supplies.

"Hey, boy," he called out to a straw-headed youngster walking on the boardwalk near the general store. "Where's your doc's office?"

"Over there, mister, next to the barber shop," the boy said. He was pointing toward a red-and-white barber sign across the street. "There he is now coming out of his office, mister."

"Thanks," Matt called back to the boy; he had already started the wagon in that direction. "Hey, doc, hold up… I got a hurt woman here." Matt shouted out louder than he wanted to, but it was necessary to be heard over the noise of the incoming stagecoach.

"What's that?" the well-dressed man in the town suit asked.

"She's hurt bad, doc. Take a look."

The doctor climbed into the wagon bed and started unwrapping the covers that had blown over Emily's head. The bleeding had stopped except for a small amount that showed on the bandage, but her color immediately worried him.

"Let's get her inside," he said, ignoring the group of bystanders that had gathered and were asking questions.

Matt grabbed the bottom of the mattress and slid it toward the back of the wagon. The doctor easily picked up the other end and shouted to the boy who had given Matt directions. "Alley, open my door and then go fetch the Loren sisters—quickly!"

The boy ran to the door and opened it and then ran off in slapping footsteps, his thin, lanky body seeming to move in all directions at once.

The two men carried Emily into a waiting room filled with chairs and a small table with old newspapers on it. The room was small but neat, freshly painted with smooth wooden floors.

"Let's put her on the floor for now, and cut those ropes," the doctor instructed.

They let Emily down gently. The doctor walked to a door in the back of the room and opened it. Matt took out his folding knife and did as he'd been told. The doctor returned and bent toward the mattress. "Good. Now help me get her on the table in the treatment room."

The two men once again lifted as one, and Emily was moved onto the surgeon's table.

"This is Emily Langer, what happened to her?" The doctor asked the question as he carefully cut away the bandage Matt had put around her head.

"I believe she was shot, doc. I didn't feel but one wound, so the bullet might still be in her."

Doc Mason looked cautiously at Matt. "Uh hum… if that's all you can tell me about her injury, wait outside and send the Loren sisters in as soon as they get here. Close the door behind you."

"I ain't afraid of seeing blood, Doc, you sure I can't help?"

"No, I need to concentrate. This woman is near gone. Now get!"

The worried cowboy backed out of the door and closed it behind him. *Damn myself! If that girl dies, it's all my fault. She was handling things just fine 'til I stuck my big nose in her business.* Matt continued to berate himself until the outside door opened and a smartly dressed woman rushed in. She hurried past Matt, her dress rustling as she walked to the door at the back of the room. She knocked once and went through the door to the room where the doctor was working on Emily.

"Who is it, Lee? What happened to her?" The woman had left the door open a bit, and Matt could see her putting her shawl on a chair as she questioned the man standing over the injured young farm owner.

"It's Emily Langer. She's been shot. It looks like the bullet grazed her head and gave her a concussion." Emily still looked too pale, and the right side of her head was shaved and swollen.

"We'll know more in a day or two if the swelling starts to go down. I'll give her some medicine that should help. I've already cleaned the wound; please put a bandage on her. Is that cowboy still outside?"

"Yes, there was a young fellow out there when I came in."

"Good, I want to talk to him. I wonder if he knows who did this."

The doctor started to push the door all the way open, then he stopped and turned back to his helper. "Stay here with Emily please, Alma. Try to wake her, but be very gentle. I'll be back soon." He opened the door and walked out.

11 Doc

Doc Mason stepped into his waiting room. He was a swarthy complexioned man with a square jaw, black hair, and dark eyes. His six foot height matched Matt's. His frame seemed thinner but didn't seem to lack strength. He called to Matt. "Please come in here."

Matt followed Doctor Mason into a small office next to the room Emily was in. Doc closed the door and pointed to a chair. "I'm Doctor Mason. Please sit down and tell me all you can about this shooting."

"I will, Doc, but first, how is she, is she going to be all right?"

The doctor lowered his voice. "I can't tell just yet, but she's been hurt bad. The bullet just grazed her head, but the concussion she suffered seems pretty severe. I'll probably know more tomorrow... unless she wakes up before then. Now, what happened?"

"Well...," Matt went on to tell the doctor most of the events that had happened since he'd met Emily Langer, and his guess that one of the three gunmen went down to the farm and shot her after he rode past them on his way to the Box T.

"Doesn't seem that anyone around here will help her, Doc, so I had to do something. I know I'm to blame for her getting shot, but what else could a man do?" Matt pleaded.

"Get out of here! Get out of here!" the woman's voice from next door interrupted the doctor's answer.

"Stay put until I get back." Doc said it as a command as he rushed out of his office door.

Backing out of the other door were two men. Alma Loren was pushing the taller of the two with her outstretched hands. "You have no right in here, sheriff," she said, her voice a whispered shout.

"Get out of there you two," admonished Doc Mason. "What's the meaning of this, sheriff? Since when do you barge into my treatment room? And what the devil is he doing here?" The doctor had grabbed the sheriff by his left arm and was pointing his finger at the short, stocky man who was with the lawman.

The sheriff pulled his arm away from the doctor's grasp. He looked angrily at Alma Loren, and then spoke to Doc Mason. "We just wanted to know what was going on. And I got a right to investigate any shooting, don't I? I'm the law in this town, Doc."

Doc Mason stepped closer to the lawman, crowding him. "Who said it was a shooting? I haven't made my mind up yet, so far as I know the young lady has a bump on her head. Besides, the injury didn't take place in town, and your jurisdiction ends at the edge of town. Isn't that what you told Miss Langer when she asked you for help with the cowards that have been harassing her?"

"Now wait a minute, Doc, you got no right to talk that way," the other man spoke up.

Doc Mason turned his angry eyes to the stocky man who stood next to the sheriff. His look was a challenge. "No one invited you into this discussion, Tanner. Mind your own business and get out of my office. You're not welcome here."

The sheriff moved between the two men. "All right, back off, Doc. We'll go for now, but I want an explanation on this later. C'mon Roy."

As the unwanted men left, Doc Mason turned back to his office and saw Matt standing in the doorway, his hand on his gun and his glare burning into the backs of the retreating men.

"Is that the owner of the Box T with the sheriff?" Matt asked.

"No, that's his brother, Roy Tanner. He's an investor. Supposed to be big in mining. But other than pushing his weight around as George Tanners' brother, he doesn't seem to do much of anything. He showed up about a year ago just when a hand on his brother's ranch claimed he found some gold in the hills up east of the Box T. The hand came in to town bragging all about it. Next day he disappeared. According to the Tanners, the cowboy just up and rode off. They spent some time looking for more gold, but didn't find anything. So the story goes. Roy went back East for a while but returned a few months ago and has just hung around since. Some say he's part owner with his brother in the Box T. Others say he's a crook, wanted back East for all sorts of thievery."

Matt's eyebrow rose… the way they did when he registered interesting information.

Doc Mason held the office door open and pointed to a chair in front of his desk. "Come in and sit down, mister. What's your name?"

Matt took his hat off and sat down in one of the two leather-covered chairs by the desk. A framed diploma from a prestigious medical school hung on the wall in front of him, behind the doctor's chair. On another wall, a large clock ticked as a pendulum swung back and forth in its glass case.

"My name's Matt Benton. I'm from Colorado Flats, Doctor," the horse rancher said as he offered his hand to shake.

The doctor took his hand and said, "Lee Mason, pleased to meet you, mister. You did the right thing helping Emily. I knew she was having trouble out there, but I had no idea it was this bad. Whenever I asked her about it she would say it was just a neighborly dispute and that it would fix itself in time. She just never let on how badly they were treating her."

Matt could tell by his handshake that this man in front of him had some sand in him. And something in his eyes said he was someone to reckon with if you got on the wrong side of him.

Doc said, "She was afraid of someone else getting hurt on her account. She's a strong, independent gal who wants to take care of her own problems. She'd sure make some man a good wife, no doubt, and there are a couple of men in town would love to court her. But she won't let herself be available. Always stays on her farm. Won't even take time for the Saturday socials anymore."

Matt leaned forward and rested his forearms on the desk. "That farm means a lot to her, Doc. Her Ma and Pa are buried on it, and I think she wants to make it work for them."

Doc Mason stood up and pulled at his chin. "I suppose that's a good reason to put up with people like the Tanners. Well, let me get back in with her and see if there's been any change. She's in good hands, Matt. Alma and her sister Beth help me all the time, and someone will stay with her until she wakes up. I promise you that."

Matt stood up and put his hat on. "I'm sure you'll do all you can, Doc. I've got some business to attend to myself. I'll check with you later and see how she's doing."

"Be careful in town, Matt, and don't trust that sheriff any. He's always with Tanner, playing cards in the saloon or strutting around town with him."

Hearing that reminded Matt of the day he'd come into town for supplies. Roy Tanner had been standing next to the sheriff, watching him as he left town that day.

Outside, the town had settled into its usual routine with people coming and going at their normal pace. Matt looked up and down the busy main street, but couldn't locate Emily's wagon. Raven had been tied to the back of the wagon, and it wasn't like him to allow himself to be led away easily by a stranger.

"Dewey took 'em, mister, if you're looking for your mule team and horse. He brung 'em all down to his livery." It was the same youngster with the hay-colored hair who had helped Matt before. He walked across the street and pointed to the end of town toward a red-colored building that was the railroad station. "It's the livery right across from the station depot. Dewey's the owner, and he's the smithy too. Had some trouble with that big horse of yours, but Dewey's mighty good with animals, so he got 'em settled down pretty good."

Matt smiled at the youngster. "Thanks again, boy. You sure make yourself useful. What's your name?"

The youngster kicked at a stone with scuffed boots worn thin on the soles and looked at Matt. "Albert, sir, but mostly they call me Alley, 'cause that's where I mostly am."

"Well, Alley, I sure appreciate your help." Matt flipped a coin in the air and told the boy, "Get yourself some pop and candy, son, you earned it."

The boy caught the coin out of the air. "Thanks, mister. If you need anything else, just call out 'Alley' and I'll come runnin'!"

Matt smiled at the scruffy-looking kid and started down to the livery barn at the end of the street.

The sign out front read, Harmon Livery, Horses Boarded and Rented, Shoes Made, and Gear Repaired.

Matt saw the wagon put up by the side of the large building, but his horse and the mules weren't anywhere to be seen. There were three horses in the corral on the other side, a roan and two pintos, but none of them was familiar to Matt. The ringing sound of metal struck against metal brought Matt inside the building. "Hello," he called out.

"Over here," came a reply. The repeated clang of a horseshoe being struck on an anvil was a familiar sound to Matt. Off to his right was an open doorway. It was filled with the rear end of a large brown-and-black mule. Matt pushed past the big animal and walked through the door. On the outside wall was a smithy's furnace, and next to it a large anvil. A big-shouldered man a few inches short of Matt's six-foot height was alternately sticking an unfinished shoe into the fire and then striking it with a heavy mallet on the anvil. When he was satisfied with its shape, he dunked it in a tub of cool water. The steam escaped the tub with a satisfying hiss, sending a small cloud of wet, grey smoke into the smithy's face. Without turning he said, "Almost finished, mister. I'll be right with you."

"Don't mean to rush you none… take your time," Matt said, as he looked around the big barn-like room. There were eight stalls in all, four on each side of the building separated by an aisle that led to a back area. The back area was dark, and Matt couldn't see past the horse stalls.

As the smithy straightened up and held the shoe up to the light with a pair of tongs, Matt could see his sandy brown hair and the beard and mustache cropped close to his face. The smithy finally spoke, "You the feller brought Miss Emily in?"

"Yes. Do you know her?"

"Some. She mostly stays to herself, though." Walking over to the front of the mule, the smithy picked up its right front hoof, tucked it between his knees, and started to nail the new shoe in place. Matt recognized Emily's Samule. The smithy continued quietly, "I noticed his shoe was loose when I brought him over here. Emily always takes good care of her animals, so I knew she'd want me to fix Samule's shoe. There won't be no charge though. That your horse was tied to the wagon?"

"Yep. Did he give you much trouble?"

"Some at first, but he's a smart one and knows a friend when he meets 'em. I put him in a back stall with some water and hay, and he's been fine."

"Thanks, what do I owe you?"

"No charge for that either. I understand you might have saved Emily's life. Your horse can stay here as long as you like."

"Thanks, I'm just going to get something to eat, and then I'll be riding out."

Holding several nails between his lips, the smithy asked in a garbled voice, "What happened to Emily? Was she shot like they say?"

"I'm afraid so," Matt answered him.

After a few more seconds the livery owner stood up and let the mule's leg down. The shoeing was finished. He looked Matt over and said, "Name's Dewey Harmon. Pleased to meet ya, mister." He extended a calloused hand. Matt reached out and shook it.

"Same here. I'm Matt Benton. I run a horse ranch up in the Colorado Flats."

The two men walked over to the large, worn doorway that fronted the livery and looked into the street. Dewey said, "I knew Emily was having some trouble with Tanner's Box T, but I can't believe they'd shoot a woman. I thought it was just a property squabble of some sort. She never let on it was this serious. Do you think they did it?"

Matt took his hat off and combed his hair with his fingers. "I can't say much right now, Dewey, but that lady helped me out of a fix, and I'm sure not going to let whoever did this to her get away with it."

Dewey undid the apron he wore for shoeing. "Well, I can handle a gun as good as most men, and I'd sure like to help settle up for Emily. She let me take her to the social a few times, before her father died, and we been friends ever since. When you get ready to collect, count me in, mister."

Matt looked at Dewey with a curious eye. "We'll see. I'm used to playing a lone hand though."

Dewey cocked his head. "If it's that Box T outfit you're going up against, you'll need someone to watch your back. They got some shifty-looking hands riding for that spread lately."

"I'll remember what you said. Can I leave the mules here for a few days?"

"Sure thing. I'll look after them 'til Emily's back on her feet."

"Thanks. I'll be back for my horse after I fill my belly."

Dewey pointed up the street. "Try the German's restaurant across the street, opposite the Three Eights saloon. He's got the best food in town."

Matt left the livery and went looking for the restaurant Dewey had recommended. He'd have to be careful of what he said around here. He was all too aware of how news traveled fast in a small town. He turned right out of the livery and started up the rutted dirt road that ran down the middle of Red Wall. A small, unpainted building caught Matt's eye. A hand-carved sign in the large window read Helmer's. Good Food and Fair Prices. *That must be the German's,* he thought.

12 Rough and Tumble

A train whistle blew and caught Matt's attention as he neared the boardwalk. He turned toward the end of town where the rail yard was. A six-car train with a locomotive, coal car, two passenger cars, an animal car, and a caboose pulled in. Matt watched the train pull into the station and didn't notice the four riders turning in toward him. Pushing their horses up to the hitching rail, two of the riders caught Matt in between their mounts. "Looks like we caught a rabbit 'atween us, Wallace. Lucky we ain't hungry for rabbit stew!" The man's voice was gruff, and he laughed out loud. His three friends joined in the laughter. The big sorrel the man named Lucky was sitting on was crushing Matt against the horse ridden by the man who had complained about his leg earlier in the day.

Caught off guard at first, the wily horse wrangler took only a few seconds to realize the fix he was in. When he saw who it was, Matt quickly thought of Emily Langer lying close to death in the doctor's office. These were the men who were responsible.

Matt knew that the horses, weighing over a thousand pounds each, could cause some serious harm to him, squeezing him as they were. He ducked quickly under the horse ridden by the man named Lucky, and came up on the left side of Lucky, grabbing his arm and cartridge belt as he did. Matt pulled with all his strength and yanked the big man out of his saddle. The two-hundred-plus-pound body seemed to freeze in mid air before landing with a dull thud in the manure-covered street.

"Ooof, what the damn blazes…" whooshed out of the loud-mouthed Lucky as he landed, sending a cloud of dust into the air.

The big man rolled over onto his belly and started to get up. Before he reached his feet, a steel-like fist exploded into his nose. Matt had stood ready. Turning his hips and rolling his large shoulders he had delivered a crushing blow to the face he now hated. One of Matt's many occupations as he looked for his father's killers had been that of water boy and go-getter for a professional boxer. King Bill Thurman had toured the country fighting local talent for prize money at county fairs and such. Part of Matt's pay had come in the form of boxing lessons, and he was a "good learner" as King Bill often told him. Matt practiced hard and took many bruising punches from his teacher until he learned to slip them and punch hard enough to back King Bill up on occasion. He was determined to be ready to punish his father's murderers any way he had to. Whenever possible, King Bill would book a fight for Matt before his own main event, enabling Matt to earn extra pay and improve his fighting skills as well.

Matt's blow caused the bloody face of the Box T rider to rock back and then forward, sending a spray of blood into the air staining the front of Matt's shirt. Only the man's huge size—at least three inches taller than Matt and at least forty pounds over Matt's one hundred and eighty pounds—kept him from falling. He had been hit before, though, and knew enough to put his huge arms up to protect his damaged nose. As Matt stepped in to follow up with another punch, the big man's right hand streaked out and hit Matt with a backhanded fist. The blow landed on Matt's right ear and was followed by a quicker left to his jaw. The pain it caused sent Matt reeling. He staggered three steps to his left and fell to one knee. A large black boot came racing toward his head. Matt rolled quickly away from the kick and got to his feet. The wallop he'd received caused Matt's ear to ring, and he had to shake his head to fight the dizziness he felt. He saw the man called Lucky coming forward, his hands balled into fists as big as he'd ever seen. Matt knew he would have to finish him quickly if he were to stay alive. He'd fought big men many times before, and he knew that their weak spot was their right side where the liver was.

King Bill had taught his young pupil a fine lesson on body punching, "Dig that left into his right side, and push it through to the other side."

Squatting low and twisting, Matt sent a terrible blow into his opponent's side. The huge frame seemed to bend in half, and a cursed groan blew out Lucky's mouth. Matt continued his terrible body assault with right and left punches until the man started falling. Lucky sat down hard on the earthen street, and fear was in his eyes. Never before had this giant been beaten, as he surely was now.

Still, he tried to get up, but, as he put a trembling hand under him to stand up, another crashing boulder struck his face. Matt wasn't thinking clearly; he was thinking of a young woman who had been terrorized by this cur in front of him, and who now might die because of his bullet. King Bill would not be pleased that his star pupil had forgotten lesson number one—always stay in control of yourself—but he would be proud of the boy he had helped become a man. Matt knew he was out of control, for he had never hit a defenseless man before. As Matt was readying a kick to the downed man's bloodied face, the boom of a shotgun roared in the air. Dropping to one knee, Matt wheeled to his left where the blast seemed to have come from. His pistol, already in his aching right hand, pointed back at the shotgun holder. It was Dewey Harmon from the livery; the shotgun was pointed past Matt and aimed at the fallen Box T man's cronies.

"Drop the guns, boys, if you want to stay in them saddles. Next one won't be in the air." The blacksmith's voice followed his gun barrel to the chests of the Box T riders. Matt stood up and looked behind him. Two of the Box T men had their guns halfway out of their holsters. Pointing his own six-gun at the one named Patch, who had dismounted, Matt grabbed the man's shirt and yanked him about roughly. "Which one of you cowards shot Emily Langer?"

"What are you talking about, mister? No one shot that lady," the visibly frightened Patch answered back.

"The hell you didn't, why I ought to—"

"Hold it right there, cowboy, don't move!" The sheriff yelled out his orders as he approached the spot where the commotion was going on. Roy Tanner followed behind the lawman with his gun drawn.

"Put that scatter gun up, Dewey. You ain't the law hereabouts. I am," the sheriff commanded.

Dewey lowered his shotgun, but it was still pointing in the direction of the Box T riders.

"What's going on here?" the sheriff barked.

"This troublemaker sucker-punched Lucky when he wasn't looking, sheriff," Wallace spoke up.

"Lucky was just funnin with this feller, sheriff, and he hit Lucky without giving him a chance to defend hisself," Wallace finished.

Wallace and Red got down off their mounts and stood next to Roy Tanner.

A woman on the boardwalk called out. "That's not true, sheriff," she said. "These men were trying to trample this man between their horses. He had to grab that big man to save his own life. I saw it all from right across the street by Doctor Mason's office."

"Why don't you mind your own business, Miss Loren? I'm sure the sheriff can handle the law in this town by himself," retorted Roy Tanner.

Matt glared at Roy Tanner who was talking to the blond-haired lady who had just spoken up for him.

"I don't see no badge on you, mister," was Matt's reply as he sent a chilling look into the eyes of Roy Tanner.

"All right, calm down, everyone. You Box T men get Lucky over to the Doc's. He ain't goin' to make it there by himself." The lawman gave the order through gritted teeth.

Lucky had been trying to get his legs under him since the sheriff had arrived and was finally having some success with the help of the hitching rack. His side was aching from Matt's punches and the fall from his horse. He knew he had cracked some ribs—he'd done it before being thrown off wild broncs.

His blood-smeared face was swollen, and his eyes were tiny slits covered with pain.

The sheriff spoke sharply to Matt. "You come in my office, mister. You got some listening to do." Matt followed the sheriff into a small building next to the restaurant. Roy Tanner followed even though Matt objected. The sheriff ignored Matt's protest. A worn desk near the back of the room guarded a hall leading to three empty cells. A barred window let a stream of dust-filled sunlight through. The sheriff sat at a cluttered desk, one leg of which had been replaced by three bricks. He spoke to Matt, asking him who he was and where he was from. The sheriff looked uncomfortable with the conversation. "Now listen here, cowboy, I don't want no trouble in this town. Maybe you ought to head outta here." The sheriff looked up at Matt who was standing in front of him rubbing his sore right hand. Matt's return look didn't agree with the sheriff.

"Sheriff, it ain't me shot that lady lying across the street in Doc Mason's office. If she dies, how are you going to hold your head up?"

Roy Tanner sent a warning Matt's way. "Don't go accusing anybody, boy. You could wind up in the middle of something you can't handle."

Matt turned to him, a look of loathing on his face. "I ain't interested in your barking, Tanner, and, like I said before, I don't see no badge on you."

The sheriff slapped his hand on the desk, cutting into the quarrel with a loud whapping sound. "That's enough, both of you. I let whoever I want into this office, cowboy. Now take care of your business in town and move on."

Matt left the sheriff's office just as Doc Mason was crossing the street. "Hey, Matt, are you all right?"

"Yeah, Doc, my hand's a little swelled up, but I'm fine."

"I heard you'd been taken to the sheriff's office. I was coming to help if I could. Come over to my office I want to talk to you."

"What's wrong, Doc, is she okay?"

"Emily's holding her own. Her color is a little better. I'd say she has a good chance now."

"Then how 'bout talking over some food, Doc. I'm starving. In fact, I was just heading into the German's when this ruckus started."

"Well, I just finished doing what I could for that no-good you beat up. I guess I could use a bite too. Let's go."

"Good, Doc. But first I have to thank Dewey. He probably saved my life today."

The two new friends walked into the livery barn where the smithy was working on the right rear hoof of a beautiful palomino stallion.

"I want to thank you, Dewey. You saved my hide back there," Matt called out to the man who had backed him earlier.

Dewey turned and looked at Matt. "It's little enough after what you did for Emily. I'd sure like to hurt that Box T bunch a lot more."

Matt was tempted to tell Dewey of his plan to do just that, but thought better of it. "Well, often enough trouble finds them that's looking for it," was all he said. "The doc and I were just going to get something to eat, how 'bout joining us?"

"Thanks, Matt, but I promised I'd finish shoeing Beth Loren's horse. She likes to ride every afternoon. That was her spoke up to the sheriff for you."

"That was brave of her to risk gettin' mixed up in that ruckus. I have to thank her too. That feller Tanner didn't seem to like her too much."

"That's because Beth and her sister Alma refused to sell their land to the Tanners and sold it to Emily's father instead. The doc knows the sisters well, and I'm sure he can tell you more about that than I can."

Doc took a timepiece from his jacket pocket and looked at it. "C'mon, Matt, I'll tell you about it while we eat. I don't want to stay away from Emily too long. See you later, Dewey." Doc Mason waved to the smithy.

The German's place was a small room with six tables and a counter that sat another eight people. The smell of coffee was strong in the air, and the warm aroma of pies baking in an oven also contended for space in the room's atmosphere. The tables were covered with clean, red-and-white-checkered tablecloths. The room was shabby but clean. All of the tables were empty, and the two men seated themselves at the nearest one. A large window gave them a view onto the street. Doc looked out at the busy street as he spoke. "Looks like things are coming to a head around here, Matt. This town's been walking on eggshells ever since Roy Tanner showed up and started throwing his weight around. He's been using his brother's ranch as a lever to get what he wants. The Box T is a big spread, and George Tanner spends a lot of money in Red Wall. In fact, he had a lot to do with the railroad stopping here. But a lot of folks didn't mind the way the town was when it wasn't as busy and had less trouble from some of the Box T hands, especially lately."

Matt looked up from his menu. "Well, Doc, folks got to stand up for themselves when they're being pushed around. Most of these townsfolk have probably been in a few battles either in the War Between the States or with Indians or stickup gangs on the way out here. Why don't they send this crew packing?" Matt's face was showing some color as he asked the question; his right ear was the color of a tomato.

"It's not that easy to get them all worked up at the same time anymore, Matt. Most of these people have put everything they have into their businesses and small spreads near town. And the Tanners are very clever about how they work their schemes."

Matt nodded his head. "I guess you got a point, Doc, but how they could let Tanner's men hoorah that poor girl like that, I won't never understand."

The two men continued talking through their meal, and Doc let Matt know he was ready to take on the Tanners whenever Matt gave the signal.

"Thanks for the offer, Doc, but I think it'll be safer for the town if I play this hand myself for now. Besides, you swore to help people not shoot them."

Doc tapped a knuckle on the table and answered Matt. "We have medicines now that kill germs and save good folks, but sometimes bad folks need a dose of lead medicine. I'm convinced now that this town waited too long to deal with the Tanners. But shooting that poor girl down is the last I'll stand for from them. You just remember there are lots of good people in this town who'll back you when the time comes."

Matt turned from looking out the window and looked at Doc. "I'll keep that in mind, Doc. Now I think I better get out to Emily's place and keep an eye on things."

Matt paid for their meal, said good-bye to Doc Mason, and went to get his horse at the livery. As he walked through the large open door, he saw Dewey talking to the woman who had taken his part with the sheriff. He hadn't realized before just how attractive she was. She was almost as tall as Dewey, but slim. She was wearing buckskin riding pants and a cowhide jacket. Her hair, honey colored, lay down across her shoulders and folded softly around them.

"Hello, ma'am, my name's Matt Benton, and I'd like to thank you for speaking up for me to the sheriff."

Beth Loren turned toward Matt and looked him over with a smile. "That's the least we can do for you, mister, after what you've done for Emily. Maybe the folks in this town will finally get their backs up straight and do something about those murdering Tanners. My name's Beth Loren, and, if there's anything else I can do for you, just let me know." The smile returned.

They sure are sisters, Matt thought as he realized how much this woman looked like the woman he'd seen earlier at Doc Mason's office. *This town certainly doesn't lack for pretty womenfolk who have courage.* "Thanks, ma'am. There just might be something you could do. I'd appreciate it if you could convince Emily to stay in town when she's back on her feet—at least 'til this trouble with the Box T is settled. Doc say's he thinks she's going to make a full recovery."

"I'm sure Lee will insist she stays with my sister and me until she's 'completely well,'" Beth said, with a wink at Matt, emphasizing the last two words. "Don't worry about Emily, cowboy. She's safe for now. Watch your own back—real carefully. There's nothing the Tanners wouldn't do to get what they want. And they want that land real bad. They were always sending some of their herd onto our land to graze even though our dad objected. That's why we wouldn't sell to him," Beth explained.

Matt tipped his hat. "I'll keep that in mind, ma'am. Thanks."

Raven whinnied in the back stall, and Matt went to him. "All right, boy, let's get you saddled, and we'll be on our way."

13 Emily's Place

Matt said good-bye to Beth Loren and Dewey and rode out of town. Once again he felt the eyes of Sheriff Brock and Roy Tanner on his back as he rode past the two men. He rode at a fast trot back to his camp on Emily's land.

The campsite looked unchanged since he had left it earlier that day. Matt unsaddled Raven and walked carefully around the site looking for any signs of recent visitors. There were no hoof prints nearby other than those of Raven.

"Doesn't look like they're on to our camp as yet, boy. I guess we're good for the night."

Matt realized he was talking to his horse just as Emily had talked to Anna Goose. A strong mixed feeling of sadness and anger came over the young horse rancher who had seen too much of both. After seeing to his horse, Matt made a small fire and put some coffee on to cook. He sat down by the campfire and wrestled with the events of the day as the stretched purple sky of late afternoon gave way to the shadows of dusk. The firelight blazed brighter as night took over the world. Settling into the same spot he had shared the night before with the pretty farm woman, Matt thought of her fighting for her life in Doc Mason's office. *They're not going to hurt her again,* was his last thought as he finally drifted off to sleep.

The night stretched on as bullets crashed around him and horses with wild red eyes and foaming mouths tried to stomp him with razor-sharp hooves. Matt woke several times to shake the nightmares out of his sweaty, cold head. Each time he fell asleep, more danger awaited him. But, when the bloody, torn body of Emily Langer was thrown on him from a rearing stallion, he woke to hear himself scream in fear for the first time in his life. Matt sat up in his bedroll and remembered his father's advice of long ago: When a monster scares you, boy, make a plan to chop its head off. And then follow your plan 'til you scare the bejeebers out of that monster. Matt did just that. That settled, he fell into a peaceful few hours of sleep.

Matt woke to a warming sun, just rising on his side of the hill. The orange light spread over the trees, somehow making them green and pushing off the morning haze. *Jacob Langer picked a beautiful estate to leave to his daughter,* he thought, as he looked around. The land was lush with vegetation, and the soil was the color of wet coffee beans—and rich for planting. The damp earth had a pungent aroma. With plenty of trees for protection from the north winds, this was a perfect spot for a family farm. He would see to it that Emily got to enjoy this place.

Carefully teasing the embers of last night's fire, Matt managed to set some small pieces of kindling to blazing. Warm coffee and biscuits would be breakfast, and then he would check on the farm buildings. He could move the newborn calf and her mother down to the Mullers' farm for safekeeping. The rest of the farm animals—the chickens and goats—could fend for themselves for a while. Dewey would take good care of the mules.

With Emily and her animals safe, the farm buildings would become Matt's big concern. Most of Emily's favorite possessions were stored at the Muller farm and should be safe there. Matt opened the large barn door to a warning bellow from the new mother. She and her calf had been locked in the barn for two days and wanted to feel the sun. Matt released them to the yard and watched for a few moments as they settled into a nearby patch of fresh grass. For the next few hours, Matt removed all the hay from the barn as the big black horse followed him around nibbling on any that fell to the ground. The buildings were solidly built with heavy timbers and logs. Free of any dry hay, and with the soaking they had gotten with the recent storm, they would still be damp enough to discourage any hastily started fires.

Matt finished his work in the barn and moved over to the cabin where he boarded up the back window and cut a heavy board to fit the front window. He cut a gun port in the board through which he could fire if he were attacked, and he started nails in all four corners of the board and set it near the window, ready for quick installation. He made sure to put some heavy timbers nearby that he could use to secure all the doors. He loosened two floorboards near the wall of the house, on the barn side. He picked up the floorboards and took them outside Then choosing a shovel from a selection hanging on the barn wall, he began to dig .When he was finished there were two crawl holes: one from the house and one from the barn. Both emptied out into the space between the two buildings. The space was usually dark, so he should be able to get in or out of either building without being seen. He covered the holes in the alley with the planks from the house. Only fool's luck would alert any Box T men to the purpose of the scrap lumber lying in the alley between the house and barn—he hoped.

The whinnying of a horse brought Matt's pistol out of its holster and his senses to full alert. Crouching low, he worked his way toward the front of the buildings. Molly and her calf were looking to his right. *That's where the trouble's at,* he thought. He backed away and moved to the rear of the buildings and peeked around the corner. Seeing nothing there, he moved around to the side of the cabin the cows were looking toward. As he neared the far corner of the house, he stopped at the sound of a walking horse. He heard only one horse. *Where are the others?* he wondered. Matt knew that the type of men he was dealing with wouldn't face him alone. The hoof beats became faster and closer; he had no time think. Ducking low, he sprang out from behind the house and looked up at Beth Loren's palomino. The horse was rider-less and hunting the freshly moved hay it smelled. Cantering over to share the bounty with Matt's stallion, the horse had Matt's attention.

"Hey, cowboy."

Matt turned to the sound quickly, and with gun pointed. He faced Beth Loren. Expressions of fear were painted on both their faces. Beth Loren knew how close she had just come to dying, and Matt knew how close he had come to killing her.

"Don't shoot!" she yelled.

Matt pointed his gun up in the air and released his breath. Then he slowly lowered the hammer on his six-gun. He was once again reminded how dangerous things had become. He certainly wouldn't want to shoot this woman, but he knew she was less than a finger's twitch from being dead.

"Miss Loren, I'm sorry," was all he could manage to say.

Beth was clearly shaken; her dark brown eyes were wide with fright. She slowly lowered her hands, which she had instinctively raised when Matt had pointed his gun at her. A nervous frown grew on her face. "It's my fault for not shouting out my arrival, Matt. Please don't blame yourself."

They smiled uneasily at each other and moved over to where their horses were feeding. Beth rubbed Raven's neck and spoke to Matt. "I used to ride out this way often to visit Emily, but, for the last few months, she's asked me not to come. I thought she wanted to be alone to grieve her father's passing, but I guess she didn't want any one else to be in danger. We have to help her, Matt. You must let her friends help."

Matt had been watching their horses feed on the hay. He turned toward Beth. "Maybe later. It's not time yet. I have a plan I think will stop the Tanners—without bloodshed. That's Emily's wish," he said.

Beth looked up at him, her slim hands on her hips. "Do you need any help here?"

"No thanks, ma'am, I'm finished here for now. I'm just going to bring her cows down to the Mullers' place where they'll be safe."

Beth started toward the horses. "I'll ride with you, if you don't mind. I usually ride Lady several times a week, but with the stormy weather lately, we haven't gotten our exercise, and I haven't seen the Mullers in a while."

Matt looked at her and a slow smile moved on to his face. "Okay, but you should start back early, I don't think it's safe in this area after dark."

The Mullers were pleased to have company, and especially relieved to hear the good news that Emily should recover from the gunshot wound. "We haven't seen you in a long while, Miss Loren, please sit down. I'll get you both a cool drink," Norma, Burge Muller's wife, said.

Burge Muller, a rawboned man hewn from hard work, placed a heavy hand on Matt's shoulder. "C'mon outside, son, we'll let the ladies catch up on the town gossip."

Burge pointed to a worn rocking chair with a tartan pillow on it. A woodpecker tapped noisy chatter on a nearby tree. Sipping the cold apple juice provided by Mrs. Muller, the two men sat on the front porch. Burge pulled on his corncob pipe and let the sweet-smelling tobacco smoke out as he asked, "What's been going on over there at the Langer place? I thought I heard gunshots from time to time, but Emily kept telling me she was shooting at wolves. With these woods that separate our properties, we're kinda isolated from each other. If that damned Box T spread has been hoorahing that girl, they oughta be run outa this territory." Burge slapped the arm of his chair for emphasis.

Matt could see the genuine concern on Burge Muller's face as he asked about his neighbor. He also saw steel in the old man's eyes. "Yes, sir, they have been shooting up her place for some time now, trying to get her to sell. I guess they figured, if they scared her enough, she'd cut and run. I may be to blame for getting her shot; I started giving them some of their own medicine the last few days. I reckon they got mad and took it out on her. She's safe now, though, and the Doc's gonna make sure she stays in town for a while."

The elder man looked at Matt and spoke up. His voice reminded Matt of a tree falling.

"Well, you just let me know when you're ready, son. I can still shoot pretty good, and I ain't never liked either one o' them Tanners much. George figures he settled this territory all by hisself. I'll give him he done a lot, but others did their fair share too. And the other one's nuthin but a lazy lout, near as I can see."

"Thanks, Burge, but I got a plan to make them leave her alone without killing anyone. That's what Emily wants."

"Well, you just remember you got backup here whenever you need it. And any help you need you'll get from the missus and me."

"I'll remember that, Burge. But, for now, taking care of her belongings and her animals is a big help. We better get Miss Loren on her way. I want her to get to town before it gets dark."

"Sure thing, Matt. Just remember what I told you—and watch your back." The two men stood and shook hands.

Their good-byes said, the two riders left the Muller farm at a quick pace. The afternoon sky had turned gloomy, and it looked as if some bad weather was on its way.

"We'll stop at Emily's farm for a few minutes, Miss Loren, and then I'll see you home."

Matt had decided it would be past dark before Beth could get home, and being with her longer wouldn't be unpleasant.

"That won't be necessary, Matt. I know this range very well, and I'll be fine. And please call me Beth."

"Okay, Beth, but I insist on seeing you home. I just have a small task to do at Emily's, and then we'll be on our way. Please don't argue with me."

"Very well. I enjoy your company, Matt, but I do ride out here 'til late in the day, very often getting home after dark."

Matt shook his head easily. "I just don't think that's a good idea now with the trouble that may be brewing on this range."

They rode up to the farm property in the creek bed that ran along the side of the house. The men moving about near the cabin didn't see them.

"Whoa," Matt's hushed instruction was for Beth Loren as well as the two horses. "Someone's by the house," Matt whispered as he pointed to the empty building.

He signaled Beth, and they both dismounted and crouched down low by the creek bank nearest the house.

Matt whispered, "It looks like three of them, and they're sure not up to any—" The word "good" was drowned out by the crash of glass as one of the intruders broke the front window.

An orange-red flame appeared from the barn side of the house as one of the men came into view with a burning rag in his hand. Matt's gun was in his hand and spitting out its own flames before Beth Loren had time to shout, "Stop that, you cowards!" which she did say, even as the cowboy next to her was firing his pistol and moving toward the big black horse.

"Easy, boy," Matt consoled his horse. "I just want to get my rifle."

Raven stood still and let Matt draw his Winchester from its saddle scabbard. The Box T rider known as Wallace managed to throw the burning cloth into the house through the broken window before one of Matt's wild shots zinged past his ear. Grabbing his ear, he ran to join his comrades who were already racing for their horses.

Matt had not fired for effect when he drew his handgun; he just wanted to stop the arson attack on the cabin. Now, with his Winchester in one hand and his reloaded pistol in the other, he fired both weapons as quickly as possible. He wanted the attackers to think they were up against several guns, hoping to scare them off. He didn't want to get into a long gun battle while Beth was with him. He'd gotten one woman shot already. He also wanted to get into the cabin as quickly as possible and put out the fire, which was now glowing through the broken window. Wallace, still holding his ear, reached the spot where his partners were waiting for him. Red, the youngest of the trio, was holding the horses. "They must have a posse over there. They was waitin' on us, Wallace, we better get outta here now!" He was screaming over the sound of three guns.

Beth Loren always carried a pistol in her saddlebags (for just such emergencies, she would later explain to Matt), and she was firing it now with a steady hand. The Box T men had been caught completely off guard by the heavy gunfire as soon as they approached the house with the fiery rag. Not being able to think of a better plan, Wallace hollered, "Let's ride!" And the three spurred their horses into a wild run toward the Box T.

As the riders galloped out of sight, Matt ran to the farmhouse and looked in through the broken window. A small flickering flame was trying to ignite a cot near the wall. Matt raced around to the space between the buildings and removed the boards that covered the hole he had dug earlier. He crawled through on hands and knees and was inside the cabin and stomping on the fire when he realized Beth was beside him, her small boots stepping on the flames that had jumped to a rug lying on the floor. "You sure do draw lightning, Matt," she said.

Matt smiled at her and said, "I suppose so." It made him think of his trail boss, Dick Stomer, warning him, "Matt, whenever a man stands tall he's likely to draw lightning to himself." Mr. Stomer was a smart man, and Matt had learned a lot from him. He'd kept his promise and written to Stomer after he bought the Cross River Ranch. The two men had continued to correspond ever since. It might not be a bad idea to write to him now and ask for some suggestions. That thought had crossed Matt's mind a few times in the last few days.

"Well, it looks like there's no serious damage, Matt," Beth said, as she looked around the smoky gray interior of her friend's house. Daylight had long since given over to dusk, and what light the fire had provided was gone.

"I guess not," said Matt, "but, if I hadn't forgotten to put this board up over the window, there might not be any."

"Stop blaming yourself for what's going on around here, Matt. This problem has been with us for some time now, and a lot of folks have been turning their backs to it. Besides, if you hadn't forgotten that board, we might not have stopped by here on the way into town," Beth chided him.

Matt turned toward the woman who was trying to make him feel better and started laughing.

"What's so funny?" a very puzzled Beth Loren asked looking up at the laughing cowboy.

"Your face is all smudged with soot, and your clothes are covered in mud. I was just thinking about how you're going to explain this to your sister." Matt reached over and tried to remove some dirt from her cheek, but he only managed to spread it more, causing him to laugh even harder.

"You're not sparkling clean yourself, mister. Your face is dirty too."

Beth then reached up and wiped the soot off of Matt's chin. Embarrassed by the touch of the lovely woman, Matt turned toward the hole in the floor. He knew his face was red, and, even though the light was dim, he didn't want to chance being teased about it.

"We'd better be going while there's still some light."

"Are you afraid of being in the dark with me, Matt?" A large grin spread across Beth's soot-blackened face.

Trying to ignore the last remark Matt said, "I'll put this board up, and then we can go."

It was Beth's turn to laugh this time. Matt was glad it was dark in the cabin. He knew the back of his neck would be red. The nails were hard to find in the dimmed light, but, after several minutes, he pounded the last one into the wall. But then the room was completely dark.

"Over here, Matt, follow my voice." Beth had moved over to the tunnel while there was still some light in the room, and now she was guiding Matt to it.

14 Taking Beth Home

Outside, Matt finished covering the hole in the ground again. The evening sky had cleared some, and a distant half moon was offering a thin glow of light to see by. The two horses seemed to be getting along well, sharing the hay Matt had moved away from the barn earlier. Matt's low whistle brought Raven out of the shadows, and the Palomino followed him.

"That's a trick you'll have to teach me, Matt." Beth said the words with a tease in her voice, causing Matt to cringe at the thought of this beautiful woman being able to see his face now. He pulled his hat low on his head and quickly stepped up into his saddle.

"I know the way, Matt, so I'll take the lead if that's all right with you," Beth said as she mounted her horse.

"That's fine," Matt said, grateful for the time to compose himself. The first few miles were on flat ground, and, with the light from the moon, they were able to travel at a good pace.

Nearer to town, the terrain turned rocky and the trail twisted several times, slowing their travel.

Almost an hour after full dark, Matt saw the dim yellow lights of town.

"Here we are, Matt." Beth turned in her saddle to tell Matt they had arrived at Red Wall just as he noticed the lights.

They rode slowly down the main street. Most stores were dark out front with some lights showing in the back or upstairs where the proprietors lived. A piano tinkled in one saloon, and a drunk came stumbling out of the other one, called the Three Eights. "Probably named for a fictitious hand of poker that the owner claims to have won the place with," Matt thought aloud. The drunk started retching in the street, drowning out the sound of the tinkling piano.

"That's what the railroad has brought to Red Wall." Beth twisted around in her saddle so she could talk to Matt. She turned forward again and kneed her blond horse to a gallop, pulling up two streets down at the last house on the right, where she waited for Matt.

"This is my house, Matt. Please step down and come on in."

It was the biggest house in town, and looked very well kept. *These sisters must be from a wealthy family*, Matt thought. "Oh, some other time ma'am," he said. "I know you're tired and probably want to get cleaned up. Thanks for the offer though."

"This time I'm insisting, cowboy. I know you're hungry, and we cook up the best supper in this county. So don't argue with me. After dinner, we'll see about finding you a place to bed down. You look like you could use a good night's sleep, and you couldn't find Emily's place in the dark anyway."

"Hi, Miss Loren. Can I put your horse up for you?" The young man, Alley, had been watching the two adults since they rode into town at the top of the street. He stepped out of the shadows that hovered in the area between Beth's house and the house next to it.

"Please do, Alley, and Mr. Benton's horse too. When you're finished, come inside and have some supper." Beth stepped out of the saddle and handed her reins to the boy.

Matt would learn later that the young boy often slept in the Loren sisters' hayloft, especially when the weather was bad. On very cold nights only, he slept on a cot in front of their potbellied stove in the back room of their house. The sisters always left the back door unlocked for him, and they had a standing offer to Alley to stay with them until he was grown. He was a proud boy and always insisted on doing chores to earn his food and some spending money.

Three years earlier, the boy and his parents had been traveling west by wagon train when his parents became ill. The train camped outside Red Wall, and Alley and his parents were brought into town and left in the care of Doc Mason. The train waited two days, then headed west again, leaving the boy in care of the town. His parents died four days later, and the eleven-year-old boy was left an orphan. All the folks in town took a liking to the young boy and helped him when they could. Lately, it was usually Alley doing the helping—working with one of the town folks to mend something or bringing in game for Helmer to butcher for his restaurant. Dewey had taught the boy to shoot, and, for the past year, Alley had returned from hunting with a white-tailed deer or a wild turkey almost every week. Dewey lent him a pony for his hunting.

Matt knew the argument was lost and dropped down off Raven. Handing the reins to Alley, Matt warned him. "If he gives you any trouble, let him go. He'll stay nearby."

"And you can whistle for him when you need him, right, Matt?" Beth Loren was smiling broadly, perfect white teeth in the middle of a big grin. Matt Benton had met his match, and he knew it.

"You win, ma'am. I'd love to stay for supper."

Matt followed the young, shapely woman into the living room of the well-furnished home. A large book cabinet and a sofa filled one wall, while a table and six high-backed chairs stood in the center of the spacious room. Standing by a grandfather clock in one corner of the room was Doc Mason, a goblet of amber liquid in his left hand. His right hand wound the brass stem that kept the clock's hands in motion. Beth didn't seem to be surprised by his presence. Doc looked twice at Beth before realizing the condition of her clothes. "What on earth has happened to you, Beth? You look like you fell into a mud hole."

"A whole lot has happened today, Lee. We'll talk about it after I get my guest cleaned up and fed. You know Matt, don't you, Lee?"

Doc, grinning, pointed to a door in the back of the room. "Yes, I do. Come on, Matt. I'll show you where to wash up." He turned to speak to Beth. "Your sister's upstairs, she's... uh, looking for something, I think."

Matt thought the doctor looked uncomfortable with his explanation of what Alma Loren was doing upstairs. He was in his shirtsleeves and looked as if he was normally very comfortable in these surroundings. "How's Emily, Doc? Has she woken up yet?" Matt asked.

"Yes, she's even sitting up and eating. She's plagued with a terrible headache though. Hopefully that'll go away when all the swelling goes down. Meanwhile, I have some medicine that helps her, and, fortunately, she sleeps well. But tell me, what happened to you two?" Lee Mason's face looked rightfully concerned. He led Matt to a guestroom in the back of the big house. An cast-iron, potbellied stove filled the back wall, and an empty basin stood on a nearby shelf. Doc picked up the basin and walked outside to a pump in a small shed. Matt followed him. Doc began pumping water into it. When it was near filled, they returned inside, and Doc turned to Matt. "Here you are, Matt, and there are towels and soap right next to the stove."

Matt started washing and began to tell the man he'd met two days ago about the day's events.

Alma Loren was sitting in her bedroom in front of a mirror when her sister went upstairs to wash and change her clothes. She heard Beth's steps on the stairs and called to her. "Is that you, Beth?"

Beth stuck her head in the room. "Yes, Alma. I'm sorry I'm so late. I hope you weren't worried. We had a bit of a problem out at Emily's place."

"What kind of problem, and who were you with? Come in and tell me about it."

When her muddy and disheveled sister came fully into the room, Alma jumped from her chair and dropped her hairbrush on the floor. "What happened? Are you all right?"

"I'm fine. I actually had an interesting adventure. I went riding over to Emily's to see if there had been any damage to her house and if I could fix things up for her before she went home. I met that fellow who brought her into town the other day—you know, Matt Benton—and he was moving Emily's cows down to the Mullers' farm for safekeeping…"

Beth continued telling her sister of the afternoon's events while cleaning up and changing clothes. She also spoke of the courageous young man who had recently come to their town.

"He's downstairs now, and I promised him a good supper, so we have to get down to the kitchen and prepare a hearty meal for him."

"I have a roast cooking now. Lee is going to join us for dinner. There is more than enough for one more."

The sisters walked down the stairs together to find the men deep in conversation, each with a drink in hand. The doctor turned first. "Well, you look a little better since we last saw you, Beth." Lee had a good sense of humor, and both sisters enjoyed his company.

Matt thought, *This gal can wear riding clothes or fine dresses and make them all look good. She's as pretty a woman as I have ever seen.* Beth had changed into a new dress that she had never worn before, and only she and her sister knew the importance of that.

"Well, I see Lee is entertaining you, Mr. Benton. I'm Alma Loren, Beth's sister, and I want to thank you for bringing her home safely. Please feel at home. We'll be serving dinner in a few minutes."

Alma turned to Beth, "Come on, sis, we have work to do in the kitchen."

Matt stopped staring at Beth and looked at Alma. "I know, ma'am. I saw you at Doc's yesterday. Thank you."

The sisters walked into the kitchen.

"They're something to look on aren't they, Matt?" asked Doc. "And they're as nice on the inside as they look on the outside. They've both helped me in my practice—delivering babies, bandaging wounds, and sometimes just holding someone's hands when they've lost a loved one. I don't think I would stay in this town if it weren't for them. And they treat that boy Alley like he was their brother, when he lets them," Doc said.

"He's a tough little poke, I'll say that for him," Matt offered.

Alma returned to the room bearing a large platter filled with meat and potatoes. "Dinner's being served in a minute. Will you tell Alley to come in, Lee? He's out in the barn caring for Matt and Beth's horses."

"Sure thing, Alma." He turned to Matt. "I'll be right back."

Doc put his drink down and went to the back door. Alma set the platter down on the table. A few seconds later, her sister arrived with another dish laden with mixed vegetables and bread and set it on the table next to the meat platter. "Can I get you a drink, Matt?" she asked.

"No thanks, Beth. That food looks so good, I want my stomach to have plenty of room for it. Can I help you with anything?"

"No thanks. We'll be ready to sit down in a moment."

Matt heard a door close in the back of the house, and soon Doc Mason and Alley came into the room.

"That horse o' yours is a handful, mister, but he sure is a special animal."

"Did he give you any trouble, Alley?"

"At first, but I got a way with horses. Dewey taught me a lot about 'em. He knows more about horses than anyone I know. Yep, he sure does have a way with them."

Matt knew his own knowledge of the four-legged beasts was pretty good, but he always appreciated anyone else who had an understanding of them as well.

The ladies returned to the room with a pitcher of water and five glasses and set them on the table. "Please, let's be seated gentlemen," offered Alma.

"You don't have to ask twice, Alma," Doc replied.

Moving quickly, Matt moved behind the chair Beth was near and pulled it out. When Beth sat down, he helped her move in toward the table.

"Thank you, Matt."

"You're welcome, ma'am."

"I thought you were going to call me Beth."

He grinned. "You're welcome, *Beth*."

Alley had been faster than Doc Mason, and he was the one who received Alma's thanks for his good manners.

"You're welcome, Miss Alma. Can I say grace now?"

"You must be awful hungry, Alley. Go ahead."

The young boy clasped his hands together and bowed his head. The adults followed suit. After the short grace, there was some small talk and several questions to Matt about his horse ranch and his past. He answered some and avoided others. They also talked of the current goings on. They ate their meal as quickly as any meal that had been served at that table, and both sisters were gratified by the compliment.

"I wish I had a ribbon to present to you ladies," said Matt. "That meal was excellent. Thank you both."

"I second Matt's opinion," announced Doc.

"Me too, Doc," Alley added.

"Why don't you men go into the parlor and smoke? We'll join you after the dishes are done," Beth said.

"I'll do the dishes, Miss Beth," said Alley. "I don't smoke anyway."

"Well then you just relax, Alley," said Beth. "You helped enough by putting the horses up."

The parlor was a smaller room behind the kitchen, with an entrance off the dining room. A single step down led onto a brightly carpeted floor. A piano filled the back wall, and a small heat box stood against the opposite wall. A settee and four cushioned chairs were placed about the room. Doc lit a thin cigar. He offered one to Matt who refused. The two men and Alley sat and talked generally for a while about horses and such, and Matt asked again about Emily.

"I do think the worst is behind her, Matt. But we'll just have to wait and see after the swelling goes down completely. Her appetite seems fine, and that's always a good sign. She's a very strong gal, and I expect that's going to help her get better.

Mrs. Kerstin is with her now—a fine woman, who also helps me out at times."

"Are you talking about Emily?" Alma walked into the room while Doc was talking and asked the question.

"Yes. Matt was inquiring about her condition, and I said I think she'll be okay."

The elder Loren sister looked at Matt and said, "Emily is lucky you happened along when you did, Matt. There's no telling what those Box T outlaws would have done to her if you hadn't helped her."

Matt wasn't so sure that was true. He was the one who had advised her to fight back. And now she was lying over at Doc's office with a serious bullet wound. Everyone in the room was looking at the young horse trader, and they all could easily read his face.

"You can't blame yourself anymore, Matt. You did the right thing." Beth had followed her sister into the room, and, if those in the room looked into her face when she spoke, they would have seen a different kind of concern on it.

Doc took a puff of his cigar and spoke. "Beth's right, Matt. Kicking yourself isn't going to change the situation now. By the way, I wired the district marshal's office today, and we should get word soon. Meanwhile, let us help you keep the Box T from doing any more damage to Emily's farm."

Matt had accepted a drink from Alma and now put it down.

"No, Doc, I have to do this alone for now. First, I just want to know who shot her and settle that score."

"I don't know, Matt... taking on that Box T gang by yourself will be awfully dangerous."

"I know, Doc, but sometimes it's easier and safer if the only ones in a fight are the main targets. Besides, I think my plan may work best this way. And I'll have a lot of help in reserve if I need it."

"Just don't wait too long to ask for it," Beth volunteered.

"I won't," Matt assured her. They shared a look.

The evening continued on with more questions about Matt and talk about the situation concerning Emily. Two hours later, Doc Mason stood up and stretched. "Well, I'm going to check on my patient and relieve Mrs. Kerstin. Good night all. Thanks for the wonderful meal, ladies. Matt, do you have a place to stay tonight? I can fix up a cot in my office for you."

"That won't be necessary, Lee. Matt will sleep in the spare room." Alma spoke with her arms folded across her chest looking directly at Matt. "I won't take no for an answer, Matt. You deserve a good night's sleep."

Lee knew there was no arguing with her when she stood that way. If this young stranger wanted to try, good luck to him. He was going home to see to his patient. Doc waved goodnight and walked out the door.

"Thank you, Alma," said Matt. "But I figured I'd bunk in the barn with Alley, if it's all right with you?"

"No, it isn't all right. Alley is just stubborn. You need a good night's rest once in a while if you're going to be out riding all day."

"Better do as she says, mister, or you won't sleep at all tonight."

"Hush, Alley. You get along to bed now, and we'll see to Mr. Benton."

"Yes, ma'am. Goodnight, Miss Alma and Miss Beth. Goodnight, sir."

The three adults answered as one. "Goodnight Alley."

Matt knew that what Alma said was true. If he was going to continue this fight, he'd have to rest as much as possible—when he could. The spare room that Beth led him to was already prepared. The covers on the bed were turned down, and a coal oil lamp burned on a dresser by the bed.

"Goodnight, Matt. Pleasant dreams."

"Goodnight, Beth. You too."

For a while, Matt could hear the two sisters moving about doing their household chores and preparing for bed. He could hear their voices, but not what they were saying. Then sleep closed the day for him.

Matt woke the next morning to the sound of someone whistling softly in the next room. He could tell immediately by the brightness in the room that he had slept later than usual. He could also tell that the sleep had been very beneficial to him. His mind and his senses were sharp. The welcoming aromas of frying bacon and brewing coffee wafted into his room. He not only smelled the food, he could hear it cooking. The whistler was moving about while whistling a popular tune. He heard the words in his head: "Buffalo Gals Won't You Come Out Tonight." The whistling continued in a low, pleasant tone. Matt thought about Beth's comment the day before when she'd said that he could teach her to whistle. He didn't know why he was so sure it was her whistling and not her sister Alma, but he was.

After pulling on his boots, Matt stomped into them a few times adjusting the fit and letting his hostesses know he was up.

"Matt, come out and have some breakfast when you're ready. There are shaving supplies and a mirror by the pump." The whistling had stopped and Beth was now calling to him.

"Thank you," was Matt's reply as he opened the door and headed out to the back shed that housed the water pump. The water was cold as he splashed it onto his face. Looking into the mirror, he saw a three-day-old beard that needed the attention of a sharp razor. He also saw Beth Loren standing in the doorway watching him. "I hope you slept well, Matt. You don't seem like a man who normally sleeps so long into the day."

"You're right about that. That good food and soft bed made me into a tenderfoot, I suppose."

"Well, I'm sure that won't last long."

"Was that you whistling before?"

"Yes, did I wake you?"

"I guess. But I haven't been woken up so nicely in a long time."

"Do you think I could teach Lady to come to me when I whistle?"

"Yes—and anyone else I expect." A small smile rolled across Matt's face and settled in his eyes.

Turning her back to him, Beth said, "Your breakfast is waiting. Come in as soon as you're ready."

Matt could see a slight reddening of her ears. *Two can play this game*, he thought.

As he walked to the kitchen, Matt saw the front door open. Alma walked in and told Matt she had just come from visiting with Emily. "She's doing much better! She's walking around and getting fidgety. It's going to be hard to keep her from going home soon. Once she takes a mind to it, she'll be difficult to stop. Emily asked me to ask you to stop by, Matt. She's anxious to talk to you."

"I'll do that, but you ladies must convince her to stay in town—somehow. She's still going to be in danger until this disagreement is settled once and for all."

Beth Loren had been standing by the kitchen door for the last few minutes, a troubled look on her face. Now she returned to the table where she had Matt's food set out. "We'll do our best, Matt, but you have to be real careful too. Meanwhile, come and sit down before your breakfast gets cold."

After eating breakfast, Matt thanked the sisters for their hospitality and promised to let them know how his plan was working. He told them he would stop by Doc's to see Emily and then pick up his horse, if that was all right with them.

"That will be fine, Matt. And don't forget to let us help you when we can." Alma opened the front door for Matt.

15 Lucky's Story

A commotion of some kind was causing the people in the street to look up toward the north end of town. Walking past the Three Eights saloon was a tall, reddish-brown horse. A rider was barely hanging in the saddle. Matt, still standing on the Lorens' porch, saw Alma's eyes squint and her brow furrow as she looked past him into the street. He turned and took in the same sight everyone else was seeing. His right hand checked the pistol on his hip and he started running to the injured rider.

Even before he grabbed the reins of the sorrel, Matt noticed the stream of blood sliding down its neck and across its chest. *This rider's been shot bad,* was Matt's first thought. And he was right.

"Who is it?" one of the onlookers asked.

"Can't tell yet—can't see his face," another onlooker shouted.

Matt could tell who it was without seeing the face, just by the size of the man. It was the man he had fought with a few days earlier—the Box T rider named Lucky. Looking up, Matt saw one puffy, blood-red eye open in a gray blue face. Matt could almost feel the pain etched in the man's face. This was a man fighting death and winning only because of his stubbornness.

The lips in the pain-carved face moved, and a guttural whisper spoke to Matt, "You're just the hombre I want to see." Then the man passed out.

"Call the Doc, quick, and someone give me a hand!"

Matt's command was answered by a familiar voice. "I'll get his feet. One of you gawkers help Matt with his shoulders." Dewy began to lift the man from his horse, then he turned down the street and yelled further instructions: "Alley... hurry!" Dewey had been coming out of the general store when he'd seen Matt running. Fearing he was in trouble, Dewey ran to Matt's aid. As he'd neared the scene, he'd seen the bloody rider and realized Matt was trying to help the man. Alley, who had been one of the first to see the horse and rider, was already running up the street to Doc Mason's office.

When Alley burst through the door of the doc's office, he saw a startled Emily Langer turn toward him, alarm on her face. "Sorry, Miss Emily, I didn't mean to scare you. Is Doc in?"

"Right here, what's the matter, Alley?" Lee Mason had been in his private office when he heard his front door bang open. Fearing for Emily Langer's safety, he'd rushed out to the outer office. He stood there questioning the breathless youngster, a Colt .45 clenched in his right fist.

"Doc, a man just rode into town. Looks like he took some lead. He's bleeding something bad. Mr. Benton and Dewey are fixin' to bring him here."

Doc Mason returned to his office and called over his shoulder. "Alley, go tell the Loren sisters. I'll need some help." Then he turned to Emily. "Emily, I need you to return to bed right now; you don't need this kind of excitement. Please do as I say."

Doc put the pistol in a desk drawer and locked it. Emily stood near the door, her arms folded. "Doc, I'm feeling much better, and I'm tired of lying around all day."

"Please, Emily, now!" Doc spoke urgently as he passed her on his way to the treatment room. He began selecting the instruments he figured to need.

"Oh, all right—but I'm not going to stay put much longer." She headed back toward her bed in the treatment room.

"Thank you, Emily." Doc Mason began to prepare for his patient.

Getting the big man off his horse was a difficult chore. Len Swelder, a wide, beefy cowboy from one of the small outfits west of town, jumped in to help Matt and Dewey. All three men tugged at the bloody clothing of the Box T man until he finally fell from his horse. They stopped him from completely falling into the street, but the move was far from graceful. With Matt and the cowboy holding the upper half of his body and Dewey holding his legs, they started toward Doc Mason's office.

After alerting the Loren sisters, Alley ran back to the men. "What can I do, Dewey?"

Dewey was struggling to hold on to the listless body. "Get the man's horse, Alley. Get him to my barn and take care of him." Alley took the reins of the now-skittish horse and began to turn him toward the stables, but the horse was scared. He reared up, shrieking, and his flashing hooves barely missed the men who were carrying Lucky. Alley pulled on the reins with all the strength he had, all the while talking soothingly to the horse. The boy finally calmed the horse and led him down to the livery.

Doc Mason was holding the door open as he directed the three men carrying the wounded man into his office. "Put him on that cot, men. I'll look at him there." Doc pointed to the far wall of the waiting room and the cot he had set up there. Working as gently as possible, the three men set the injured man down. As Matt was moving away from the cot, his right arm was caught in a vise-like grip. The huge fist of the injured rider held Matt's arm from moving. "Stay put. I rode a long way to talk to you. Tell these others to leave," Lucky's raspy voice demanded.

"See here, this is my office and you're my patient. You'll do as I say," Doc ordered, as he began to cut away the man's bloody shirt.

Lucky looked past him at Matt and said, "Doc, there ain't nothin' you can do for me. I'm finished. But, before I go, I got to square things up about that lady getting shot."

"You do look in grave shape, mister, but I'm a doctor and I can't let anyone just die without trying to help. You're in no condition to argue—you might not have much time."

The door to the treatment room opened suddenly, and Emily Langer entered the waiting room. She looked at the wounded man and seemed overtaken by a sense of apprehension. She folded her hands together and leaned against the doorjamb, her eyes focused on her tormentor.

"Doc, please put him in the treatment room, I'll stay in your office."

Doc looked at Matt then back to Emily. "Very well, Emily, but you must go in there now and stay there."

"All right, Doc," Emily answered even as she was opening the door to his office.

"Okay, men, let's pick up the cot and carry it into the room on the right," Doc said. The room Emily had been staying in contained an operating gurney and a bed, along with the other necessary furniture. The gurney was prepared with a fresh sheet, and the bed was made up with fresh linens as well. The four men managed to get the cot with the heavy-bodied man in it next to the operating table. Working as one, on Doc's orders, they placed the man on the table. With the man on the table, Doc spoke to the three men. "Thank you all very much. Now please wait outside and send the Loren sisters in as soon as they get here."

Once again the big hand of the wounded Box T man caught Matt's arm. "You stay, pardner. I got to talk to you right now. That girl's still in danger." The voice was getting weaker, but the words gripped Matt's insides. "I don't have much wind left so listen close." Lucky grimaced as he said the last words.

In a stumbling pattern filled with gurgling coughs and grunts of pain, the gravely, whispering voice told his story: "Late yesterday afternoon Roy showed up at the Box T and went into the main house where George was. We could all hear them shouting at each other. They was in one of their worst fights yet. For the last few weeks they fought each time Roy came out to the ranch. Some time later, Roy came out and told Wallace to take a couple of men and burn down the Langer place. He usually gave me those jobs, but he knew I was still stove up from the beating you gave me. The three men left, and soon after Roy settled down to play poker with some of us, as he often did. About an hour or so later, the three of them rode into the yard like the devil was chasing them. Wallace told Roy that a posse was waiting on them at the Langer farm and nearly killed them all. He showed Roy a knick taken out of his ear. Roy jumped up and turned the card table over. He grabbed Wallace by the shirt. 'So you didn't burn down her house?' he screamed at him. Wallace said he didn't think they had, but he did manage to throw a burning rag through a window.

"Roy let go of Wallace and went out into the ranch yard. He walked around a bit, then he came back into the bunkhouse and offered five hundred dollars to anybody who would kill that Langer woman. He said he didn't care where she was, he just needed her dead."

The wounded man coughed a few times then wiped his mouth and continued.

"Most of the men looked at him like he was crazy, but Wallace said he'd finish what he started for that much money. I didn't know it was Wallace that shot the woman, but then I remembered him going back to the farm alone to get something to ride after you set us afoot the last time." The large man coughed again, the pain of the exertion carved on his face. He struggled to continue, "He must have had a hide-away gun on him. I went up to him while he was saddling a fresh horse and told him he was one of my men and I didn't want him killing no woman. We got into arguing about it, and I knocked him down. I thought it was settled so I turned away, but he came up pulling his iron and put two bullets in me before I could go for my gun. I sat down there at the corral, and some men came to help me, but Roy told them to leave me be. I was done for anyway, he said. When Wallace rode out, I dragged myself onto my horse and started for town. I heard Roy tell the men to let me go. He said the buzzards would pick me clean—save them from digging a hole for me. They were George's men and didn't care for me and my men no how. I must of passed out a few times on the way. Once, I woke up hanging onto the saddle horn and my horse was grazing on some grass. I musta slept for a while." Lucky grimaced, closed his eyes, and opened them again. "Anyway, that's how I ended up here. You got to protect that girl." He coughed painfully again. "Wallace is going to kill her if he can."

Matt was leaning over the big man listening intently. "Why does Tanner want her dead now? After just trying to scare her for so long." Matt wanted to know.

"Scaring her was my idea," said Lucky, his voice becoming weaker. "Roy wanted to kill her from the beginning. I didn't want to hurt no woman, so I convinced him to let me scare her off. Said it would be less trouble in case the law got involved—even though he knows the sheriff will back him when he takes over the abandoned farm… whether she runs away or gets buried on it. I think he killed the girl's pa and turned the wagon over on him to make it look like an accident." Lucky's eyes were closing even as he spoke.

Matt looked at Lucky; he was confused. "Roy don't seem to be a real cowman, why does he want her property so bad?"

"He thinks there's gold on the land where that stream comes out above ground. Talk is, he has some big investors back East. I heard him talking to George about it once. Sounds like they gave Roy a goodly amount of money up front and he lost it gambling. Talk is, these fellas that gave him the money ain't used to being the ones stolen from." Matt thought Lucky was through speaking, but Lucky had a question. "She kin to you, mister? Why'd you get involved?"

Matt was still digesting Lucky's story, but he answered him. "I got a strong hate for bushwhackers, and I don't think much of men who pick on defenseless women."

Lucky's face twisted in pain. "I don't either, mister," he said through another coughing fit. "But you got to believe me when I tell you I was trying to save her life in my own way. I ain't a good man, mister, but I ain't no snake neither."

Matt looked down at the man he had learned to hate. "Well, I reckon there's some truth in that, Lucky. You showed some courage in what you did to help her. Don't worry, I'll take care of the lady and finish what I started. The Tanners have got an awful lot to lose, and, one way or another, they're going to be sorry they started this trouble. Now, let the Doc work on you. He's a pretty good doctor, and you're a tough hombre. When you're better, I'll have an honest job offer for you on my ranch." Matt patted Lucky's shoulder and stepped away.

From the treatment room, they heard the door in the outer room open with a whooshing sound. Footsteps clattered across the wood floor, and then soft taps on the treatment room door announced the arrival of Alma and Beth Loren. The two sisters had been tending their garden. It hadn't taken them long to wash up and head over to Doc's office.

Beth was the first one to enter the room and asked the questions as she walked toward the men. "What's happened, Lee? Who's been shot now?"

Doc Mason, head down, was busy tending to the injured Lucky, so Matt spoke up. "It's one of the Box T men, the man called Lucky, and he had an interesting tale to tell."

"Beth, I'll need some probing tools and swabs, first, then plenty of bandages," Doc instructed.

"I'll get them, Beth, you stay and help Lee." Alma had followed her sister into the room and was already gathering the items the doctor had asked for.

Doc looked up at Matt, his hands covered in blood. "Matt, there's not much you can do here, and we'll need the room. Will you wait outside please?"

"Sure thing, Doc, but let me know if he has anything else to say."

"He's unconscious now, and he's lost a lot of blood. He won't be talking for a while, if at all."

Matt left the room and closed the door behind him. The door to Doc Mason's office opened at the same time, and Emily Langer stepped into the waiting room where Matt stood. He looked at her closely for the first time since he'd brought her to town. The bandage on her head was clean and almost covered one eye. The dark purple bruise spread from her eye down to her chin, but her face seemed less swollen. "What's happened, Matt? Is this more trouble concerning my farm?"

"I'm afraid so, Emily. That feller in there is the man who was leading the raids on your spread. The one named Lucky." Matt continued talking to Emily for almost an hour, telling her most of what had happened since she'd been shot. He finished by asking her how she was feeling.

"Oh, I'm fine now, but Doc wants me to stay nearby so he can check on me for a while. I'm real anxious to get home, though, and I want to see my animals."

"Well, considering what Lucky just told us, I'm pretty sure you should stay in town for a while longer. You'll be much safer here until this trouble is settled. Dewey has your mules, and the Mullers are taking good care of the cows. Beth Loren and I stopped by there yesterday."

Emily pressed her lips together and blinked slowly. There was a silent moment, and then she spoke. "I don't like others doing my fighting for me, Matt. I have to hold that land for myself if I'm to be worthy of it."

"We all need help at times, Emily. Some problems are just too big for one person."

"But you're taking this on all by yourself, Matt, and I can't let you get hurt for my sake."

"Emily, these are the same kind of skunks that killed my pa. They want what don't belong to them, and they don't mind killing good people to get it. I'll have help when I need it— I'm confident of that. Meanwhile, it looks like they're getting desperate, so it's important that you stay out of sight. There are plenty of good people in this town who'll help us if need be."

Matt and Emily talked a little while longer. Emily looked toward the room where a man lay near death… a man who had been harassing her. "I hope he makes it. He doesn't seem to be such a bad man after all."

Matt nodded his agreement. He touched Emily's arm and said good-bye to her. He went out into the street where a light rain was beginning to fall.

16 Sending for Help

Matt crossed the street and made his way to the train depot. He peered through the empty telegrapher's window and found the man dozing in a chair, his feet propped among the papers on a messy desk. Matt had to speak several times to rouse him. "Hello! Hello!"

"Yes, sir," said the sleepy man, yawning. "What can I do for ya?" He blinked several times and finally looked awake. He uncurled his legs, rubbed sleep from his eyes, and combed his long stringy brown hair back with his fingers. Finally, he approached his small window and looked directly at the stranger.

Matt leaned on the red-painted board that served as a counter. "I need to send a telegram." Matt recited the words he wanted sent over the wires and paid the man. He told the telegrapher he would stop in later that day for his reply from Orville. Even though the man told him that might be too soon to expect an answer, Matt knew that Mr. Hubbleman, the key man at the Colorado Flats telegraph office, would make sure his message got out to his ranch as soon as possible. And he was sure Orville would waste no time sending his answer. Matt then headed over to Dewey Harmon's livery.

Despite the soggy weather, the large, barn-like building was alive with the business of the day. Dewey was removing a horseshoe from the fire and dipping into the cooling bucket of water nearby. The sizzling smoke from the process filled the air. A chestnut gelding stood between Matt and the smithy and slurped water out of the bucket that hung in front of him. Matt walked over to stand in front of Dewey. The smithy looked up. "Hey, Matt, how's that gunman doing?"

"Doc says he don't have much of a chance, but he was still working on him when I left a few minutes ago."

"Well, Doc Mason don't brag on himself much, but he's a pretty fair sawbones when need be."

"I hope so. I think this Lucky fella might a been trying to do the right thing in the wrong way."

"Huh? What are you getting at, Matt?"

"Well, when you finish shoeing that horse, maybe we can sit down somewhere and I'll fill you in. We gotta talk about protecting Emily too."

Dewey wiped his hands on the worn apron hanging around his waist. "Okay. Give me ten minutes. Why don't you make yourself comfortable in my quarters back behind that door?"

Matt turned and looked in the direction Dewey was pointing. A small, heavy door was situated by the back wall, almost out of sight. Matt walked to the door and walked into a well-kept kitchen area. A table and two chairs stood in the center of the room; a potbellied stove and a small cook stove stood against one wall, and shelves against another. Wood planks covered the floor, in contrast to the rest of the building, which had dirt floors. Matt sat in one of the chairs and started shuffling a deck of cards that was lying on the table. A few minutes later, Dewey came in. "Bring me up to date, Matt, while I heat some coffee for us."

Matt shuffled the cards again. "Well, you know that this fella that rode in all shot up is one of Tanners' gunmen—the one I had the fight with. Seems he objected when Roy Tanner talked about murdering Emily. Another gunman named Wallace got the drop on him and cut him down…" Matt then went on to tell the town's smithy the rest of Lucky's story. "So we're going to have to find a safe place for her to stay," said Matt, finishing up his tale. "The Doc's office will be the first place they'll look."

"And next will be the Lorens' home, if they're as determined to kill her as Lucky says they are," Dewey offered. "Emily's going to have to be well hidden so they can't find her."

Dewey got up to pour their coffee, and Matt looked around the room. "Where do you sleep?"

Dewey set the coffee down on the table. "Right in there," he answered, pointing to another solid door at the end of the room, just past where the cook stove was. Matt couldn't see it from his seat, so he stood up and walked past the other man to the door that was along the same wall as the stove.

"I built that room when I first took this place over. There's nothing behind it outside but thorny bushes. You couldn't get near it without losing most of your hide," Dewey said, chuckling. "Are you thinking the same as me? But would she be willing to stay here?" The livery owner looked at Matt with doubt on his face.

"We'll have to ask Emily," Matt said. "It sure would make a good hideout for her. We could sneak her over here at night."

Dewey continued with the plan, "She'd have a ready gun hand near her all the time. The Loren sisters are always in and out of here, so it won't be suspicious if they come over to visit with her."

Matt added, "We could get Doc to fix a small bandage on your arm—kinda make it look like you hurt yourself. Then he could come over to check up on you—and Emily—whenever he wants."

"Good idea, Matt. I'll get the room tidied up right away just in case you can talk her into staying here."

Matt looked at Dewey and shook his head. "Not me! I'll leave that up to the doc or the Loren sisters. Maybe we could make the move tonight?"

The men drank their coffee in silence, each thinking through his next move. Matt put his cup down and wiped his mouth with his hand. He stood up and thanked Dewey once again for the coffee. "You're more than welcome on my next drive, Dewey," he said laughing. "Coffee like that would keep a man working sun-up to sun-down!"

Dewey smiled. "Thanks. What's our next move, Matt?"

"Well, while you prepare for Emily's visit, I'll see if Doc can arrange the move. Then I'm going to give the Tanners something to think about besides killing Emily. Make them worry about protecting their own property."

Dewey sipped at his coffee and said, "Be careful, Matt. And don't worry about Emily. We'll take good care of her."

"I know that, Dewey. Keep a gun handy, but don't make it obvious. The trick is for them not to be able to find her."

Matt left the stable and headed for Doc Mason's office. The townspeople were moving about in their normal routine, and nothing seemed out of place. A buckboard rumbled up the soggy street laden down with farm goods for sale. The rain was turning the dusty street to mud. Matt entered the waiting room of Doc Mason's clinic and knocked quietly on the door to the treatment room where he had left the doctor working on Lucky an hour earlier.

"One minute," Beth called out softly.

A slow minute went by before Beth walked out and spoke to Matt. She was drying her forearms and hands with a white towel. A small, stray lock of hair lay across her forehead. She brushed it back with the back of her still-damp right hand.

"He's a very strong man, Matt, and Doc thinks he has a chance if he makes it to morning. Do you think they'll really try to murder Emily, right here in town?"

Matt looked directly at Beth. His eyes joined hers in worried thought. "Yes, I do. From what Lucky told me, that Roy Tanner is awful desperate. He may have borrowed money from some tough customers to get Emily's land. And they might be expecting payment in full—soon. Anyway, I'm glad you're still here. I have a plan to hide Emily, but I'll need some help convincing her to go along with it."

"Sure, Matt, what's your plan?"

"Well, I might as well explain it to you and Doc and your sister at the same time."

"All right, let's go into the treatment room. We were just cleaning up. Lucky's asleep, and Emily is busy in Doc's office doing some paperwork for him."

The two stepped into the treatment room as Lee Mason and Alma Loren were stepping away from each other.

"Matt, have you found out any more news?" Alma asked the question as she brushed her hands over her apron.

"No, but I want to talk to you all about a plan to protect Emily."

Doc Mason rolled down his sleeves. "Go ahead, Matt, we're listening."

Matt looked at the wounded man and then back to Doc. "Let's go in the other room so we don't bother your patient."

In the waiting room, Doc walked to his front door and locked it. He turned back to the group, his back to the large window that looked out onto the street. "Go ahead, Matt," he said.

Matt laid out his plan to them, explaining along the way why he didn't think it would be safe for Emily to stay at the doctor's office or in the Lorens' home. He then explained more of his plan in detail. "The way Dewey told it to me, there's only one way into his rear quarters and that's through the front. He doesn't think anyone even knows he built the room in the back. And, since he's always there anyway, everything'll seem natural, and no one will suspect he's protecting Emily. You'll have to make the move tonight. I'll find Alley before I leave town and send him over to tell Dewey to expect her."

Doc Mason stepped away from the window. "Whoa, everybody. Let's talk to Emily first. She's going to have to agree to this plan."

"You're right, Doc, and that's where you come in. Good luck!" Matt smiled and gestured with a wave of his hand for Doc Mason to go and confront his stubborn patient.

Matt walked back into the treatment room and looked over to the table where the Box T gunman lay with his eyes closed. His chest was rising and falling slowly, but his face was still a sickly grey. "Good luck to you, big fella," he said. Matt walked back out the door, said good-bye to his friends, and kept going out through the outer door as well. He took one look back and saw Doc Mason walking into his private office.

The rain was still falling, and the town looked dreary. Matt looked up the street. A few horses stood at the hitching rail of the Three Eights saloon, their heads hanging down, wet tails flicking idly at some invisible flies, as they waited for their owners. Two of the horses looked familiar to Matt, and he walked over to them. *Box T sure enough,* Matt thought. *I wonder if that Wallace is in there.*

17 A Challenge to Wallace

Matt looked through a dirty window as he walked to the entrance to the saloon. He pushed open the swinging doors and took in the place with a quick glance. It was typical of most saloons. Dirty sawdust covered the floor, a small stage held a piano, and several card tables were strewn loosely about the room. A large, baldheaded, red-faced man tended the bar. His hands were too small for his size. A few men sat at several of the tables, some playing cards, others idly gossiping—about Lucky's arrival in town, Matt was sure. He didn't see the man he thought was Wallace, but he recognized the man he had strapped to his saddle and sent down into Tanner's yard. Lucky had called him Patch. He was sitting with another man who could have been with the ambushers at Emily's farm, but Matt couldn't be certain.

Patch watched Matt enter the saloon, and fear gripped his stomach immediately. He knew this was no man to go up against alone, and he didn't intend to go against him ever—even with backup—if he could help it. He kept his eyes down looking at a spot on the whiskey-stained table between him and his companion. Matt knew he'd get no information from Patch—at least not in front of others—so he ignored him and kept looking for Wallace. Satisfied he wasn't in the room, Matt leaned on the bar and asked for a beer. The big barman placed a schooner of the golden liquid in front of Matt and took his payment.

"You seen Wallace today?" Matt's question was directed at the barkeep, but it shouted in Patch's ear. Patch couldn't help reacting. His face looked ashen as he stared at the tall man at the bar.

Matt turned and looked down into the scared eyes of the man he had sent home from Emily's farm tied to his horse. "How 'bout you, pardner? You know Wallace, don't you?" Matt's right hand was on the pistol in his holster. *Sometimes frightened men do stupid things,* Matt was thinking. *Hopefully he'll go tell Wallace and force him out in the open. I'd rather have him concentrating on me than Emily.*

"I ain't seen him in a while, mister. But this'd be the place to find him when he's in town." Patch surprised himself with the tone of his voice. It had much more bravado in it than he felt. But, Matt's grin quickly chilled the Box T rider. Patch knew this man in front of him could easily kill him without losing his smile.

"Run along and tell him I'm looking for him. Tell him I want to know if he can shoot at a man who's looking at him."

"Sure... sure thing, mister, I'll tell him." Patch was speaking even as he was getting up from his table. He banged one of the table legs with his knee and stumbled sideways, knocking over a chair on his way to the door. Without looking back, he flung the two swinging doors apart and rushed out into the street. His companion—Porter, another Box T rider—got up slower and followed Patch out of the saloon.

Looking back at the still-swinging saloon doors Patch stepped into the stirrup of one of the waiting horses. The two men had hoped to wait out the rain in the saloon before heading back to the ranch. A cold wind had picked up that didn't help Patch's spine feel any more comfortable. The other Box T rider was an older hand who had hired on with George Tanner to tend his herd and didn't like getting mixed up in Roy Tanner's schemes. Sitting their horses, they moved away from the hitching rail. Porter shouted across the wind to Patch. "You better stop in at the doc's and flat-out ask if Lucky's gonna make it. That's what Roy sent us to town to find out, and we better have some kinda answer for him when we get back."

The news of Lucky's arrival in town all shot up had been brought out to the ranch by one of the town loafers who knew Roy Tanner would be interested to know about it. *There might be a nice reward for such a piece of information*, he'd thought.

Knowing the man would just take the few dollars he gave him and get drunk, Roy Tanner sent Patch and Porter into town to find out about the wounded Lucky. After they arrived in town, Patch told Porter he was going to get some tobacco and then meet up with him in the saloon.

Patch then slipped down the alley alongside the doctor's office and peeked in a window. The shade was drawn nearly all the way down, but he could see Lucky was alone. He quietly tapped on the windowpane. When no answer came back, he pushed the unlocked window up several inches and called for Lucky.

"I'm here, Patch, but I'm too tired to talk."

"Okay, Lucky, just listen to what I got to say." He told Lucky that Roy Tanner knew he'd made it to town and that Wallace was in town and was going to be given the news by the sheriff. "You know he's going to try to finish the job. He's also bound and determined to kill that Langer woman. Here's your gun Lucky. I brung it with me in my saddlebag." He tossed the pistol onto Lucky's bed. As he closed the window, he whispered, "Good luck, pard."

Patch then met up with Porter in the saloon, where he would later be confronted by Matt.

The two men rode over to the hitching rail in front of the doctor's office.

"You go on in, Patch. I'll watch the horses." Porter spoke through the rain that was running off the front of his hat.

"Yeah, thanks for the pleasure, Porter. I'll be right out." Patch handed Porter the reins to his horse, walked up to the front door, and knocked twice. He hooded a hand over his eyes and looked in through the window; he couldn't see anyone in the waiting room. Patch opened the door and stepped into the quiet office. "Hey, Doc! Doc Mason!" he called out.

A door at the far end of the room opened, and Emily Langer walked into the room.

"The doctor's busy. What do you want?" she asked.

Patch was shocked and relieved to see who it was. He recognized Emily as the woman they had been harassing. He didn't want to believe he was involved in killing a woman.

"Ma'am, I just wanted to ask about Lucky, the man who was brought in all shot up."

"The doctor's still working on him, and he can't be bothered. I know they don't think he has much of a chance." Emily had no idea who she was talking to, but she figured it would be best, in case the man was from the Box T, that he thought Lucky was dying.

With a clicking sound, the door to the right opened. Alma Loren walked into the room and walked directly up to the Box T man. "What do you want here, to finish the job?" She spoke loudly in Patch's face.

"No, ma'am. Lucky's a friend o' mine. I hope he makes it. Does he have a chance?"

"Not much. Doctor's working on him as best he can. You'd better leave now."

"All right, but please tell Lucky Patch's still one o' his men. And I'm waiting for his orders. He'll understand." Patch didn't wait for an answer; he just turned and left the office.

Outside, Porter tossed the reins of Patch's horse to him. "How's he doing, is he gonna live?"

"Naw, not much chance o' that. Wallace shot him good. They just waitin' for him to die. Doc told me hisself. Let's go tell Roy."

The two men rode their horses at a slow gallop out of town, mud splattering up around them as they went. Patch's brow was knit tight in serious thought. He mumbled to himself, "I know Wallace will try to finish Lucky if he thinks he's gonna live. I gotta convince him Lucky's 'bout dead as he's gonna get... in case the doc brings him through."

Two men watched the Box T men ride out. Matt stepped out of the Three Eights saloon just after they passed by, and Sheriff Brock watched them through his office window across the street. After Matt watched them for a while, he walked along the boardwalk toward the other end of town. The sheriff's eyes left the two riders and followed Matt's progress down the street. The horse wrangler's long stride quickly took him out of the sheriff's view.

Matt looked around for the young town boy for a few minutes, then gave up and walked over to the Lorens' barn to get his horse. The boy was there, currying Beth Loren's horse. "Hello, Mr. Benton. I already done that big one of yours. He didn't give me no trouble at all."

"Thanks, Alley. Now I need you to do me another favor."

"Sure thing, sir." The boy tapped the two curry brushes he was using and watched the dust fall to the ground. Matt told the youngster some of the plan concerning Emily, and instructed him on the importance of secrecy in the matter.

"You can count on me, Mr. Benton. I know how to keep things to myself, sure enough."

"I know that, Alley, but I also need you to be real casual when you go over to Dewey's. I've already been there today, and I don't want people—especially the sheriff—to think something's going on over there."

"I understand, sir."

"That's good enough for me. I've got to ride out of town in a little while. Will you saddle my horse for me, please? I'll be right back."

"He'll be ready when you get back, sir."

Matt put his hand on the boy's shoulder. "Thanks, friend," he said.

Matt left the young man and walked down to the train depot. A train had just arrived, and some passengers were still climbing down onto the platform. The steam hissing from the engine hid others in a cloud of vapor. The same, sleepy man was at the telegraph keys, and Matt waited for him to stop sending a message before he asked about his reply from Colorado Flats.

"No, nothing yet, mister," the man told him.

Matt's forehead wrinkled at the answer as he thought about it. *It's only a short ride out to the ranch. And I know Orville would send the messenger racing back with his answer. I'm sure he'd understand my meaning—and know I needed his help.*

Matt's message had read: "Still in Red Wall. Need your backing. Like on our first train ride."

"Well," he told the telegrapher, "maybe Mr. Hubbleman couldn't get anyone to ride out and deliver my message yet. I'll stop back in the morning." Matt spoke even as he was walking away from the window.

Back at the Lorens' barn, his horse was saddled and ready to go just as the youngster had promised. Matt flipped Alley a coin and thanked the boy. He stepped into the saddle and patted Raven's neck. "C'mon, boy, we have some work to do," Matt whispered to his horse as they rode slowly out of town. Once out of view, Matt set the black to his normal fast gait. The rain had stopped. The afternoon haze was giving in to dusk, and the shadows were stretching into darkness. As night fell, he reached his destination.

18 Alley's Walk

"Okay, Alley you're as pretty as you're ever going to be," Beth Loren said as she finished tying a bow under the young boy's chin. She had helped him fit into one of her dresses, and now she was securing a large bonnet on his head. "Remember, keep it pulled low in the front and walk slowly over to Doc Mason's office." She was having a hard time not laughing out loud at the young man, but couldn't keep a smile out of her voice. "We don't want anyone recognizing you."

"Well, I sure don't want that either, Miss Loren. If anybody sees me like this, I won't be able to show my face ever again in this town."

"Don't fret, Alley. What you're doing is very brave and it may well save Emily's life. We're all very proud of you."

Alley shifted around nervously while Beth made final adjustments of her clothes on him.

"You're right, I guess. I just hope I can walk like you. Well, wish me luck, here I go."

With those words trailing behind him, Alley walked out of the front door of the Loren sisters' home and made his way across the lamp-lit street to Doc Mason's office.

It was still early in the evening, and a few townspeople were walking about. Henry Willard, the barber, was just closing his door and called out, "Good evening, Miss Loren."

Alley kept walking but remembered what Beth had told him and waved his white-gloved hand at the man. The glove was a tight fit on his growing hand, but it looked fine in the dim light. He didn't respond to the two cowboys riding by, on their way out of town, who said good evening.

In his office, Doc Mason had closed his curtains early and now waited. Peeking out of the corner of one curtain, he watched Alley's approach, a small grin on his face. As soon as the boy neared his door, he opened it

"Great work, Alley. If I didn't know the plan, I would think Beth was coming over to visit with Emily. Now let's get the rest of the plan underway. Go into my office and take off the dress. I'll tell Emily to get ready."

A few minutes later, the switch was made, and Emily was standing in the outer office with the two men.

"Thank you very much, Alley. I know you were probably embarrassed wearing Beth's dress in the street."

"Not just in the street. But if it'll help you stay safe, it was worth it, Miss Emily. Good luck."

"Thanks. I'll leave now, Doctor Mason, and I'll meet Alley over at Dewey's place."

"Okay. Dewey's waiting for you with those clothes of yours we sent over earlier. Stay out of sight, and I'll stop by tomorrow and see how you're doing. Remember—walk slowly with your head down. And, if anyone calls to you, just wave your hand and keep moving. Good luck."

Doc Mason held the door open and watched as Emily started her walk to the stables at the end of the street. The rest of the plan would have Alley, dressed once again in his own clothes, which he had worn under Beth's dress, scurrying through the backyards and wooded lots to the side entrance of Dewey's shop—hopefully unseen as he usually was. There he would once again put on Beth's dress and walk to the Loren home, making it seem to anyone watching some or all of the activity as though Beth had just gone to spend some time with Emily and then stopped in to the stable to check on some other business before going home. If all went well, Emily's true whereabouts should be known only to her few close friends.

"Well this is it, Emily. I hope you'll be comfortable here. I fixed the room up as best I could." Dewey had been waiting for Emily's arrival ever since he'd watched Alley walk over to the doc's office. Now, he was showing her around the back area of his business, where no customers were allowed.

"I'm sure I'll do fine. Thanks for all your trouble."

"No trouble at all, Emily. I'm sure you'll be safe here 'til we can get this problem fixed with them Tanners."

While Dewey and Emily talked, Alley arrived, changed back into the dress, and returned to the Loren home. Beth greeted the young man with a hug. "Alley, you were great! I never looked so good walking across the street. Is everything set at Dewey's?"

"Yes, ma'am. Dewey had everything ready. Miss Emily should be comfortable there for a while."

"Good, now let's hope Matt's all right."

Matt rode over the crest of a small hill and spotted the herd of cattle he had seen a few days earlier. They were settled in a small bowl-like park that emptied through a narrow valley into the vast prairie that comprised most of this country. When he had seen the prairie earlier, he had noticed the rich green grass and the stream running across it. This was Tanners' main herd, but he had only two men guarding it. Matt spoke quietly to Raven. "I guess Tanner's pretty sure of himself. He don't figure anyone will bother anything that belongs to him. Well, I guess it's up to us to let him know that times have changed. C'mon, boy. Let's ride down there nice and easy."

Matt nudged the big horse and trotted slowly toward the two outriders, who had met up for a chat. He drifted into the area where the men were sitting their horses. Keeping his head down, he shielded his face with his hat. After the rain had stopped, a slight wind had picked up and brought a bright half moon out of the clouds. It wasn't likely these drovers would know him, but Matt figured, if they saw he wasn't from their outfit, they might get cautious. He meant these men no harm.

The two riders, seeing a man approaching them so casually, cloaked in the evening gray, thought he was coming to relieve one of them early. Matt had drawn his six-gun earlier, and now had it in his hand, which was draped lazily across his saddle horn, with the gun away from the view of Tanners' men. When he was close enough to talk quietly to them, Matt pointed his pistol at them and ordered them to unbuckle their gun belts and let them fall. One of the men was Porter, the man who had been in the saloon with Patch. His eyes held Matt's for a while. A tough-looking cowhand with grey, intelligent eyes, he complained, saying, "I got no part in any of Roy Tanner's tricks, but George Tanner's paid me to watch his cattle for a long time. I ain't never let a cow get lost yet."

"I know how you feel, partner, but I got the drop on you, and there ain't no sense you dying for Roy Tanner's bad ways. I'm just going to scatter these dumb cows out into that valley yonder so you can spend a few days—with some help—rounding them up."

The man's eyes appeared to see the reason in what Matt said, and they changed from dangerous to understanding. "All right, young fella, but you know I gotta tell Tanner who you are."

"How do you know who I am, mister?"

"I was in town when you whupped that dog Lucky, and I saw you earlier today when you scared the beejeebers out of Patch in the Three Eights. But, like I said, I work for George Tanner—not that skunk of a brother of his."

Matt recognized the cowboy from the saloon earlier in the day. His lips pulled together and he said. "Don't be so sure how you judge that fella Lucky 'til this is all over. Now drop your gun belt and get off your horses and start walking."

The men did as Matt ordered and began walking toward the Tanner ranch. Matt slapped their horses and sent them running into the herd.

Moving back and forth behind the herd, Matt started the cows moving toward the valley that led to the prairie. He wanted to have them moving forward before he started them running. *It isn't as easy as some think to get cattle running*, he thought. *They're basically a lazy lot.* Once the herd was moving at a good pace, Matt started firing his six-gun at the bright silver moon. Waving his hat and hollering, he soon had a stampede going. "Har, har, gidyap! Har, har! Keep moving, you lazy steaks!" Matt was shouting at the top of his lungs. Galloping alongside the now thundering herd, he kept firing his pistol as he aimed the frightened beasts into the narrow valley. Their large, white eyes, wild with fright, reflected the light of the thin moon.

As the first of the herd reached the closed-in walls of the valley, Matt slowed down and got behind the cattle. In the valley, the night was black dark, the high walls cutting off the light from the moon. Matt holstered his pistol and drew his rifle from its scabbard. The darkness frightened the cattle even more, and the noise from their deadly hooves reverberated against the walls of the narrow valley into a thunderous symphony that sounded like falling mountains. The noise from their hooves drowned out the rifle shots; Matt stopped shooting and reined in the big black horse. The first cattle to make it through the valley started spreading out over the vast prairie in front of them. Out of the valley, the sky was lit with moonlight once again, but the sounds of the cattle that remained in the valley kept those already out of it running fast. Matt patted Raven's neck. "Okay, boy, we've done our job for tonight. Let's get to our camp and settle down. Tomorrow will bring more excitement, I'm sure."

The bright silver moon guided Matt back toward his camp. He moved through the woods high above the house and barn and surveyed Emily's property. There was no evidence of any further damage to the buildings. He concentrated on the area near his campsite. Matt and Raven quietly skirted the site where they had been bedding down and found no signs of disturbance.

"It looks like they ain't found our spot yet, big fella. I don't see any hoof prints or footprints that ain't ours. Let's get some rest while we can."

After he saw to his horse, the tired drover checked out his tent. *Don't want to lie down with any snakes or varmints in here*, he thought. His bedroll was damp and cool, but Matt settled in and finally slept until morning.

Dawn was a grey curtain lifting out of the black night. Matt had been lying awake for some time contemplating his next steps. He moved slowly out of his bedroll, listening carefully for any unusual sounds. The creek was continuing its rush over the smooth, slippery rocks that lay under its water. The gurgling creek and the wind blowing through the trees were the only sounds he heard. Thoughts of the last few days were flowing through his head as he was trying to figure out his next moves. Emily's safety was his first concern, and he wondered if his new friends in town had been able to get her into Dewey's room without her being seen. If that was successful, he could concentrate on protecting her home and property from the Box T crew.

Matt rode into Red Wall just before noon. He had spent the early morning hours scouting the Tanner ranch and its crew. For a while, he'd hidden by the fallen trees and watched a few men hanging around the main house, most likely waiting for him to attack again. Later, he saw most of the hands scattered throughout the plains gathering the herd he had stampeded during the night. Matt then followed a back trail Dewey had described to him earlier and entered town from the little-used road that led into town by the train depot. He crossed the tracks and walked his horse quickly into the alley next to the Loren home. He tied the reins to a post, walked around back, and knocked on the rear door.

Alma Loren opened the door before Matt finished knocking. She wiped her hands on the flour-covered apron she was wearing. "Matt, we've all been worried about you. Are you okay? Come in. Come in. I was just looking out the window for Beth and I saw you ride by."

"I'm fine, Alma. Where is Beth?"

Alma moved aside for Matt to enter. Matt stepped in and removed his hat. "Oh, she's just out riding Lady."

Matt looked concerned. "How did the move with Emily go?"

Alma smiled. "Oh, I think it went very well. I don't think anybody took notice." She went on to tell Matt every detail of how their plan had worked. "And even though poor Alley was embarrassed to death," she finished up, "he did everything we asked of him and performed real well. If I didn't know it was him I would have thought it was Beth walking around."

Matt told Alma about his doings, including the cattle stampede he'd started. He also told her that Emily's place seemed intact so far. "Now that I'm sure Emily will be protected here in town, I'll stay out by her place and keep watch out there."

Alma removed her apron and placed it on the back of a chair. She took a grey shawl from a wall peg and put it across her shoulders. "All right, Matt. But, before you go anywhere, rest up for a while and I'll get Doc Mason over here. I'm sure he wants to talk to you, and I'll make you some lunch. It won't look strange to anyone. Lee often has his lunch here."

Doc was just coming back from seeing a patient when Alma flagged him down in the street. She casually walked over to him and asked him to lunch.

"Sure thing, Alma, and I do want to talk to Matt," he said.

Doc put his horse up at Dewey's livery and checked on Emily while he was there. She seemed in good spirits, and her wound was healing nicely, he thought. He left after only a short visit, but promised to return later and bring Emily and Dewey up to date on what Matt had been doing.

Beth saw Raven in the alley and tied Lady next to him. She would put her horse up later. Right now, she was anxious to see Matt. Doc met Beth on the porch and walked in with her. Matt was sitting at the table deep in thought. Beth said hello to Matt and received a smile in return. She excused herself and walked into the kitchen. Doc sat down across from Matt. "I just visited with Beth," he told Matt, "and she's doing fine. Her headache is gone and so is the swelling on her face. She seems to be comfortable. I guess Dewey's doing his part real well."

Matt's face brightened. "That's good news, Doc."

"Yes, it is."

"And Lucky had a visitor last night. A friend of his stopped by," Doc said. He went on to tell Matt how he found Lucky's six-shooter on his bed. Lucky had fallen asleep soon after talking to Patch, and the gun was lying on his chest when Doc went in to check on him. When he woke up, Lucky told the doctor about his friend's visit and what he'd said.

While the men were talking, Beth and Alma put sandwiches and coffee on the table and sat down to listen. Both men reached for their coffee. Doc asked Matt about his recent activities. Matt sipped his coffee and then put his cup down. He started telling them about the events of the last night. "I think I gave the Tanners something to think about. I'm sure some of their men are still busy rounding up those cows! The way I figure, it will go one of two ways. Either they'll think it's not worth the trouble, or they'll show us just how desperate they are."

Matt had a strange look on his face as he said the next few words. "You know, Doc, I've been thinking—maybe it would be easier if we just killed that Lucky feller off."

"What!" Doc was obviously incredulous.

Matt chuckled. "Not really, Doc—just a pretend funeral. You could say he died and order a box. We'll fill it with stones and nail it shut. Then tomorrow you get a few people to take it out to the cemetery and bury it. That will at least give us one less person to protect."

Doc's face relaxed and he smiled. "That *is* a good idea Matt; I'll see it gets done." The two men returned to their coffee.

Beth, who had been out riding for several hours that morning, now told the small group sitting at the table that she had been out to the Langer spread. All three looked at her with stern looks on their faces. Matt spoke somberly. "Beth, didn't I almost kill you a few days ago when you were traipsing around out there? And you promised not to go out there until this is all resolved. You must stay away from there—all of you. I have to be free to shoot fast when I sense danger and not worry that I'm going to shoot a friend. There's plenty of work here in town protecting Emily, and you all have to be vigilant for any sign of trouble."

Beth looked down at the table and then at Matt. "I'm sorry. I don't want to do anything that would put you at more risk. I thought I could help, but I see your point. I won't go out there again 'til this is over."

Matt stood and looked at her, and raised his voice as he spoke. "You told me that before, Beth. I hope you mean it this time."

Beth looked back down at the table; her eyes were wet. Alma and Doc looked at Matt with curiosity at the young horse wrangler's stern rebuke of Beth. He had always spoken in a quiet, respectful tone. These last words to Beth had been like a slap to her face. Matt felt bad about his words, too, but he would rather hurt her with words now than with a possibly deadly attack later.

"Matt, can I see you outside please?" Doc Mason stood up and started for the back door. His face was hard, and his eyes narrowed as he said the words.

The two sisters stayed in the house, but could hear the men's angry voices coming through an open window. The words weren't clear enough to understand, but the women were sure the conversation was about Beth. The two men stood face to face, inches apart, intense looks on both faces.

"Doc, I just want to be sure she stays away from there. When this is all over, I'll apologize. Meanwhile, sometimes a sting is remembered longer than a few light words. I'm sorry, Doc, that's the way it stays."

"All right, Matt. I guess you're right. The most important thing is that she doesn't go out there while it's still dangerous. But remember, we're all a little nervous about this, and we're all trying to do what we can to help."

"I just don't want any of you hurt on my account, Doc."

"Funny, that's what Emily has been saying to you, Matt." Doc patted Matt's shoulder.

Matt looked toward the house. "Doc, I have some errands to run. Please thank the ladies for lunch for me." Matt untied the reins of his horse and started out of the alley. His first thought was to visit Emily, but then he thought better of it. *No sense in drawing any attention to Dewey's place,* he realized. *If anyone is watching me I might draw suspicion toward the stable.* Matt rode out of town the same way he'd entered and headed for Emily's farm.

The next morning was dull and overcast. A perfect day for a funeral, Doc Mason observed upon waking. Over coffee the day before he, Matt, and the Loren sisters had discussed the plan to "bury" Lucky. Doc had then filled in Dewey and Alley. All except Matt and Emily would attend the "funeral." Dewey was right on time with the wagon, and he helped Doc load the casket into back of it. Doc had hired two men to dig the hole the evening before. The funeral procession left town under the watchful eyes of the sheriff. Doc Mason had paid him a courtesy visit the night before to tell him of Lucky's passing. The sheriff didn't seem too sad, and, more importantly, he had asked no questions. Doc Mason and the rest of his acting cast were all properly somber. They marched behind the casket and watched it as it was lowered into the ground by the two men Doc had paid to dig the grave. Alma Loren led the group in a prayer, and they returned to town. Later, when she was asked why she'd attended the outlaw's funeral, Alma said, "Even the bad should have someone pray over them when they die."

Lucky, though still weak, thought the whole idea was very funny. "I wish I was well enough to attend," he offered when Doc Mason told him about his demise and funeral arrangements.

After the funeral, the group of mourners went their separate ways to attend to their daily chores. It was understood that they would tell no one else of the ruse, and Lucky would stay out of sight.

19 Wallace

Wallace rode into Red Wall the night after he shot his former partner, Lucky. He was determined to get the five hundred dollars from Roy Tanner for killing Emily Langer. As the dull afternoon dragged on, he was sitting in the room he'd rented above a small furniture and woodworking store, smoking a cigarette. He looked out the dusty, cracked window at the street below. The store was located on the same side of the street as the Loren home, so he didn't see Matt enter or leave. He'd spent most of the time since he'd arrived watching the comings and goings of the townspeople. Last night he'd seen the woman he thought to be one of the Loren sisters go into the doctor's office across the street. When she came out, she then went to the livery. This morning he'd watched Lucky's casket taken up to the cemetery. The sheriff had stopped by the night before and passed along the news Doc Mason had given him about Lucky being dead. "One less job to finish," he replied to the sheriff. And then forgot about it.

The night before he'd also watched silently as the young, yellow-haired kid moved quietly around the town, long after dark. "Why, that little scratch is probably peeking in windows," he mumbled to himself.

Earlier, Wallace had opened his door to get some air in the stuffy room and had overheard the carpenter's wife Sarah talking to him in the shop downstairs. Wallace's room was at the top of the stairs that led directly into the shop behind the store. "That woman that was shot musta got well enough to go home, Jesse. I just finished cleaning Doc Mason's place, and there ain't no one there but some old tramp, must be sick. I called out to her 'cause we usually talk some, but she didn't answer. And the clothes I cleaned for her were all gone." The woman stopped talking for a second and then continued. "Doc said the baby's doing fine, but he doesn't want me cleaning there anymore 'til after the baby's born. Said I already worked off more'n the baby will cost in a year."

The couple was expecting their first baby, and Doc had let her do some cleaning chores to offset the cost they would incur with him for her care and the baby's care. Though he'd have been happy to deliver the baby for free, the independent couple wouldn't hear of it. They had opened the store six months earlier when they learned they were going to have a baby. Jesse didn't want his wife to have a baby on the hard-scrabble farm they had been renting. "Town's the place for us now," he'd said, and his wife had agreed, tired of seeing her husband so worn out, and tired herself, from the sun-up-to-sun-down farm work. Jesse was a man of many skills. He had even been a lawman at one time, but that was their secret.

"They hidden her somewhere. Most likely right here in town," Wallace went on. "That Doc ain't goin' to let her go all the way out to her farm so soon. They got to get up earlier if they want to fool me."

As he listened from his upstairs room, the killer mumbled to himself; it was a habit he'd picked up in prison. He'd pay particular attention to Doc Mason, that meddlesome liveryman, and them two sisters. If anyone knew where that Langer woman was, they would. "Oh, and one other troublemaker…" he whispered as he nodded his head. The evening shade started drawing down on the dusty window glass.

That night, Alley was making his usual rounds. Most nights after the town got quiet, the young boy would pretend to be the sheriff. He'd patrol the streets and back alleys of the town that had taken him in and cared for him. He would make sure the doors were locked in all the businesses and no crooks were lurking about.

Alley was in the back of Doc Mason's clinic when a rough arm grabbed him around his throat and pulled him into the small stand of willows behind the buildings. The young boy was taken off guard, but fought back bravely to free himself. Only seconds from passing out, he managed to kick his attacker in the shins and break free. He was a tall boy without much weight, but he had long arms and big hands. He folded his left hand into a fist and struck out at his attacker. The punch caught Wallace by surprise, knocking the older man back. Alley then swung hard with a right hand, but missed. Wallace regained his composure and once again pounced on the boy and began pummeling him with his own, much heavier fist, hitting the boy in the body and face. Punch after punch rocked the boy's head back, his blonde hair flailing about like a dust mop being shaken out. Finally, Wallace knocked Alley to the ground and began slapping the left side of his head over and over. Only the bees stinging his ear kept

Alley from passing out. His whole face was swollen and sore, and his ear had been ripped by a ring Wallace wore. Every slap sent waves of torturous pain throughout his head. The young boy could barely see through his swollen eyes, but he could tell the man was talking to him. Finally the beating stopped, and the man grabbed Alley's shirtfront and pulled him close to him. "Where's that woman hiding? Where's that woman hiding?"

The man's breath stunk of stale whiskey and tobacco. The look on his face terrorized the boy, but Alley shook his head from side to side in answer to his question.

Wallace wouldn't give up. "You know where she is, and you'll tell me, you little street rat," the killer growled.

Wallace had left his room earlier and lain in wait for Alley. He had seen the boy involved with all the adults concerned with the Langer woman and figured he must know her whereabouts too. He raised his hand again as if to strike the boy, but Alley put his hands up to try to protect himself.

"Oh, you're still tough, are ya?" Wallace grabbed Alley's left hand and placed it on a flat rock that was lying next to the boy. Holding the boy's wrist, he kept the hand there and picked up a cragged rock, the size of a turnip. A sudden swoosh of night air was the only warning the young orphan had of the terrible pain that was coming. When the rock struck his hand, a stream of choking sobs burst through the boy's lips. Wallace pushed his forearm into the boy's mouth to silence him, but small grunts of hurt still seeped through. The rock smashed down on the boy's fingers again, and the pain tore apart what inner strength the boy had left.

"Where is she, where is she?" Wallace was somehow managing to scream at the boy while making very little noise.

The night had been mostly dark with cloud cover, but now a bright half moon broke through the clouds. For the first time, Wallace could see the boy clearly. Alley's face was a tortured mask of swollen eyes and lips. The lower portion of his ear was hanging against the side of his face. "You're a tough little bug, but you'll tell me."

Wallace saw something in the boy's look that scared him. It was death. But who's? Again, Alley heard the swooshing sound. Somehow, in the breath it took to feel the pain again, Alley was able to consider lying to his torturer. But he realized that, if he said she was in the Lorens' care or someone else's, he would only get them hurt too. This time the pain found a new place in the young boy's body, and he couldn't bear it. The pain in his fingers traveled throughout his veins to hurt the very blood in his body. "Dewey's livery," he blurted out.

"The livery!" Wallace congratulated himself.

Wallace stood over the boy, and the clouds rolled across the sky and stopped the moon from witnessing any more. He still had the rock in his hand, he flung it at Alley's head and walked away.

Lucky was lying in bed trying to think of a way to help Matt, but he knew he still wasn't strong enough. He heard a thump on the side of the building and then another. Straining, he managed to get out of bed, pull the curtain aside, and look out the window. The light from the room showed him a grotesque image. Only the yellow hair, now matted with blood, looked familiar. It was the kid they called Alley. He had been around often, helping the Doc and Emily Langer.

Lucky managed to open the window slightly and told the boy to go to the front door and come in. "I'll get the doc," he said.

"No, the livery, the livery, hurry! He knows, hurry! I'm okay. Go! Hurry!" The tormented face pleaded.

"Doc! Doc!" The big man was almost crying at what he had just seen as he screamed out for Doc Mason. And then he remembered the doctor was seeing a patient somewhere at the end of town. While he was hollering, he reached the table where his gun was. Not able to find his boots, he went out barefooted but with his gun tucked in his belt. "Good thing I told them I wanted to wear my pants and not that nightshirt they gave me." He laughed to himself as he reached the street.

Lucky had walked only a few doors down the street when the weakness and nausea took hold of him. The big man had to grab onto a hitching rail to keep from falling. He knew he had to rest, but he didn't have time. He started for the livery again.

Wallace had left the boy for dead and headed to the end of the street and the stables. "Damned urchin, givin' me so much trouble. I could be out of this town by now," he mumbled. The gunman cursed under his breath as he walked behind the buildings toward Emily Langer. A creaking noise and the slap of a door hitting its frame cautioned Wallace, and he froze next to a large crate behind the milliner's shop. A man walked out from an alley up ahead and went into an outhouse by the tree line.

"Shut the door you damn fool!" Wallace screamed to himself in silence. The man had left the outhouse door open and would easily see Wallace if he tried to get by. The gunman flattened himself against the box and waited. The man finished sooner than Wallace thought he would, and the sound of the door once more slapping its frame told Wallace he could be on his way again.

Wallace reached the rear of the barn-size building near the railroad tracks and started making his way through the bramble bushes. The thorns tore at his skin and ripped his clothes so he backed out. "Ain't worth the trouble," he said to himself. Instead, he sidled up to a nearby side window and looked in. The strong back of the livery owner was facing him. He was sitting on a bench with a leather harness over his knees. Dewey was replacing the buckles for a customer who needed the harness the next day. Wallace crouched under the window and moved toward the small side door. He pulled easily on the handle, but the door was locked. Normally, Dewey wouldn't lock that door until he was turning in. But, because Emily was there, he'd locked it at nightfall.

Wallace took a breath and knocked on the door. Dewey turned toward the door and called out, "Who's there?"

"I'm a cowboy with a lame horse. Young boy up the street told me you'd help. Said you wouldn't turn away a hurtin' horse. That's what he said."

Dewey stood up and hung the harness on a nearby peg. He reached out to the next peg and drew his pistol from the holster that was hanging there. "Just a minute," he called out as he stuck the gun in his wide belt, behind his back.

Wallace burst in as soon as he heard the bar slip away from the hasp that secured the door. He hit the door hard and caught Dewey by surprise, knocking him back. The crazed gunman came through the door with his gun ready and pointed at the startled Dewey. "Back up and shut up," he commanded.

Dewey did as he was told, but tried to get his hand behind his back as he was moving.

"Hold it, put them hands up or I'll shoot," Wallace warned. "Stand still!"

"Is everything all right, Dewey?" Emily had been sitting in the back with the door open. She was darning some of Dewey's socks when she heard the commotion. Now she was walking down the dimly lit aisle between the stalls. Only the light from her room and Dewey's work area illuminated her. Her hands were in the pockets of her dress. Emily saw Dewey standing with his hands in the air and stopped.

"Keep coming, lady." Wallace barked out the command when she stopped. He was standing next to Dewey holding a gun to his head.

Even with the worried look on her face, Emily looked very pretty again. Since regaining her health and resting, she had returned to looking like a beautiful young woman. This wasn't missed by Wallace. Even before he saw Emily, he had been thinking of kidnapping her and taking her to Roy Tanner. If they could get her to sign away her property before they killed her, it should be worth more to Tanner. And maybe he would take a bonus for himself before he killed her. Wallace knew Roy would make up a story about her signing the deed before she was shot. Some outlaw shot her would be his story, Wallace was sure. He knew they had the only lawman around on their side. Wallace would just take his money and head for Mexico.

Wallace pointed his gun at Emily. In the silence, he looked her over more closely and ordered her to saddle the horse in the first stall. Dewey slipped his right hand behind his back and tugged at his hidden gun. Wallace saw the movement and clubbed Dewey behind the ear. He looked down at the fallen man. "You're lucky I don't want to make any noise, or I'd shoot you dead. Don't get any ideas though, lady. I'll shoot if I have to, and I'll kill the both of you."

Wallace went to the horse next to the one Emily was saddling, pulled the saddle from the shelf beside the stall, and threw the saddle onto the back of the horse. "Hurry up with that saddle, lady, and mount up," he yelled.

Emily was hurrying; she wanted to get the killer away from Dewey as quickly as possible. When Wallace had the horse saddled, he walked to the big door and opened it. "C'mon, let's go, miss, and stay close to me." Wallace mounted his horse and moved to the right side of Emily. He warned her. "Nice and slow, and don't try to call out to anyone."

They turned right and trotted a few paces up the street and stopped.

Emily saw him first and gasped. Lucky had had to stop at almost every hitching rail and post in order to catch his breath and gain a little more strength for his journey. Now he was resting on the boardwalk steps. He was almost to the livery; he needed to gain just enough strength to make it a few more yards. The street was graveyard quiet save for the clip clop of the two horses leaving the livery stable. Lucky's face was bathed in sweat despite the cool night air that was blowing on it. His breath was labored. He gulped in as much of the cool air as he could and stood up.

"Hold it right there, Wallace. We ain't finished yet." The voice sounded like it was coming from a cold, wet cave. It was weak and scratchy, but Wallace knew immediately who was talking. His pistol was still in his hand, but a quick movement from Emily distracted the ruthless killer. The gunfire, according to an eyewitness who described it later, was "like a pack of Chinese firecrackers exploding at midnight."

Before she left her room, Emily had taken the small pistol Dewey had given her when she first arrived. She'd put it in her dress pocket, but hadn't wanted to endanger Dewey when she saw that Wallace was already pointing his gun at him. The first chance she got to use it was when Wallace was surprised to see Lucky. As soon as Lucky spoke, Emily pulled the gun out of her pocket and fired at Wallace. Lucky got two shots off before a bullet tore into him and sent his body tumbling to the ground. Wallace had looked back at his prisoner, but fired at his former partner. His first two shots missed their mark he was sure, but, with his last shot, he saw Lucky fall. A sudden wooziness overcame him and he realized he himself had been shot. He spurred his horse to a gallop and raced down the street. Emily watched him ride away as she jumped off her horse and ran to Lucky.

Other watchers, who had come out at the sound of gunfire, saw a man ride up the street bent over his saddle. Trying to stay in the saddle, Wallace gripped the pommel with both hands. The stolen chestnut horse was skittish. The weakness in the hands that had been so brutal to a young boy only a short time ago caused Wallace to let go of the pommel, which was slick with blood. As he tried to reach again for it, he slipped down the side of the horse and fell under the prancing legs. The startled horse tried to avoid the obstacle, but its hind feet trampled the body. The horse fell. The sharp hooves cut deep into the gunman as they drove his body into the soft ground. The frightened horse rose up again and wandered, unharmed, over to a nearby water trough. Wallace's body lay in a crooked heap on the ground. People ran out of their homes, some with lanterns, to gather around the two fallen men.

Doctor Mason said goodnight to his patient just as the gunfire erupted. He gathered his things quickly and walked outside just in time to see Wallace fall from the saddle right in front of him. Doc rushed to the sloppy mass on the muddy street and knelt down. He didn't recognize Wallace, but he checked him and determined he was dead. He then stood up and spoke to some men in the crowd of bystanders. "Move him over to the sheriff's storage. We'll bury him tomorrow. Where is the sheriff, by the way?"

"I don't know, Doc," said one of the bystanders, "but there's more casualties down the street. I think one o'them is that big fella was supposed to be dead."

Lee Mason looked up and saw that the speaker was Howard Rohls, the owner of the general store—a respected member of the town council and a usually responsible man. "Thanks, Howard. See this body gets moved off the street, will you?" Doc was running down the street by the time Howard answered.

"Move—move out of the way and let me through," Doc Mason hollered as he pushed through the crowd.

Once Doc got through the crowd of onlookers, he could see Lucky lying half in the street and half on the boardwalk steps. His head was nestled in Emily's lap, and she was talking to him.

"Emily, what's happened here?" He spoke to Emily, but his eyes were on his patient lying in the street, bleeding again, the front of his white linen shirt a dark crimson stain. The doctor felt his neck and his chest and could tell that Lucky was once more at death's door. Without waiting for Emily's answer he shouted into the crowd. "Where's Alley?"

"I don't see him around, Lee," Alma Loren said. Alma and Beth had heard the shots and had seen Emily climb down from her horse just as they opened their front door. They had run over to her along with the rest of the crowd. Alma spoke to her sister even as she continued looking through the crowd.

"Beth, I'll help Lee. Ask some of the men to help you look for Alley."

"Where's Dewey?" Doc had his hands on Lucky's chest as he shouted into the crowd. Blood was flowing through his fingers, maybe taking Lucky's life with it.

"He's in the livery!" Emily shouted. Her heart was torn between the two men who had tried to help her, but she knew Lucky was more seriously hurt, so she'd stayed with him. "That villain hit him in the head with his gun. Please someone help him."

Lee Mason stood up and took a deep breath. Things were spiraling out of control. He closed his eyes and then opened them. He looked over the crowd of townspeople who still gathered around. Howard Rohls was one of them. Howard had seen to the moving of the dead man to the storage shed and then headed down the street to help Doc Mason again, if he could. Doc reached into his pocket and called out to Howard. He gave him the key to his office. "Howard, in my back room there is a stretcher. Please fetch it here and get some volunteers to carry this man back to my office. It has to be done very gently but quickly." Then he turned to Alma. "Alma, get the bandage material out of my bag. Lucky's been shot again. The wound's on his right side. Keep the bandage tight on him 'til I get back."

Doc gave the orders matter-of-factly and precisely. He wanted to take control and get Lucky and Dewey to his office as soon as possible. He started to stand up and head toward the livery.

"Doc! Doc!" Lucky called out, his voice a strangled whisper, as Doc started to leave. "Important! Come here." The sound wasn't much more than a grunt.

Emily wasn't sure if the doctor heard him and she called out too. "Doctor Mason, he's calling you."

"Yes, Yes. I heard. Why don't you and Alma go check on Dewey. I'll go with Lucky to the office."

Emily stood up and joined Alma, and they ran for the stables. Doc could see the strain in Emily's face and wanted her to keep from thinking about Lucky. He walked back to Lucky and leaned down near his mouth to make it easier for the wounded man to talk. Lucky leaned forward. The veins in his neck were blue rivers on his pale white skin. "The boy, Doc, he's in real bad shape in the alley by your office. Help him first." Lucky spoke as loud and fast as he could and then passed out. Lee Mason leapt to his feet and motioned to a man in the crowd. "Stay with him 'til the stretcher gets here."

Doc ran up the street to his office. Howard Rohls and some men were heading back to get Lucky. Doc called out for one of the men, who was carrying a lantern, to come with him.

The yellow glow from the lantern flowed over Alley's feet first and then illuminated the rest of Alley's crumpled body. Lee Mason cursed out loud for the first time in many years. Even in the dull yellow light from the lantern, he could see the damage done to the young boy's face. Lee picked up the almost lifeless body and started for his office door. The man with him said "Dear God," and ran ahead to open the door. As Lee went through the door, the boy's long arms and legs hung down and swung like loose ropes. The man took hold of Alley's legs, and they carried him into the treatment room. "Up on the table... gently, Bill," Doc said.

They put the unconscious youth on the table, and Doc walked around the room and lit all the lamps to full light. He was trying to get the anger in him to subside. Before he looked back at Alley, he stared out the back window into the darkness. He reminded himself that he was a doctor, and that's what this boy needed now. *You can be his friend again later*, he consoled himself.

Doc walked back to the table and saw the full damage done to this lovable kid who would always do whatever he could to help others. Doc thought how odd it was that, when he needed to put things in order, while he was tending to Lucky, the first person he called out for was Alley. He would have told this young waif to open his office and get the stretcher, knowing that he would do it quickly. Then the boy would have run back and begun preparing the operating room for him. The lamps would all be lit, the bed would be turned down, and all the doors would be open when he got there. Instead the boy lay broken on the table.

Four men marched laboriously up the street. The man they carried on the stretcher was heavy and large. His body barely fit in the carrier. Still they walked slow and steady to keep from jostling their burden. Howard Rohls, a man of medium stature, was at the front giving instructions to the other three men. He had taken over the job of organizing the move to Doc Mason's office.

Beth had gone to the stable looking for Alley. She wasn't aware of Alley's condition and just assumed the boy had been sound asleep somewhere and missed all the commotion. It would be a rare occurrence, but she wasn't thinking clearly. She saw Dewey on the floor and went to him.

When the two women ran into the stable, Dewey was sitting up and leaning against Beth, who was kneeling on the straw-covered floor. Beth was holding a wet cloth to his head, and his hand was on hers. "How are you Dewey? Are you all right?" Alma Loren spoke as she leaned down to look in Dewey's eyes.

"I don't think he has a concussion, Alma. I checked his eyes earlier and I've been talking to him. He is going to have a terrible headache though, I would guess." Beth spoke to her older sister as she moved the cloth over Dewey's forehead.

Emily stood back watching the sisters administer to the man who had been ready to die for her. She had been getting to know Dewey more each day, and knew she was very fond of him. Seeing him leaning against Beth and holding her hand unsettled her for a moment.

Emily spoke her words through trembling lips. "Dewey, I owe you so much. I hope you're going to be all right." The violence she had been a part of tonight was getting to her. Besides worrying about Dewey, she couldn't rid herself of a dreadful thought that kept slipping into her mind. *Suppose one of my bullets missed that gunman and hit Lucky instead. I could be responsible for his death.* Emily shook her head and bent down close to Dewey. "I'll wet that cloth with cold water if you like, Beth." She reached out and took the cloth offered to her by Beth.

Outside in the cool air, Emily worked the green-painted handle on the water pump. The familiar squeaking of the handle was a relief from the noise of the blood pulsing in her ears. So much had happened in the last few weeks—and now this.

After the cloth was wet, Emily wrung out the excess water and returned inside. Dewey was sitting in a chair, and Beth and Alma Loren were standing nearby. Alma spoke as she and her sister both patted Dewey on the back. "We're going to leave him in your hands, Emily, if you feel up to it. Don't let him sleep for now though, I'm sure Lee will want to look at him later."

The two sisters hurried up the street to Doc Mason's office to help care for Lucky. After he had told Matt how he was actually trying to save Emily's life by scaring her, they had begun to like him. Now that they knew he was responsible for saving her again, even most likely at the cost of his own life, they wanted to help him as much as they could.

The front room of the small clinic was filled with townspeople when the sisters arrived. Beth and Alma squeezed through the crowd to the treatment room. The people in the crowd were murmuring quietly with a mix of sad and angry voices. Some of the comments didn't make sense to the sisters until they opened the door. "Lee what can we—Oh! My God!" Alma screamed and fell back into Beth who was still coming through the door. Doc Mason was leaning to his left reaching for a cloth. On the table in front of him was the brutalized young body of Alley. Neither sister had had any idea that anything had happened to him. The boy was lying on the table naked from the waist up. His slim body was covered in bruises, but it was the condition of his face that wrenched their hearts.

"Alley! Alley!" Beth's voice was a loud sob as she ran toward the boy she thought of as her younger brother.

Doc Mason spun quickly and grabbed her. Looking over Beth's shoulder, he saw Alma, tears flowing, her eyes wild with fright. "Listen to me, both of you. It's bad, but maybe not as bad as it looks. I need your help—and right now. But you must find a way to get hold of yourselves." With one arm around Beth's shoulder, Doc took Alma's hand and led the sisters to a bench in the far corner of the room. "Sit here for a few moments and compose yourselves. Later, when we have time, I'll tell you what I know. When you're ready, I'll need you to follow orders without question. Now, I need to keep working on Alley."

Doc left them and returned to his young patient. The sisters did as Lee told them. They consoled each other for a few moments, and then both sisters drew deep breaths and stood up. They wiped their eyes and reached for aprons. Alma said, "We're ready, Lee. What can we do?"

Doc Mason looked over his shoulder and gave his orders. "Beth, change Lucky's dressing. He already had an infection from the last bullets. We can't let it get worse. And make sure it stays tight. He can't afford to lose any more blood."

Beth walked to the smaller bed across the room where Lucky was and started working. His huge frame was almost hanging off the bed in places. Before he passed out again, Lucky had insisted that Doc Mason work on the boy on the big table. "Ya got to do right by that boy, Doc, he's a good 'un," was how he had put it.

Lucky told Doc Mason he was sure Wallace had beaten the boy. The big man was shot in the right side of his chest. The bullet had entered less than two inches away from one of the earlier bullets holes. This one had hit something vital, Beth knew. She didn't have to be told how grave his condition was. She knew from her experience working in this very infirmary that a man as weak as Lucky was would probably not survive this latest wound.

In a quiet voice, as his skilled hands probed and massaged Alley's face and body for the next four hours, Lee explained what he was doing. "This boy took a fierce beating trying not to tell that fellow Wallace where Emily was. I believe two of his ribs are broken, and one may have cut into his lung, but I can't detect any bleeding there. It may just be pressing against it. His face also has some broken bones, and he's having a hard time breathing. What I'm trying to do is maneuver the bones back where they belong so they can knit back together properly. His hand is going to be the most difficult because so many of those bones are very small. But, if we don't do it properly now, he may be left with a useless hand. We have several hours of work left, so let's keep at it."

The room took on a solemn character. There was very little talk except for the proficient instructions from Lee to his two assistants. For the next several hours, Doctor Lee Mason worked on his two patients, moving from one to the other as the situation allowed. When he went to the smaller table, he would check Lucky's pulse and heartbeat. Most times he would shake his head somberly and then pat the man's shoulder. Beth did her best to stop the bleeding and keep the wound clean. Fortunately, both patients remained motionless for the rest of the night.

Meanwhile, the authoritative voice of Howard Rohls took control of the situation in Doc's waiting room. He knew the talking was getting louder, and that the doc and his assistants needed as much quiet as possible. "Okay, everyone, let's move out of here and let these people work in peace." He put his hands on two of the loudest men and began ushering them into the street. When he had the room cleared, he opened the treatment room door and caught Beth's attention. He whispered, "The waiting room's cleared, but I'm going to stand guard out here 'til you're finished. Tell the doc, if he needs anything done, I'm out here."

"Thank you, Howard." Beth nodded her head and closed the door.

20 More Trouble

The following morning, the citizens in the town of Red Wall were somber. The sky reflected their dismal mood. Dark, smoky clouds smoldered across the horizon, and the dampness it held scented the air. Doc Mason and his staff had taken turns sleeping in short stints until late in the morning. Their sleep was fitful at best, but it helped. They had worked on Alley and Lucky until past dawn. Doc Mason finally announced, "That's the best we can do for now. The rest is up to them and the Good Lord."

Alma went home to cook some breakfast, and Howard Rohls went to open his general store. The sun finally broke through the clouds directly overhead as the westbound noon train pulled to a hissing stop at the station. More than twenty men stepped down from the first car, emptying it. Dewey, his head still sore, was repairing a broken board in his corral and watched the men from the train walk toward him. He figured their number at twenty-six. He put the nails he was holding into the pocket of his smithy apron as they approached. They were a strange-looking group.

Some were dressed in eastern, city-type clothes, and some in western gear. They seemed to be an evenly mixed bunch. One of the men addressed Dewey. "Hey, you the fellar's gonna get our horses outta there?" The man was tall and lean with a sharp, pointy nose and wide jaw. He spoke the words quickly, like an Easterner. He was pointing at the last car of the train. Larger than the others, it was the one used to transport animals.

"Sure thing, mister." Dewey put down his tools and walked across his corral. He had made a deal with the railroad several years ago to load and unload any livestock they carried. As Dewey spoke to the stranger, railroad workers were lowering the stockcar ramp, which connected to Dewey's corral. Dewey walked up the ramp and pulled up the lever that locked the door. As he pushed the big red door open, Dewey couldn't help but notice that the horses were an odd group, too, just like their owners. One after another, he brought all the animals down the ramp and into his corral. A porter was unloading their saddles from the baggage car and bringing them over to the corral on a cart.

"You gents are welcome to saddle up in the corral if you like," Dewey said, and went back to work on his fence.

"Where's a good drinking spot around here?" This time one of the western-dressed strangers was asking the question.

"There's a water trough right there," Dewey answered and pointed at a wooden trough filled with water along the fence.

The cowboy laughed, joined by several of his friends. "No, you fool, I mean for us to get some liquor," he said.

Dewey's eyes tightened, and he walked toward the man in western dress. "No need for insulting me, mister. I thought you wanted to look after your horse after a long trip."

The cowboy spat a dark tobacco stain on the ground near Dewey's boot and spoke back to him. "I don't need no horseshoe maker to tell me how to take care of my animal." As he talked, he rested his hand on a six-gun he had strapped to his waist.

"Hold it, Evans," wide-jaw said. "We don't need trouble in town. You may have your hands full soon enough. Sorry, smithy, he gets cranky on train rides. Is there a good saloon in town?"

Dewey looked at the stranger with the eastern clothes and wide jaw. "The Three Eights is just up the street on your right," Dewey said. He took his apron off and tossed it on a fence rail, his stare challenging the tobacco spitter.

"Thanks," said the traveler. "And how 'bout the Box T, how can we get there?"

Dewey gave the man with the wide jaw the directions to the Tanner ranch. He also took more careful stock of the bunch in front of him. He noticed they were all armed. The group seemed equally divided. The men in eastern dress wore shoulder holsters under their jackets; the others all had iron strapped to their waist. Rifles filled the scabbards on most of the saddles.

Sheriff Brock was sitting by the window eating an early lunch at Helmer's restaurant when he saw the rowdy-looking bunch walking up the street. The men dressed like Easterners interested him the most. He knew that meddlesome horse wrangler, Benton, was expecting help. But his friends would not be dressed the way some of these men were. Besides, he reminded himself, those telegrams to Colorado Flats never were sent. The telegrapher, a lazy lout, who was prone to drinking too much, depended on the sheriff's friendship to stay out of jail most nights. When Matt had given him the message to send to Orville Piker, the telegrapher had taken it to the sheriff instead. Brock had told him to forget to send it, along with any others the cowboy might give him.

Brock stared out the window at the strangers, deep in thought, his chin leaning on his fist. A half-eaten lunch plate sat in front of him. He was remembering a heated argument he'd overheard the Tanner brothers having recently. He had been sitting on the front porch of George's house. It was a warm day and the windows had been open. The two brothers were going at it. "Listen George, I'm telling you, if we don't get that girl's farm—and soon—that syndicate back East will send trouble this way," Roy had said. George had shot back harshly, "Don't talk to me about trouble, I've had my house and my bunkhouse shot to hell and almost burned to the ground. My cattle were scattered halfway to Texas. I told you from the beginning that chasing that woman off wasn't going to work. Now she probably figures we killed her father too. I ain't so sure you didn't, and I ain't sure there really is much gold on her property anyway." Roy had responded, "What are you talking about, George? Didn't you see the gold your rider brought in here that night? I followed him back to that creek and found some more traces in the same spot, right there where the stream comes outta the ground from the high country." George continued, "Yeah, a trace is all you ever found. You bought that gold nugget you took back East from that miner going home from California. You tricked them crooks into lending you all that money, and then you lost it in Dodge City—gambling! Now you got me in it up to my neck too. All I wanted was her grazing land and water so I could raise more cattle. I should have offered her more money like I wanted to." Roy had been adamant, "Well like it or not you're in it with me, George," George had responded, "Listen, Roy, if they send someone out here for your neck, they can have it. But, if they try to take my ranch, I'll fight them off just like I did Indians and rustlers alike." Roy had ended the conversation, shouting, "All right! You take care of your ranch. I'll tend to the Langer farm business." The sheriff remembered Roy storming out of George's office, slamming the door, and pounding out onto the porch. He and Roy had then ridden into town.

The bunch from the train was nearing the Three Eights saloon when Brock called to them. He had paid his bill in Helmer's and now stood on the boardwalk in front of the restaurant. "Just a minute, gents," the sheriff said as he stepped off the boardwalk and walked toward the men, a hard look on his face. "What brings you to Red Wall?"

"We came for a beer, sheriff. Heard the Three Eights had the best in the West." Once again, the man called Evans was laughing, and some of his friends joined in.

Brock sent a scowl his way. "I asked you a civil question, mister." Sometimes Brock surprised himself with the amount of iron in his backbone. He could guess who these men were, but he wanted to tell Roy Tanner he was sure. Brock knew he was finished in Red Wall after several of the townspeople had questioned his whereabouts when the young boy had been beaten and Emily Langer had almost been kidnapped. None of them had seemed satisfied with his story that he'd been staying overnight and fishing at Wild Dog Lake. It was a popular fishing place for a lot of the townsmen, but no one ever remembered the sheriff going there. Truth was, he had guessed what Wallace was up to and wanted no part in it, so he had stayed out at the Box T, as he often did. He hadn't figured on the boy getting hurt, though.

The man with the wide jaw spoke up. He seemed to be in charge. "Sheriff, we're just going into the saloon to get a beer, and then we're going to look up an old friend. We'll be out of your town within the hour."

"Who's your old friend? Might be I know him." Brock was standing firm, and it felt good.

"Well, ain't he the nosey one?" Evans was talking, and his hand was once again sitting on top of his pistol.

"It's my business to be nosey, mister. If you look close, you'll see this here's a sheriff's badge." The sheriff pointed to the star on his shirt. "Now who's your friend?" he asked again.

"Whoa, everybody." Wide-jaw stepped in front of Evans and looked at Brock. "No need for getting your back up, sheriff. We're here to see our old friend Roy Tanner—owns a spread near here called the Box T. That right?"

Brock didn't show his surprise that the men thought that Roy owned the Box T. "Could be," the sheriff said. "You men have your drink and move on."

The man with the wide jaw, whose name was McKiernan, turned to Evans and took hold of his shoulder. Under his breath but sternly, he scolded Evans. "Ain't the time for trouble yet. I told you that before. Now keep that gun holstered and your mouth shut." He pushed Evans toward the saloon doors. "Come on men, let's see how good that beer is. I'm buying," McKiernan said.

McKiernan had come west with orders from his bosses to protect their investment. He had picked up Evans and his men in Kansas City where they were spending their loot from a bank robbery they'd pulled in Texas. McKiernan had been sent by the syndicate to take over Roy's ranch and set up a headquarters for future expansion of the syndicate, including gold mining.

In the saloon, the men from the train busied themselves at the bar ordering large amounts of beer and whiskey. They were too busy talking and drinking ten minutes later to notice the sheriff ride out of town. He was riding to the Box T to warn Roy Tanner. Brock knew he didn't have a big reputation as a gun hand, but fact was he was pretty good. Rifle or pistol, he could hit what he aimed at. And he could get his six-gun out pretty quick if need be. Remembering the argument he'd overheard between the brothers, he judged George to be the stronger of the two. Roy was ruthless, he knew, but, when the chips were down, he bet George would be the one left standing. His plan now was to tell Roy about the strangers in town. Then he would offer his gun to George. Roy had only a few men left of Lucky's gang, including that worthless Patch. But George had some good men who had ridden for him a long time. They were scattered for miles across his ranch, but could be brought to the main house in a few hours.

Matt had spent the last two days watching the Box T and, occasionally, Emily's place. He was unaware of the events that had taken place in Red Wall as he looked down on the Box T ranch yard from his hiding place behind the two fallen trees. Matt was getting ready to ride to town when he saw a rider rapidly approaching the ranch from that direction. As the rider got closer, he could see the white foam spraying from the chest and neck of the chestnut horse. The rider was Sheriff Brock. "What's got him so hell bent for leather, I wonder." Matt spoke to himself as he continued to watch Brock. The sheriff rode into the front yard of the Box T at a reckless gallop and just barely managed to stop his horse before it collided with the hitching rail in front of the main house. The sheriff jumped from the lathered animal and ran into the house. Matt watched for a while longer and then mounted Raven and headed for town. *I better get to town and find out what he's so all fired anxious to talk to the Tanners about,* he thought.

Matt was almost to town when he spotted the riders coming toward him. His first thought was that it might be Orville and some Cross River riders. *That might explain the sheriff's hurry,* he thought. As the riders got closer, he could tell some of them weren't sitting their saddles very well. "Orville didn't hire them boys," Matt said to his horse as he patted Raven's neck.

Matt moved Raven to the side of the road to let the group pass. A man riding up front, wearing clothes from back East, put his hand up and stopped the group. Matt could sense the man's discomfort on horseback. "Whoa, damn it!" The Easterner shouted at the smallish dun-colored horse he was riding. "You a Box T man?" he asked Matt. The rest of the riders milled about in a discordant group. Some of the men had little control of their mounts, and they were causing other riders to pull away from the group to gain control of their own horses.

"No, sir, can't say that I am," Matt answered. "If you're looking for their spread, though, you're headed in the right direction. It's about six miles that way," Matt said, pointing back toward the direction he was coming from.

"Well, thanks, mister," the Easterner responded.

Matt wondered if these men were the reason for the sheriff's hasty ride out to the Box T. "You fellas here to sign up for roundup?" Matt asked.

The man with the wide jaw that Matt had been talking to now had his back turned to Matt—his horse was turning in circles, and he was struggling to bring his mount's head around under control. A man who was sitting his horse calmly urged his horse a few steps nearer to Matt's big black. "You funnin' with us, cowboy? Maybe you think some of these boys is here for the rodeo too."

Matt tried not to, but a small laugh came out anyway. "I guess you're right, partner, no offense meant."

"Evans, let's go!" The man Matt had spoken to first finally had his horse facing in the right direction and didn't seem to want to waste any time. McKiernan watched their confrontation and saw Evans' hand move toward his pistol. He also saw that the cowboy he was talking to was watching Evans' hand too. The cowboy didn't seem worried.

Matt left the disorganized crew and rode toward Red Wall. When he arrived a short time later, he went directly to the livery stables, figuring the riders he'd passed must have come in by train. *They certainly didn't ride them horses from back East*, he told himself.

Matt hoped Dewey would have some information for him. The large door was open and Matt rode in and dismounted. The livery was cool and dark and looked empty. He wondered if Emily was in the back. "Hey, Dewey, where are you?" he called out. After a few seconds, he shouted louder, "Dewey!"

"Out here, Matt." Dewey was in the yard saddling a grey horse.

Matt walked out and waved to him. "Hello, Dewey."

Not having any idea of the recent events that had happened in town, Matt started to ask about the riders, but Dewey interrupted him. "Matt, where've you been? I was just going to ride out to look for you—a lot has happened since you been in town last."

"Is Emily all right?" Matt asked, a worried expression took over his face. Little did he know his worry should have been for other people.

"Emily is fine, but some others aren't. Come on back here and I'll explain." Dewey took the saddle off the grey and led him to one of the back stalls.

The men went in to Dewey's private quarters. "Sit down, Matt, I've a lot to tell you," Dewey said as he pointed to a chair.

The two men sat at Dewey's table for half an hour. Dewey told Matt about moving Emily to his place and about the fake funeral. He also told Matt about the strangers that had arrived earlier. Then he explained fully about Alley and Lucky being hurt. He'd started off by telling Matt that they were hurt, but then had to tell things in the order they'd happened, so they'd make sense.

Matt wanted to run up to Doc's office as soon as Dewey told him about Lucky and the boy, but Dewey stopped him. "I was just there, Matt, and they're both sleeping. Doc's been giving Alley laudanum to keep him quiet. He puts a little in a glass of sarsaparilla soda for him. Doc and I were just talking, that's why I was going out looking for you. We believe those men that came in on today's train are hired guns. We think it best if someone rides to Fort Wilson and asks the army for help."

Matt shook his head. "I'm afraid that won't work, Dewey. When I was there, I heard Captain Alpern talking to a settler from just north of the fort. He told him that he was short handed and had been forbidden to send any troops out of the fort. It seems there have been rumors of unrest in the Indian camps east of Darby. He advised the settler to bring his family into the fort."

Matt was reminded then about his men from the Cross River. Orville should have replied to his wire by now. He was also reminded of how often he had seen the telegrapher drinking with Sheriff Brock. He rubbed his chin and squinted then put his hand on Dewey's shoulder.

"Dewey, walk over to the station with me, please, and follow my lead."

"Hey, you, wake up!" Matt wasn't polite when he was angry, and he was plenty angry now. His shout woke the snoozing telegrapher.

"What do you want? Ain't no answer yet. You just gotta wait." The man talking back to Matt was rubbing the whiskey spider webs out of his eyes. His stringy brown hair was stuck to the side of his head. That side of his face was red from lying against his desk.

Matt leaned in the window. "Listen to me, mister. Dewey here was a telegrapher in the army and he's going to listen to your signal. And if it ain't sent right, I'm coming in there to talk to you personally. And don't look for the sheriff to help you—he's long gone from this town. Now start sending what I tell you."

The telegraph operator sat upright and began tapping on the keys as Matt recited his message to Orville once again. Dewey leaned into the window and listened to the code the man was clicking. When the tapping stopped, he looked at Matt, doubt on his face. "I might be a little rusty, but that sounded correct."

"Well, if I don't get an answer by tonight, I'll know he's tricking us and I'll come back bringing trouble." Matt said the words loud enough to get through the cloudy brain of the man at the key. He slammed his hand hard on the counter, and the two left.

In the doctor's office a few minutes later, the rooms were quiet. A lone fly buzzed the window in the outer office where Dewey stood looking out into the street. Matt was talking to Doc Mason. "Doc, what's their chances? Can they pull through?"

Doc put down a pad he'd been writing on. He rubbed his forehead and closed his eyes for a moment then looked at Matt. "I'm not sure about Lucky, but I think Alley will live. His hand is what I'm trying to save now. There's a lot of damage to the bones and the nerves. I'm working with it several times a day to keep the blood circulating, and I'm hoping the bones will knit properly. If they do, and the nerve endings heal themselves, he may get full use out of it again. He's a young man, and it would be hard for him to get by with one hand. We just have to hope for the best. He also has some broken ribs that worry me. I thought one of them might have pierced his lung, but now I don't believe that happened. His body was banged up pretty badly, but he seems to be mending well."

Doc Mason turned and looked down at the hulking body on the other bed. "Lucky is another matter though. He's so weak now that we have a hard time keeping him awake long enough to get any food down him. And he needs the nourishment to get his strength back. He may be bleeding inside, but I can't operate on him unless he gets stronger."

Matt looked at the floor and then back at his friend. He nodded that he understood. "Let me know what I can do, Doc. He's a lot better man than most folks think he is. We gotta pull him through this."

Doc Mason put his hand on Matt's arm and looked directly into his eyes, "I feel the same way, Matt, but it doesn't look good right now."

Matt and Dewey walked out of the office and headed across the street. Doc Mason had told them the women were at the Lorens' home. Matt's eyes were searching the street, looking for any Box T hands that might be around. Seeing none, he focused on Dewey. "We have to convince Emily to stay with you again; it's still the safest place for her."

"Well, I didn't do such a good job last time, Matt. I can't blame her for not trusting me now."

"I doubt that's the reason she left, Dewey. Let's go talk to her."

The Loren home was the largest in town and usually looked friendly and hospitable. Today it seemed different. The windows were down and all the shades were drawn tight against the windowsills. A dark uneasiness covered the house like a ghostly shroud. The men stood at the front door, hats in hand.

Dewey rapped on the glossy brown wood below the glass panel. A small hand appeared by the curtain and pulled it back. Alma's face looked out; it was worn and very tired looking. "It's Matt and Dewey," she called to the back of the room as she unlocked the door. "Come in, come in," she said with forced cheer in her voice.

Alma opened the door and ushered the men into the living room. It looked the same as Matt remembered, but gloomy. "Matt, we've all been worried about you. I guess you've heard what happened here?"

"Yes, I did. I'm fine. How are you all doing?"

"We're all right. We're just worried about Alley and Lucky."

"Yeah, I know. I just spoke to Doc Mason. Is Emily here?"

"Right here, Matt." Emily spoke up; she and Beth were standing in the shadows by the dining room table.

There was a lamp lit on the cupboard, but the wick was turned down low.

"Sit down, Matt; I'll put some food out in just a bit. You too, Dewey, please sit down. We were just going to eat lunch."

Beth pulled one of the large chairs out as she spoke. She then walked out of the room and into the kitchen. Emily came forward and hugged Matt.

"I'm glad you're okay, Matt. So much has happened, I don't know if it's worth it anymore. That poor boy and Lucky are hurt so bad. And now more gunmen arrived on the train today. Where will it end?"

Matt put his arm around Emily and guided her to the chair Beth had pulled out. "Let's sit down and figure out some things," Matt said.

Alma left the room to help her sister. Dewey and Matt sat in chairs opposite Emily. Matt spoke quietly. "Emily, none of this is your doing. The Tanner brothers and their greed is what's causing this trouble. If we stick together, we'll beat them."

Dewey stood up and started toward the kitchen. "Here, let me help you with that." Beth was coming through the kitchen door with a serving tray filled with sandwiches. Alma followed with the coffee.

"We're fine, Dewey, thank you," Beth answered. Beth moved to the table and set the tray down. Alma placed the coffee down and then some cups. Beth brought another chair to the table and sat down. They all began eating.

"Matt, I know Lee and Dewey have brought you up to date about the goings on around here. What have you been doing?" Alma spoke while putting her coffee cup to her lips. Matt told the group about seeing the sheriff ride into the Tanner's yard. He then told them how he'd met up with the bunch from the train. "I've also been checking on your farm, Emily. Everything seems fine there."

The conversation continued while they ate lunch. Matt drank some coffee and put his cup down. "What's confusing me now," he said, "is that, with everything out in the open, what's their next move?"

"Maybe they don't know themselves," Alma answered.

"That's real likely, I expect, Alma. I think it's best if we all hunker down a spell and watch." Matt spoke to Alma and then turned his attention to Emily. He was trying to figure out a polite way of speaking to her alone but couldn't come up with any. Finally he gestured toward the back of the room and said. "Emily, can I see you out back for a minute?"

Emily looked up at Matt, and a slight blush rose in her cheeks. Matt stood up and started walking to the back door.

"Sure, Matt," she answered him. Looking around the table, Emily stood up and said, "Please excuse us."

"We'll be right back and I'll explain," Matt said holding the door open for Emily.

"Well I'll start clearing the table," Beth said, a curious almost hurt look on her face, as she looked toward the back door.

The Lorens' backyard was quiet in the late afternoon. Small chirpings from the birds that found refuge in their trees were the only sound. Large oaks shaded the far areas of the yard, while smaller redbuds, which produced beautiful reddish pink blooms in late spring, grew nearer to the house. The street traffic of wagons and horses went mostly unheard thanks to the two giant oak trees that guarded either side of their house in front. Once they were alone in the backyard, Matt put his hands out and held Emily's arms. "Emily, Dewey says you won't stay with him in the livery anymore. He thinks you've lost faith in him."

Emily looked up at Matt. "Oh no, Matt, it's not that at all. I just don't want to put him in danger again. That man— Wallace—almost killed him." She sat down on a bench that was placed between two of the redbud trees and put her hands on her lap.

"Dewey's a grown man, Emily. He knows what he's doing— he wants to protect you."

"Matt, Dewey's very brave, and I appreciate what he wants to do for me, but I'll be fine in the hotel."

"Hotel!" Matt yelped. He couldn't help being startled by Emily's revelation that she intended to stay at the hotel. "I thought you were staying here with the Lorens!"

"No, I couldn't do that either. That would only put them in danger too."

Matt walked over to a small rail fence that separated the food garden from the walking area. He put his foot on a rail and leaned against it. "Emily, I believe you're still in danger, and I would worry a lot less if I knew you were with Dewey. It won't be much longer, and, if you were with Dewey, Beth and Alma would be able to concentrate on helping Doc Mason. You could help out there during the daytime too."

Emily stood and walked over to the fence by Matt. She seemed to be studying the ground, and then looked up at him. Their faces were inches apart. "All right, Matt, but only for one more week, then I'm going home."

Matt looked back at her. Her determined face worried him; he wasn't sure a week would be long enough. He decided to leave it there for now.

Dewey was standing by the front door looking out at the street when Emily and Matt returned to the house. He'd become a very vigilant man of late.

Matt walked up to the big smithy and slapped him on the back. "Dewey, you'd better run across the street and clean up that bachelor's room. You're gonna have company again." Emily stood between the men.

Dewey looked carefully at Emily. "Are you sure, Emily? I'll be more careful this time."

Emily managed a small smile and said, "What happened wasn't your fault, Dewey. You couldn't refuse to care for an injured horse."

"Thanks, Emily, I'll go tidy up a little—see you a little later. I have some shoes to shape too. Good-bye all; thanks for the lunch, ladies." Dewey grabbed the last cookie off the plate on the table and left.

21 Trouble on the Box T

Brock was sitting on the porch of the main building at the Box T when they rode in. His hat was pulled down over his eyes, and his chair was leaned back against the log wall so the front legs were up off the floor. He was thinking about what he had told Roy and George a short time earlier. "There's twenty-six of them far as I counted. Some don't look like they're from around here. Back East, I'd guess. Came off the train little more'n an hour and a half ago, or so. Leader's a man named McKiernan. The city-dressed ones is carrying their guns in shoulder holsters. The others is packing 'em on their hips. Said they was commin' out here to see you, Roy."

George had thanked the sheriff for riding out to tell them. Then he'd sent the sheriff in to the kitchens to get some grub before he headed back to town. George had been very civil, but the sheriff had decided just to rest up on the porch for a spell. What Brock really wanted was to stick around and try to speak to George alone and make his offer—and maybe even hear the brothers arguing again. He'd learned a lot that way before. They hadn't disappointed him.

Brock hollered into the house that company had arrived.

The ragtag group rode up to the hitching post in front of Brock. Some of the cowboys rode up close to the rail and sat their horses. McKiernan and some of the city men dismounted awkwardly, pulled their mounts up to the post, and tied them.

"Well, sheriff, you get around, I see." The man called McKiernan was looking over his shoulder at Evans when he spoke. "You men wait here. Where will I find Roy Tanner, sheriff?"

"Right here, McKiernan." Roy spoke up as he stepped out onto the porch. Forewarned of the visit by Brock, the brothers had stayed back in the doorway until McKiernan asked for Roy.

"What brings you way out here? I wasn't expecting you." Roy Tanner spoke as he stood next to George, who had joined him on the porch. Roy was dressed in a brown suit. No gun was visible. George had on his usual range clothes—including the six-shot Remington he always wore on his hip. McKiernan looked over both brothers. He didn't miss the frayed leather holster and the worn-down walnut handle on George's pistol. They both were obviously well used. McKiernan leaned over and spoke under his breath to a man in a bowler hat who was standing next to him, "Anyone who carries a gun for that long and has used it that much must be pretty good with it."

"Who's your friend, Roy?" McKiernan asked.

"This is my brother, George," Roy answered.

McKiernan put a smirk on his face. "Well, Roy, I'm here to look over that gold mine you borrowed the syndicate's money for. I brought Harry here with me." McKiernan pointed to the man in the bowler hat. He was a smallish, pale-looking fellow with an extremely long face. Along with his hat, he was wearing a black jacket that seemed too big for him. "He's a geologist... knows something about gold mines. These boys is here to help us pick it up. Got some more men comin' in a day or two... also figured to look over this ranch you put up for collateral."

The last words rang like gunshots in George's ears. They felt like a punch. His face was contorted with rage as he looked at Roy. The look wasn't missed by McKiernan. George noticed McKiernan's interest and made himself relax as he looked over the assembled men in front of him. Besides being a good gun hand, George was also smart. He studied the bunch in front of him and figured them out quickly. The cowboys were gun hands who probably only punched cows when they had to. McKiernan and the other city slickers—except for the geologist—were probably pretty tough too. Besides the sheriff, whom he wasn't too sure of, he had only Roy, his cook Will, and the two men left of Lucky's crew nearby. George wasn't a man to back down from a fight, but he didn't bet into a pat hand either, if he didn't have to.

George turned to Roy. "Roy, it's getting late, but, if you ride out now, you might can show these gents some of that gold before it gets dark, I bet."

It was Roy's turn to be shocked. He blurted out, "What... uh, no... I think it's too late, George. The sun'll be down in an hour."

McKiernan stepped forward and looked at George, "I think that's a good idea, George." He turned to Roy. "Saddle up, Roy, you said it wasn't far from your ranch." The way McKiernan said it, it sounded like an order. Then he turned to Evans. "You men settle down here. I'm sure brother George will find you something to drink. You know, western hospitality, right, George?" McKiernan had a sly grin on his face.

"I guess we could do that," George answered. He aimed a steely look at McKiernan.

Roy looked back over his shoulder at his brother, a stunned look on his face, while he walked over to the barn where his horse was stabled. McKiernan and his geologist walked their mounts beside him.

George set his eyes on Evans. "Have your men put up their mounts in the corral. I'll put a couple of bottles on those tables." George pointed to three, long, rough-hewn tables with benches on either side of them that sat in the side yard between the main house and a work shed.

George looked over at Brock who had been standing to the side watching Evans and his men. As the men started toward the corral, he called to him quietly. "Brock!" When Brock looked his way, George motioned with his head for the sheriff to follow him inside.

In the large room the Tanners used as a parlor and also as George's office, George turned toward Brock and spoke quickly. "Go down to the bunkhouse. Two of Lucky's men are there repairing equipment. Tell them I want to see them pronto."

"Sure thing, George," Brock said, and immediately headed for the bunkhouse. He knew this was not the time to talk to George about joining up with him. If he had George figured right, the Box T boss was already working on a plan in his head.

Patch and Red were sitting quietly at a scarred table, leather straps of all kinds spread out before them. The dates and names carved in the table, along with cigarette burns and the scratches from men's spurs, told of its age. Each man held a pair of pliers as they worked at pulling rawhide strings through the straps. They were working in the dull light from two dirty windows along with a bit of late afternoon sunlight that peeped through the bullet holes Matt had put in the door. Brock walked into the bunkhouse and held the door open with his boot as he spoke to them. "You two men, George wants to see you right now, up at the house. There's some strangers by the corral, but don't pay no attention to them. Let's go."

Patch didn't like the way Brock talked to them at all, but he seemed sure of himself. "C'mon, Red, let's get up there and see what the boss wants," he said.

As they walked to the house, they saw Roy and two city-dressed men riding out of the yard. They also took in the men unsaddling horses in the corral, but they weren't obvious about watching them.

As soon as Brock left, George went to the cold shack where the salted meat was kept. The gray-plank building was in the back of the main house. Will Albrecht, the ranch cook, was out there curing meat. A wiry, baldheaded man, he had been a top rider for George until he was trampled by a rank bull. The bull had been acting crazy, attacking several steers in the herd. Will rode in to the herd to separate the ornery bovine from the more peaceable ones when his horse stepped in a prairie hole and stumbled. Will was thrown to the ground. "The bull got me good," was the way Will described his injuries. Another cowboy shot the bull dead, stopping it from killing the fallen cowboy.

Will walked with a limp now, and he couldn't sit on a horse long enough to chase one cow.

George walked into the shed and put his hand on his old friend's shoulder. "Will, I need you to hook up the buggy and take Liz into town. I want her to catch tonight's train," is all he said.

As all Box T riders knew, when the boss asked them to do something, it was an order, and, if he wanted to explain it, he would. "Okay, George, I'll git right on it." Will wiped his hands on an old towel, put away the meat he was cutting, and left.

Liz had been George's wife for twenty-two years. She hadn't been married to him when he was building the ranch, but she had fought alongside him many times defending it. She was a pleasant-looking woman with brown hair turning to grey. When she wore riding boots, she was almost as tall as her husband. Her face, though mature, still kept the prettiness of her youth. She was upstairs in a room she used for sewing and other household projects. It was in the back of the house, next to their bedroom, where she could look out on the mountains off in distance. She was unaware of the men who had ridden in earlier.

George tapped on the door and stepped in. He spoke in a sincere voice. "Liz, I just had a telegraph message come out from town. Your friend Annie, in Denver, is sick and is asking if you could go there and stay with her."

A look of surprise came to Liz's face. "Why that's awful sudden. I just got a letter from her last week, dear—and she was fine."

"Well, you know Annie wouldn't ask if she didn't need help. I already told Will to hitch up the buggy. He'll get you into town for the night train, if you hurry."

His wife still looked uncertain. When Matt had shot up their property, George had told Liz it had just been some drunken cowboy who managed to get away. She hadn't asked about it anymore, but she was skeptical. "Are you sure, George? I hate to leave you here alone. Why don't you come with me? It would do you good to get away from the ranch for a while."

George avoided his wife's eyes and said, "I'm sorry, I can't. I just had some fellows stop by looking to buy some breeding stock. I'll be showing them cattle for the next few days. Why don't you get ready? Will should be calling for you any minute." George kissed his wife on the cheek and left her to get ready.

As George walked down the stairs, he saw Patch and Red standing on the porch just outside the open door. "Come in here, men," he called out to them. The two men walked in to the house and took their hats off. George stood in front of the men and spoke in voice that took them into his confidence. "I've got an important job for you two. Listen closely. I want you to ride out to the big basin and find Porter. Tell him I want all the Box T riders rounded up and brought to town. He's to make arrangements for them to eat at Helmer's, drink at the Three Eights, and stay at the Drover House Hotel. They can put their horses up at the livery. I'll stand good for any cost. Tell him we might have shootin' trouble here soon, and I want all the boys that are able here—two hours after first light tomorrow morning. Get my message to Porter—he'll know what to do from there. He'll know what to say to the men."

"We're on our way, boss." Patch nodded his head to George and pulled on the shirtsleeve of his partner.

"Stay clear of them fellas that rode in here earlier." George pointed out the window as he spoke.

"Sure thing, boss." Patch did the talking again as they walked outside. The two men saddled their horses quickly and were riding out of the yard when they saw the men sit down at the tables outside the main house.

George got several bottles from the hutch and brought them out to the men. He plunked them down on the table. "Enjoy," he said, with little hint at pleasantness.

Evans grabbed one of the bottles and looked up at George. "We need glasses, " he said.

"People in hell need cold water," George replied through a sneer.

Evans started to stand.

"You need me to do anything boss?" Will had brought the buggy to the front of the house and then had walked around to the side. He moved to the table and was standing behind Evans when he spoke. He wore a Colt pistol on his good hip. His hand was resting on it. George looked at Evans. "No, Will," George answered his good friend, "there's nothing here I can't handle, come on inside."

Evans sat down, a sour grin on his face.

Once inside, George walked to the staircase that rose along the left-hand wall of the big room. He stood still and listened until he was sure his wife was still in their bedroom packing. Then he moved to a large desk made of finely sanded oak. A picture of Liz sat on the corner near the wall. George sat down and offered his old friend a seat near the desk. He told Will about the men who had just ridden in. Then, in a conspirator's voice, he said, "Listen, Will, I need you to make sure Liz gets on that night train. There's trouble brewing here, and I want her to be far away when it starts. I told Liz her friend is sick. That's a lie, but, by the time she finds out, she'll be in Denver. After she gets on the train, meet up with Porter in town, and tell him what I told you about these fellas sittin' outside."

"Sure thing, boss," Will answered and started for the door.

Both men turned as they heard Liz coming down the stairs. "Will, I'll be right out," she said. Will turned to look at Liz. He touched his hat brim and continued out the door. Liz walked over to her husband. She was wearing a blue-and-white traveling dress. A small brown suitcase was in her right hand. "George, are you sure you'll be all right?"

"Yes, I'll miss you, but I'll be fine. Let me put you in the buggy, or you'll miss the train." George took the bag from his wife and kissed her. He walked Liz outside and helped her into the buggy. He put her bag in the back and then walked to the front of the buggy. George slapped the rump of the near horse. As the buggy began to move, he looked up at Liz and waved good-bye. Liz returned the wave and blew him a kiss. Evans and his men watched.

After Brock had brought the two Box T men up to the house, he had sat back down on the chair on the covered porch and leaned it once again against the side of the house. From there he had been keeping an eye on the men from the train. George, having seen his wife off, turned and walked up the steps of his porch. He glanced over at the men drinking his whiskey. Evans was staring at him. The rest of the men were busy passing the half-empty bottles around. Evans' lips were set in a sneer as he looked up at George. George turned toward the sheriff and motioned for Brock to follow him into the house.

Inside, the room was getting dark. Shadows were starting to form in all the corners. George set about lighting several lamps. When he was finished, he walked behind his desk and sat down. He pointed to the cupboard and told Brock to get a bottle and two glasses. An open wooden box sat on his desk; he reached in and brought out two cigars. "Cigar, Brock?" he said, as he held a cigar out to the sheriff.

"No thanks, George." Brock waved his hand.

Pointing to a chair on the other side of his desk, George said, "Sit down." George struck a match on his boot and lit his cigar. He drew in deeply before he spoke. "Brock, I figure you to be one of Roy's men. Why're you hanging around here?"

Brock poured two drinks, handed one to George and sat down. "True enough, George. I was taking orders from Roy. But I seen things turn around here lately, and I don't figure Roy's the one to be backing now. This looks to be shaping up as a fight for your ranch, with Roy and those city fellas on one side and you on the other. I figure you to be the one sittin' at that desk when it's over."

George leaned forward, his right elbow on the desk. The hand holding his drink was steady. He pointed it at Brock. "You just give Roy some information from time to time and settle some small squabbles. What do I need you for?"

Now Brock leaned forward and put his drink down on the desk, his eyes on the owner of the Box T. "George, I never did brag much on my gun. But I can use it better'n most men. When I took the job as sheriff in town all they wanted was someone to put the lights out at night. No one never did ask about my handiness with my gun. So I kept it to myself. An ace in the hole never hurts, George. I figure you can use a good gun hand long about now. And I swear to you, you can count on me as much as you trust that old gimp you sent your wife off with. When this is over, all I want is a stake to get me to California and a new start."

George put his glass down and looked directly into Brock's eyes. "Fair enough. You're hired, but know this, if I find you're double dealing, I'll shoot you down, front or back, like a cur dog the minute I find out." He offered Brock his hand.

The two men shook hands and stood up. George gave orders. "Now, I want you to go to the bunkhouse and find any guns and ammo my men might have lying around, and hide them."

Brock had learned quickly from watching Box T men. He left for the bunkhouse as soon as George stopped talking.

Matt left the Loren home and walked over to Doc Mason's office. He stepped through the outer door into the waiting area, and started walking to the back of the room. The whole building seemed eerily quiet. The last rays of the late afternoon sun slid in under the lowered shades, lighting up his boots but leaving the walls to their solitude. Matt's footsteps on the grey-painted board floor alerted Doc Mason, and he opened the treatment room door. Doc looked into Matt's eyes and shook his head as he spoke.

"Matt." Doc murmured, his voice was somber as he lowered his head. "He didn't make it, Matt. Lucky died. I'm sorry."

"Oh, no!" Matt blurted out, his voice matched Lee Mason's anguished tone.

Doc put his hand on Matt's shoulder. "Come inside, Matt."

Doc opened the door wider and let Matt pass by. He spoke in a whisper. "About five minutes ago he tried to sit up and then fell back on the bed. I heard him gasp and went over to check on him, but he was already gone. I was just going to get Jesse to help me move him. I don't want him here when Alley wakes up." Doc was standing next to the bed Lucky's body lay on. Matt stood next to him with his hat in his hand, his head bowed. On the other side of the room Alley lay sleeping.

"Damn them Tanners. I'm gonna cut both of them down first time I see them," Matt hissed to the floor.

Doc remembered the angry look on Matt's face when he had brought Emily to him and told him what happened to her, so many days ago. But hearing him talk now and seeing his face told Doc Mason all the more of the violence Matt was capable of. Doc couldn't blame Matt; he'd had the exact same feeling only moments ago. Now, after just calming himself, he knew he had to calm Matt too. Only a short time ago he'd said to himself, "Vengeance, fueled by blind rage, would most likely get more good people hurt."

Pointing to Lucky's feet, Doc said, "Matt, if you'll grab his legs, I'd like to move Lucky next door until Jesse can get here with a casket. The boy's liable to wake up any minute. I've been weaning him off the laudanum since he's feeling better and has less pain."

"Sure, Doc," Matt replied and took hold of the big man's legs.

They took Lucky's body to the room on the other side of the office where Emily had stayed before moving to the livery. Doc Mason pointed to the bed near the back window, and said, "Let's put him down here for now."

"Okay, Doc. Then I'll go arrange things with Jesse. I think it would be best if you told the women and Dewey. The women are up at the Lorens' house. Dewey just went back to his livery."

Lee Mason's eyes showed the dread he had been feeling about bringing this news to them. They had all grown very fond of Lucky. "I guess I should get it over with. It's going to hit them real hard though, Matt."

"It sure does hurt, Doc," Matt agreed.

The two men started for the front door. Doc stopped before opening it and turned to Matt. "Hold it, Matt. I can't leave Alley alone for too long; he's likely to wake up any minute now."

"I won't take long with Jesse, Doc, and then I'll hurry back here and stay with the boy."

"Okay, Matt, just tell Jesse to start building the casket, and say I'll stop in to see him later. Oh, and Matt, ask Jesse what kind of sidearm that Wallace fella carried. Jesse took care of his burial and he holds all personal effects for the sheriff. Keep the answer between me and you, please."

Matt nodded his head and stepped out of the door. "I'll meet you back here later," he said over his shoulder as he stepped into the street.

Both men wore sober looks on their faces. Matt looked up and down the street as he crossed over to the carpenter's shop. No sign of any Box T men.

Patch and Red wasted no time after leaving the ranch. Their horses were thoroughly lathered with sweat when they spotted Porter. He was sitting on his horse, one leg hanging lazily over the saddle horn, watching over a herd of grazing cows. Smoke rose lazily past his eyes from the cigarette he held between his lips. The cattle looked content, eating the deep green grass at their feet.

Patch, hands together at his mouth, shouted out to him as they rode up. "Porter, we got to talk to you."

Porter looked up and unhinged his leg. He pulled his mount to the left and started riding toward Patch and Red, his hands waving to them to slow down. When he was close enough to be heard, he spoke to them with an irritated voice. "Keep your voice down or you'll start them runnin'. What's so important anyway?"

Patch reined his horse in next to the Box T foreman and began to speak, hurried words tumbling out of his mouth. "We got important instructions for you from George."

"Well, calm down and gather yourself so's I can understand you," Porter told him.

Patch took a deep breath and then told Porter everything George had told him to say.

When Patch finished, Porter nodded his head to himself as he stepped out of his saddle and looked at the ground. "Damn that Roy. I knew it would come to a shooting war," he said, as he knelt down in a patch of dirt and began to draw a map with his folding knife. His map showed the location of the Box T men he wanted Patch and Red to roundup. When he was finished, he stood up and dusted his knees with a strong weathered hand. He looked at the two messengers. "You men gather up these boys and I'll get the rest. And don't burn up that horseflesh no more'n you have to to do it. You're likely to be needing them ponies in the next few days. Now ride easy away from here and make sure you tell each man to leave his cattle in a draw or some low ground so's they'll be there when we get back to 'em. See you in town."

All three men mounted and rode off. Patch and Red rode together for a short distance then split up heading to the places Porter told them they would find other Box T riders.

"Why, it was a forty-four Navy Colt. It's hanging right there behind me." Jesse the carpenter was twisting his body to his right and pointing to the six-gun and holster hanging on a wall peg behind him, as he answered Matt's question. The gun belt—an old cracked, brown leather rig—looked to be hanging there forever. It had already gathered a covering of sawdust and plain old ordinary dust. It didn't look dangerous.

"Thanks, I was just curious." Matt didn't feel like explaining about Doc asking the question first. Matt had already told Jesse about Lucky.

Jesse looked at Matt and scratched at the stubble on his chin. "I'll get some men busy digging the grave first, then I'll start on the box. Tell Doc it'll be ready in about two hours. Sure too bad about that man dying."

"Sure is, Jesse. Thanks," Matt said and left the shop.

Outside the carpenter shop, Matt looked up and down the almost-deserted street again. A small, brown-and-white dog ambled alongside a piece paper blowing across the dusty road. Still no Box T men were to be seen. He hurried back over to

Doc Mason's office. Inside, the front area was quiet, but Matt could hear a low moaning noise from the back room. He moved quickly to the back. Alley was sitting up holding his injured hand next to his chest. "Hey, boy, you have to stay down 'til Doc says it's okay to get up." Matt moved over to Alley and helped him lie back down.

"Where's Lucky, Matt? Is he all better already?" The boy seemed too skinny, and his face still looked hurt as the words seemed to drift crookedly out of his mouth. Matt didn't know how to answer his questions. Hat in hand, scratching his head, he stalled for time to think. No good answer came to him. He was trying to think how Doc might handle it. Still stalling, Matt walked to the rear of the room and picked up one of the two chairs lined up against the back wall. He brought the chair over to the boy's bed and set it down so the back was facing Alley. Matt straddled the chair, and leaned his arms on the chair back. He knew Alley deserved an honest answer. His mind was searching for a way to tell the boy about Lucky's death as painlessly as possible. Still, no good ways came to him. Matt knew this boy, who was barely fourteen, was going to be hurt no matter who told him or how. He was growing up fast just as a lot of young people had to sometimes. He remembered starting out to look for his father's killers when he wasn't much older than Alley.

Matt leaned forward and looked into the boys damaged eyes and sighed. "I'm afraid our friend passed on, Alley. Lucky died a short time ago. He squared away his business here and left us for a better place. The Doc did all he could, but Lucky's injuries were just too much for even him to fix."

A groan too mournful for someone so young erupted from Alley's still-swollen mouth. He turned his back to Matt and began to sob. Matt put his hand on the boy's heaving shoulder.

Doc Mason had gone to the livery first and told Dewey the bad news. Then both men went to the Loren home. The sisters and Emily took the news hard, but, as Doc expected, they were able to regain their composure after a few minutes. The three women had all seen their fair share of hardship, and Doc knew they would want to help plan Lucky's real funeral. They all left for Doc Mason's office.

Matt heard them enter the front door and got up to greet his friends. He met them in the waiting room and stopped them. Hands on his hips, he shook his head side to side and said, "Doc, I had to tell Alley about Lucky. He woke up and asked me as soon as he saw the empty bed."

Doc Mason looked past Matt at the treatment room door and nodded his head. "Well, he had to be told, Matt. Thanks. How'd he take it?"

"Not real good, Doc. He's trying to buck up, but I think he's still blaming himself for what happened at Dewey's."

Doc spoke decisively. "Come inside, all of you!" He led the way into the room. Alley was lying in the bed with his back to them. His thin shoulders shook with every sob. Doc walked over to Alley and put his hand on the boy's back. "Turn around, Alley. We have to talk." He patted the boy's shoulder and then stepped away from the bed.

Beth walked to the bed and put her arms around the boy and spoke soothingly. "Alley, Lucky was a good man, and he died doing what he thought was right. He wouldn't want you to be sad because of that. He did the brave thing he did for the same reason you took such a beating from that snake, Wallace. He was trying to help a friend."

Alley turned toward Beth and wiped at his wet eyes with his sleeve. His face was red and blotchy. His hair was a tangle of wet straw hanging on the side of his face. "I know that, Miss Loren. Lucky told me a few days ago that he could die happy if we were all still safe. He said he was glad to be friends with decent people again," the boy said between sniffles.

"Listen, everybody, please!" Doc Mason was standing near the bed Lucky had been in when he died. The bed hadn't been touched since they had moved his body. The covers were bunched off to one side, and the pillow still held the impression of the big man's head. Doc was looking at the group of friends in front of him. He had his hands raised and spoke a little louder than usual to get their attention. When he spoke, his voice was steady and firm. "The terrible events that have happened here in the last few weeks are not the fault of anyone in this room. The Tanners are the ones who set these things in motion, and they'll have to answer for it. I'm sure there are some questions we don't know the answer to yet, but the finger has to point at the Box T. Now, let's concentrate on giving Lucky a respectful funeral tomorrow, and then we'll discuss our plans to resolve these problems. We have to figure on ways to protect each other while forcing the Box T to answer for their crimes."

All members of the somber group looked at Doc and tried to mix his words in with their own thoughts. Beth was rubbing Alley's back, and spoke up first. "I think Doc is right. You can't blame someone who's trying to do what's right if others keep causing the trouble to get worse. Maybe we—"

Beth's words were cut short when the outside door opened and hurried footsteps sounded in the outer office. "Hello? Anybody here? Doc, you here?"

The voice was unfamiliar to most of those in the room except Alley. He said quietly. "That's Corliss the telegraph man. I recognize his voice. I deliver messages for him sometimes."

Matt let his gun slide slowly back into its holster. "He must have my answer from Orville," he said. Matt stepped past the others and opened the door.

Corliss stopped short when he saw Matt, and started stammering. "I... I... I th... thought you'd be here. You weren't at the livery or the Lorens' house, so... so I figured you'd be here. I know you're friends with the doc. I mean... umh... a... well I got your reply from Colorado." He stuck a trembling, thin hand out at Matt and offered him a wrinkled piece of paper. His squinty eyes scanned the room behind Matt and the people in it.

Matt took the paper from his hand and replaced it with a two-bit piece. "Thanks for your prompt delivery," Matt said with little disguise of the sarcasm he meant. "If I were you, I'd just do my job and stay out of this fight." Matt had the man scared, and his words were intended to keep it that way.

"Yes, sir, I get your meaning, mister." Corliss turned and walked out the front door. He looked to the right for a few seconds and then headed left to go back to his office at the depot. Matt straightened out the wrinkled paper and began to read the short reply: "Received message. Be there soonest. Orville."

Matt walked back into the room with his friends; his face looked relaxed. "Well, I guess you did a good job of acting, Dewey," he said, holding the telegraph in the air. "Some of my men will be here inside a few days. We should be able to move on to Emily's farm and secure it—with your permission, of course, Emily. I think, if we show the Tanners we're determined to hold your property, they might back off now," Matt said.

Emily had been standing next to Alley's bed and now walked up to Matt. Her hands were tucked in the pockets of the brown dress she was wearing. "Matt, what about all those men that rode out to the Box T earlier?"

Matt didn't disguise his puzzlement. He looked at Emily, his head slowly shaking side to side. "I don't know how to figure them yet, Emily. I've been thinking about what Lucky told us about that syndicate from New York—the one he said Roy Tanner was mixed up with. Could be it's them, I guess. Anyway, if you'll agree, I think putting my men on your place will make the Tanners think twice about trying to move onto your spread."

Emily sat back down by Alley and looked up at Matt. "All right, Matt. I agree with what Doc said earlier. We can't let the Tanners or anyone else steal and hurt people without fighting back. I won't question what you do from now on, but I do want to help protect my own land."

Matt left it there.

Alma walked over to her sister and said, "Come on, Beth, let's go home and see if we can find one of Dad's suits that will fit Lucky. I think he'd like to be buried nicely dressed. We'll be back as soon as we can, Lee."

Beth nodded agreement, and the two sisters left.

When they stepped through the outer door of Doc's clinic, both sisters turned their heads to the right. Beth then turned to Alma and said, "Some of those horses have Box T brands on them. I hope Matt waits until his men get here before he goes after that Box T bunch."

The horses were tied to the hitching post in front of the Three Eights saloon up the street. Looking back into the outer room, Alma saw Doc talking to Matt. "I'm sure Lee will calm Matt down until the time is right," she said to her sister. "Let's go get that suit."

The sisters turned left and started for their home. Emily pulled her chair closer to Alley's bed and began talking to the boy trying to console him about Lucky's death.

Matt and Doc stepped out into the waiting room. Matt reached back and closed the door. He kept his voice low. "Wallace wore a forty-four Navy Colt, Doc. Why did you want to know?"

"Emily was concerned that her bullet might have done Lucky in—she was firing the gun Dewey gave her."

"I don't think Dewey would give her a forty-four to handle. Did he, Doc?"

"No, she had a twenty-five caliber. She'll be glad to hear that. I already told her it was a heavy caliber weapon that killed Lucky. I'll go tell her now."

"Okay, Doc. I'll stop back in a little while."

Matt finished his talk with Doc and stepped outside. He was curious at the way the Loren sisters and the telegrapher had looked toward the saloon when they left the Doc's office. He too looked to his right. Several of the horses he saw at the saloon's hitching rail bore the Box T brand. Matt's temper flared at the sight of the brand, but he remembered the conversation he'd just had with Doc Mason. He had agreed with Doc to hold off any confrontation until his men arrived. But he hadn't agreed not to go into the Three Eights for a beer.

22 Porter

Porter rounded up the men he'd been sent to find and led them into town. He told them little, except that there was trouble brewing in the town of Red Wall, and the Box T was in the middle of it. He promised to explain everything when all the men were gathered together in town at the Three Eights. He expected everyone in within the hour. Porter stood at the bar, one foot resting on the boot rail. He was talking to another long-time Box T rider named Cal. Some of the other men sat at nearby tables, bottles of whiskey in front of them. A cowboy with a thick, black mustache dealt poker hands to the others at his table. Some townspeople were scattered about at tables and at the bar. An uneasy peace existed in the room.

Porter spotted Matt first as Matt walked through the swinging doors. Porter stepped away from the bar and looked into Matt's eyes. His hand moved slowly as he laid his shot glass on the bar. Matt saw Porter move as he swept the room with a glare. He didn't see anyone who looked like the man he remembered as Roy Tanner, and he didn't know what George Tanner looked like. He looked at Porter and said, "Where you hiding the Tanners?"

Matt recalled his meeting with Porter when he'd stampeded the Box T cattle. Porter seemed like an honest cowboy, working for the brand, and Matt knew he'd be loyal to the Box T and fight for it if he had to.

Porter gently moved Cal away from him with his left hand and positioned his right hand above his gun. He said, "George Tanner's at the ranch, not hiding from anyone. I don't know where Roy is, and don't care. You had the drop on me last time we talked, mister. Things is different now. Why don't you turn around and walk out of here?"

Matt moved easily and set himself into the stance he'd want for a quick draw, if need be. The large, dusty mirror behind the bar became busy with ghostlike figures getting out of harm's way. Table and chair legs scraped the floor. Most had seen lead flying about in shootouts before and didn't want to be hit by any stray bullets.

Outside, the sound of horses galloping disturbed the quiet, early-evening air. Another bunch of Box T riders was arriving. When the group pulled up in the street outside the saloon, Patch dismounted and tied his horse to the rail across the street from the saloon. He waited for the men he'd gathered to dismount, and they all walked over to the bar. Swinging the doors open, he stepped in and quickly figured out what was shaping up. He hollered out, "Hold it! Stop! Don't nobody draw!"

Matt was able to see Patch come into the saloon from the corner of his eye. He backed up to the wall so he could keep both Patch and Porter in view. Patch waved his hands over his head and walked in between the two men. He stood directly in front of Matt. "Ease up, mister. Porter here, and the rest of us, are George Tanner's men. Roy's the one you want. He sent Wallace to kill that woman, and he's the one got Lucky all shot up. George's gettin' ready to tangle with Roy's friends from back East right now."

"That's enough, Patch!" Porter had been listening impatiently and now spoke up sharply.

Matt relaxed his hand and looked past Patch at Porter, who still stood, tense, at the bar. "I'll back off on George for now, but he must have known what was happening at the Langer farm, and he's going to answer for that."

Porter relaxed his hand, and signaled for his men to sit back down. It was clear to everyone there that they were prepared to back up their boss—with guns if necessary. Several townsmen in the bar, angry about the treatment of Emily Langer and the beating of the boy, were also standing ready for gunplay. Jesse was sitting by himself, quietly watching. He had stopped in for a beer before finishing up Lucky's casket and closing up his shop for the night. He slipped his pistol back into its holster and left.

Matt realized, by what had transpired, that Patch didn't know his good friend Lucky was dead. He looked at him and said quietly, "Step outside with me for a minute, mister."

Patch was surprised by Matt's soft tone. His face wrinkled in confusion. He followed Matt outside. On the boardwalk in front of the saloon, Matt turned and put his hand on Patch's arm. His eyes were sad and his voice was hurting. "Fella, I hate to tell you this, but Lucky died a while ago—for real this time, I'm afraid. Doc did all he could, but his wounds were just too bad. I'm sorry."

Patch took the news hard. Matt saw his face turn white and watched his eyes well up with tears. The heartbroken cowboy wiped at his face with his shirtsleeve, not wanting Matt to see him cry. Matt patted him on the back and suggested he walk around for a while and then stop in at Doc's to say good-bye to his friend. Patch, his head down, nodded and walked off. Matt crossed the street to check on Lucky's casket.

Just after dark had fallen, Roy, McKiernan, and the geologist returned to the Box T. The rest of the gang had settled in the bunkhouse. Evans had asked George for more whiskey for his men, but he'd refused, saying they would be on their way soon. Evans and his men were in a foul mood when McKiernan entered. "What the hell's goin' on here?" Evans' words attacked McKiernan. "We're sittin' here all afternoon with a couple of empty bottles and nothing to eat," Evans hollered out.

He stood up from the card game they were playing and pushed the table back roughly. He was now facing McKiernan with a scowl on his face. McKiernan looked hard at Evans, and his eyes narrowed. "Back off, Evans, this is me you're talking to." He growled his words and walked back outside.

Roy walked into the main house and found George and Brock playing poker. They sat at the round table where George and his wife usually ate their dinner. An open bottle of whiskey and two glasses sat on the table. George was smoking a cigar, and both men still wore their guns. The picture didn't look right to Roy. "What are you still doing here Brock? Why ain't you back in town watching things?" Roy spoke as he headed to the hutch to get himself a glass. *A few whiskeys are just what I need*, he figured.

"Don't you worry about that right now," George yelled harshly at his brother. "What are you going to do with them hombres you brought to my ranch?" Cigar smoke puffed out of his mouth with each word. And each word sounded like a curse word. George slapped his cards on the table and slid them over to Brock. "Deal," he said. Brock kept his head down and dealt the cards.

As Roy reached for a glass in the cabinet, his hand quivered and he knocked the glass on its side. He tried again, picked up the rolling glass, and looked at his brother. He stiffened his back. Roy knew he wasn't as brave as George, but thought he was a much better bluffer. "We're in this together now, George. No sense puttin' your anger on me, least not 'til we get this problem settled. As you figured I'm sure, by the time we got to the creek it was too dark to see much, so we're goin' back in the morning. Now what's he still doing here?" Roy pointed his chin at Brock as he asked the question.

George picked up the cards he'd been dealt and then flung them onto the table and stood up abruptly. His chair slid back and caught on a rough plank. It teetered on its back legs and fell over, clattering across the floor until it hit the chimney and came to a rest. George fixed his gun belt so it was comfortable. "Roy, get this between your two ears and keep it there—as far as you're concerned, Brock works for me now. He takes orders from me and answers to only me. You, on the other hand, as far as I'm concerned, work for *them*." He jerked his thumb over his shoulder in the general direction of the bunkhouse.

Roy was surprised that Brock was now working for George, but he had already figured he had run his string out with George.

"George!" Brock spoke under his breath urgently as he pointed to the main door. He had seen McKiernan walk past the front window. The doors were open to allow the cool night air into the house. McKiernan stopped in the doorway and looked at the three men. Without asking, he walked in. "George, you surprised me, and you embarrassed me in front of my men. When the syndicate we work for lent all that money to your brother, Roy told us we would always be welcomed here and treated like family. Isn't that that right, Roy?" McKiernan stopped talking and turned slightly to stare directly at Roy. Without letting Roy answer he continued. "Now my men tell me you refused to give them any more whiskey and you haven't even offered them supper. That's not very hospitable." He turned to Roy, "Is it, Roy?" McKiernan took the empty glass from Roy's hand and set it hard on the desk in front of George.

Roy looked at George. His whole scheme was coming down around his ears. He knew George must have a plan by now, but George obviously wasn't sharing it with him. Roy started to stammer an answer when George cut him off. "I wasn't sure what your plans were. I thought you might be more comfortable in town. As far as giving your men more whiskey, some folks might not like their men getting drunk when they're not around to watch out for them." George presented a reply that made some sense to McKiernan, but still didn't please him. It was exactly what George wanted to do—get McKiernan to think he was running the show himself… letting McKiernan think he was getting away with telling George what to do. And it worked.

"Well, we're accepting Roy's invitation to supper and a bunk to sleep in for the night," McKiernan said.

George's answer sounded reluctant, as he poured whiskey into the glass McKiernan had set in front of him. "All right, you can set up in the bunkhouse. My men are all on night watch anyway. This time of year our weather turns bad in a heartbeat. Now, as far as supper, I had to send my cook into town with my wife. She had to catch the evening train to visit with a sick friend in Denver, but, if you got someone can cook, I'll provide the food. There's a cook stove right near the tables your men were sitting at outside, and a woodpile in the back of the house."

McKiernan picked up his drink and looked at each of the three men in turn. A fake friendly grin formed on his face. "Maybe now we can all work together. I'll find someone to cook and send him up here." He drank the whiskey and placed the glass back on the table with a slow, almost gentle motion, then turned toward Roy. "Now, how 'bout them bottles for my boys?"

Roy looked at George, who nodded. The exchange between the brothers wasn't missed by the city man. Roy walked to the hutch and pulled down two bottles of whiskey and handed them to McKiernan, who accepted the bottles and left.

When Matt walked into the carpenter's shop, Jesse looked up from his sweeping and motioned to a pair of sawhorses near a side wall. Lucky's casket sat on them. "It's ready, Matt," he said.

The two men carried the coffin across the street and down the alley to Doc Mason's side door. With Doc's help, they brought it in and put Lucky's body into it. Patch was still sitting in the outer office after a brief visit with his best friend's body. He sat on a chair, head hanging down into his hands. Matt went out to talk to him. "I'm glad I got to know the real Lucky. He was quite a man," Matt told Patch.

Patch looked up slowly his eyes red from crying. All he could manage to say was, "Yep, he sure was."

Lucky's funeral was set for early the next morning. Posters were put up around town for any or all to attend.

23 Good-bye Lucky

The following morning Matt, Doc, Jesse, and Patch loaded the coffin into the funeral wagon and began the trip to the cemetery. They would all act as pallbearers. The Loren sisters and Emily rode in the Lorens' buggy along with Alley, who had been given permission by Doc Mason to attend—only because he had agreed to return to bed directly after the service. Dewey and Howard Rohls followed behind the wagons on horseback; several townspeople accompanied them. The morning was dreary with grey, gloomy clouds hanging just above the rooftops. A misty rain was falling.

With the coffin in the ground, a local reverend said some prayers over the grave. He then asked for someone to step forward and say something about Lucky. Emily, wearing a plain black dress borrowed from Beth, her eyes looking red and troubled, moved to the grave and spoke. "This man we bury today saved my life at the cost of his own. I don't think any of us could ever do more or wish to be braver than him. I pray he's in heaven now." She struggled to keep her voice steady. "Thank you, Lucky." Emily walked quickly away from the grave, her hands covering her face. The Loren sisters joined her and put their arms around her.

Patch stepped forward, his hat crushed in his hands. He cleared his throat and spoke hesitantly. "Uh… uh… I'd like to tell you something about my partner." His voice was quiet but strong. He looked down at his friend's coffin. "His real name was Bill Stewart. He was the best partner any man could ask for. I met Lucky when I was glad to eat six days out of the week. I didn't own a horse and couldn't find a job. My clothes were threadbare, more in need of patches than pockets. He gave me a spare horse he owned and let me ride with him. Taught me how to work cattle and take care of myself. Mostly we did honest work, though sometimes we did stray off the right trail at times. He was gruff and harsh talkin' at times, but he'd never hurt no one didn't look to hurt him first. What he did to get hisself killed don't surprise me none. He felt terrible about scarin' that lady, but he believed he was savin' her life. He really did. Amen."

The preacher said some final words, and the crowd started moving away. As the procession left the hill, two men began filling the grave. The rain was falling harder, turning the dirt into mud.

The Lorens invited everyone at the funeral to come back to their house for refreshments. Most of the mourners went there. Matt and Patch stood under the overhang in front of the sheriff's office, talking. The rain cascading from the roof formed a curtain in front of them before it splashed into the street. The two men had talked earlier in the morning before putting Lucky's casket in the wagon. According to the plans Patch had explained, he was supposed to catch up with Porter and the rest of the Box T riders and head for the ranch. Patch also told Matt as much as he knew about the men from the train and about the sheriff staying at the ranch. The whole situation seemed very confusing to Matt. Patch shook Matt's hand and left town amid a slurry of mud splashed up from his horse's hooves. Matt pulled his collar up, bent his hat against the rain, and walked to the Lorens' home.

24 Patch Takes a Stand

A fast-moving rivulet of muddy water ran down past the side of the Box T's main house. George watched as it followed a course under the tables the syndicate men had been sitting at yesterday. Whenever there was a heavy downpour of rain that lasted this long, the dry wash came to life. It was fed from a natural pool that formed on the high ground in front of his house. George stood on his porch for half an hour considering the changes the rain had made to his plans. He'd sent Roy down to the bunkhouse earlier to rouse McKiernan and his men. George was hoping to convince McKiernan to take all his men with him to scout for the best places to get at the gold.

Roy returned quickly, telling George that McKiernan wouldn't budge. "He says he'll wait for the rain to stop, George… honestly that's all he would say."

Roy stood under the porch roof and waited for his brother's reply. "Damn, that spills the pot," George muttered angrily.

Roy backed away and took off his raincoat. He slapped his hat against his leg to rid it of as much moisture as possible, and went inside. Brock was sitting nearby in the shadows; he wasn't noticed by Roy.

George also walked inside and watched Roy go to the cupboard for some early morning courage. He walked over to Brock and spoke quietly. "Ease out of here and meet up with Porter and the men; they should be halfway here by now. Tell Porter the plan has changed and he's to wait for my instructions back in town. He'll know what to do."

Brock stood up and said, "I'm leaving right now, George." He walked leisurely to the barn, stepping around puddles when possible. He knew George wanted him to leave quickly—but unnoticed if possible. Brock saddled his mount in the dim light of the large barn. The lone rider walking his horse out of the main gate wasn't seen by anyone except George.

George stood on his porch staring at the small stream rushing by. He was deep in thought. *If I had one more creek on this property, I never would have got involved in this mess. I just needed more water and I got greedy at that poor woman's expense. I can't blame Roy on that. I'm the one agreed to it after I heard that fella Lucky's idea. But I never told Roy to get involved with that damned syndicate. He did that all on his own.* George looked up at the sky out to the west where the weather was coming from and went back to his thoughts. *Now with this rain falling so hard, them lazy louts won't move 'til it stops... probably tomorrow at the earliest. They outnumber us pretty good. Holding them off from inside the buildings won't be hard, but digging them out of that bunkhouse before the rest of their gang gets here would cost too many good men. We'll just have to wait 'til they're out looking for Roy's gold. Then I'll*

Joe Bryceland

get my men inside with plenty of provisions. We'll be prepared for a long standoff.

George took a cigar from his shirt pocket and lit it. The smoke wafted slowly upward and became part of the soggy air. He walked across the porch, sat in the chair Brock had recently vacated, and called to Roy to come outside. Roy finished the whiskey he was drinking and walked out to his brother. George looked up at him from his chair and spoke. "Listen, Roy, I want you to ride over to the Langer spread and find a likely spot to bring that fella McKiernan and his cronies to tomorrow morning. Make sure it's at least an hour's ride out from here. Then, tomorrow morning, you make sure you get them all out there."

Roy's moaning complaint was cut short by the murderous look on his brother's face.

Before noon, most of the guests had left the Lorens' home. Alley had been allowed to take part in the gathering, but now Howard Rohls was escorting him back to his bed in Doc's clinic.

Once again, Matt and Doc were in a sober discussion. Emily and the Loren sisters listened in. Matt was sitting at the table, a cup of coffee in front of him—a dark liquid crystal ball he was studying. His hands surrounded the cup. Doc leaned against a wall, his right foot crossed over his left. Dewey stood next to him, his eyes fixed on Matt who was telling them all he'd learned from Patch and about all the confusion brought on by the appearance of the men from the train. He finished by saying, "I think we have to sit tight for a while and see how the wind blows. Meanwhile, I'm going to stay out at Emily's place 'til my men get here."

Doc pushed off the wall and moved to stand at the table across from Matt. He leaned forward, his hands pressing on the tabletop. Blue veins pulsed on his thick, muscular hands and wrist. He looked at Matt. "Matt, we'll keep an eye out for your men and send them out to you as soon as they get here, but I hope you're going to stay away from the Box T 'til then."

"Sure thing, Doc. Right now, I just want to keep an eye on Emily's place. At this point, I don't think anyone knows what's going to happen next, so let's all keep our eyes and ears open." Matt stood and stretched. "I'm going to get going now. Good-bye all." He waved to the group. Before he turned to open the door, he received a concerned smile from Beth.

Patch was anxious to catch up to Porter and the rest of the Box T crew. He whipped his horse fiercely as he raced across the uneven ground of the shortcut through some woods he and Lucky had used often to get to town. The shortcut would take several miles off the trip, but he lost sight of the road many times. There were also many dangers in the shortcut—gopher holes and hidden vines on the wet grassy floor. Somehow, he made it through and arrived at the road just shy of the turn into the yard at the main house. He pulled up his mount and looked around the quiet area, then waited for Porter and his men to appear. After ten minutes, he decided they must have gotten in without any trouble and were now staying out of the rain in the bunkhouse. In fact, however, they had been intercepted by Brock and were on their way back to town.

Patch rode easily into the yard, head down to avoid the rain. He dismounted by the corral and walked into the bunkhouse. He was startled by the sight of all the strangers occupying the bunks. Evans and several hard-looking men were seated at the table he and Red had been sitting at just yesterday. A man wearing only his long johns and a holstered pistol was dealing a hand of poker. Patch recovered quickly and walked past them to Lucky's bunk under the small back window. A short, heavyset man was snoring in it. Patch reached under the bed for the saddlebags Lucky kept there. When Patch couldn't feel anything with his hand, he lay on the floor and peered under the bed. The saddlebags were gone. Lucky had kept an extra pistol and two boxes of cartridges in them along with most of his personal effects.

Evans had been startled by Patch's appearance and was just now recovering. He stood up and approached Patch. "What the hell do you think you're doing?" Evans had been in a bad mood ever since they'd arrived at the ranch, and now he had someone to take it out on. He stood in front of Patch, pistol in hand. "Answer me, damn it! Who are you, and why are you bustin' in here?" The veins in his neck were straining to stay under his skin. Evans' intent was clear in his voice; he was going to humiliate Patch.

Patch stood up and looked Evans square in the eyes. He wasn't scared at all, and surprisingly felt very calm, as he spoke. "Where's my partner's saddlebags was under that bunk?" His left hand pointed to the floor near Lucky's bunk. His right hand moved to his gun.

Evans poked him in the chest with his shooter. "I ain't seen no saddlebags. You accusing us of stealing, mister?" Evans' left hand shot out and punched Patch in the face.

Patch let his chin roll with the punch and took the blow easily. He let a slow smile form across his face. He remembered Matt doing that in the Three Eights saloon and how it had unsettled everyone. A question flickered across Evans' eyes, and Patch used that moment to slap the gun out of Evans' hand and draw his own. He pointed his gun at Evans' chest and shouted. "Stand still, everyone. One move and he goes to hell first."

Patch got behind Evans and, using him as a shield, started for the door. He didn't see the man in the long johns slip Evans a gun as they passed by the now-crowded doorway. As they walked backwards across the yard to Patch's horse, Evans twisted his gun hand behind him and fired. The bullet hit Patch in the side. Patch felt a burning sensation and instinctively pushed Evans away from him and ran for his horse. Shots rang out at him from the bunkhouse porch, and a bullet hit his left shoulder spinning him around. Patch faced three gunmen and Evans, who was still running with his back to him. The one in the long johns was pointing a barking rifle at him. Patch aimed at him and fired. Two black holes appeared in the man's dirty grey shirt near its top button, and he fell to the porch floor. More bullets whizzed around Patch as he tried to reach his horse. Suddenly, gunfire erupted from the main house, and Patch saw George Tanner firing a rifle at the men by the bunkhouse.

Evans fell into the room with George's bullets chasing him. McKiernan and several others were trying to give him covering fire, but George split his fire between the one window in the front and the door. The bunkhouse was built to withstand attack from outside, and that door and window were the only two ways out or in. There were other openings, but they were too small for a man to get through; they were used as gun ports. Most of the men were lying on the floor trying to protect themselves from flying glass and ricocheting bullets.

McKiernan knelt by the window next to Evans. When he heard the shooting change from the heavy rifle shots to the pistol Patch was firing, he ordered his men to get outside.

"Get out there and quiet them guns! You think I brought you here to lie on that floor?" McKiernan yelled.

Three cowboys bent low and ran to the door. Evans waved two other men to the window. He looked at the men by the door. "When we start shooting, get out and around back and then make your way to the house."

George had been writing a letter to his wife when he heard the shooting. He'd grabbed his always-loaded Winchester and run to the porch where he'd seen the fix Patch was in. He began firing at the shooters, a steady, withering fire that sent them all ducking inside. George was shouting as he fired. "Over here, son, get over here!"

Patch grabbed his horse's reins and stumbled to the main house. He fell on the porch floor and lay on his belly facing the bunkhouse. George saw the blood on the young man's shoulder and knew he was in serious trouble. "Can you shoot, son?"

"Sure thing, Mr. Tanner, but I'm low on ammunition. I figure I got two more rounds in my gun."

George's rifle was empty, so he threw Patch his six-gun. "Here, take this. I'll be right back with more ammo. Don't let them out of the bunkhouse."

Patch had emptied his own gun and was using George's when they started out the bunkhouse door. The man in the lead was a small, wiry cowboy named Brant. He came out low and running fast. Patch's pistol shots didn't deter him, but the second and third men exiting the door were met by more accurate rifle fire. The second man out was hit in the chest, stumbled into the yard, and fell dead to the muddy earth. The next man was hit in his left arm and right leg. He fell against the wall and started crawling back into the bunkhouse, leaving a smudged trail of blood on the worn-out porch floor.

Brock heard the gunfire on his way back from his meeting with Porter and the Box T men. He spurred his horse and raced back to the ranch. Now he was hunkered down behind the corner post of the corral. The rifle in his hands was blazing away, and he stopped anyone else from leaving the bunkhouse. The second man he shot was crawling back into the crews' quarters, but Brock concentrated his fire on the window to stop the return fire that was closing in on Patch.

George returned to the doorway with two rifles and another pistol. He dropped two boxes of shells on the floor and slid one of the rifles to Patch. "Did any of them make it out of the bunk house?" he asked Patch.

"Yes, sir. One got around back a few minutes ago," Patch answered.

"Aw, hell," George complained as he began firing on his own building again.

A bullet plucked at his sleeve, tearing his shirt and searing his arm. George looked over at Brock; he realized what had to be done. He cupped his hands over his mouth and shouted to Brock. "Brock, you two hold them off for a few more minutes then we've got to get out of here. When I call to you, cover us with all you got." George bent down and picked up a box of shells and tossed them across the yard to Brock. They were forty-five caliber, the same as Brock was firing. The box landed near Brock and split open, spilling some shells at his feet.

"Keep 'em pinned in there, son, I'll be right back." George shouted his words to Patch as he ran to the back of the house.

George opened the back door slowly and wasn't surprised to see the man who had escaped from the bunkhouse sneaking toward the house. Both men fired as one. The syndicate man's bullet flew over George's head and thunked into the doorframe. George was used to firing on the quick, and he hit the man in the middle of his belly with his first shot. The gunman cursed and stumbled into the brush, disappearing in the overgrowth. The Box T owner sent several more rounds into the brush after him. The wounded man stumbled deeper into the woods away from the house. Two more of George's bullets had hit him. He died sitting against a tree a few minutes later.

George rushed back into the house and headed for the steel safe that sat on the floor behind his desk. He worked on the combination and opened the heavy door. A black leather satchel sat on the bottom; it contained all the important papers in George's life. He kept them gathered up in the bag for just such an emergency—although he always imagined the emergency would probably be a fire. George scooped the rest of the contents of his safe into the bag—several stacks of paper money, most of his wife's better jewelry, and some gold and silver chunks he had gathered over the years. He ran back outside to join Patch.

His two men had done a good job containing the syndicate crew, but George knew come nightfall they would be able to slip out and surround the Box T men.

"Can your horse carry two, son?" he asked Patch.

Patch was lying prone on the porch floor; he was firing the rifle one handed. The pain in his shoulder stopped it from being of much use. "I reckon he can if he has to, Mr. Tanner," he answered through clenched teeth. The wounded cowboy continued firing as he answered. George couldn't see the weakness in his eyes.

Patch's horse was hiding on the far side of the house away from the flying bullets. George leaned against the doorjamb and fired an intense fusillade at the bunkhouse. His rifle barrel was smoking when he called out. "Brock, we'll be making a run for it in a minute. Be ready to cover us. Keep their heads down for a while and then follow us. We'll head to town."

Brock waved a slight acknowledgment to George and reloaded his rifle from the shells lying at his feet.

George looked at his man lying on the porch floor in front of him. The blood from his shoulder wound formed a small puddle next to him. George called down to him. "Son, I'm going to bring your horse up here. When I do, get in the saddle and I'll climb up back."

Patch nodded his head and waved his rifle in acknowledgment. "Okay, Mr. Tanner, I'll be ready."

George moved easily toward the skittish horse. As he reached for the reins, the horse reared and struck out at him with its sharp hooves, but the Box T owner had handled horses all his life and had expected the reaction. He grabbed the reins and spoke soothingly, calming the excited horse. He tied his satchel to the saddle. Brock and Patch were keeping up a steady stream of fire at the men in the bunkhouse, keeping the return fire to a minimum. George led the horse to the porch steps and called for Patch to get mounted. Patch stood up slowly, his weakness now very apparent to George. "Come on, boy, don't give up now!" he called out.

George was holding the frightened animal with two hands and not firing his rifle so as not to scare the horse any more. The men in the bunkhouse were waiting for them to try to run. As soon as he had seen George lead the horse up to the front porch, McKiernan had told his men, "Get ready—they're going to make a run for it!" Evans and two men were kneeling on the floor by the door, rifles ready.

When Patch stopped firing, the men at the window fired non-stop at Brock's position, pinning him down. George and Patch were standing in the open—easy targets for the men by the door. The door banged open, and a deadly rush of bullets flew through the rain at George and Patch. Brock was doing his best to keep them from firing accurately.

"Come on, boy, get up in the saddle!" George was holding the struggling horse with one hand now; the other held his smoldering pistol.

Patch reached for the saddle horn, but a bullet smashed into his left side. *That felt like a kick from a mule,* he thought, as it sent him to one knee. He turned back to the bunkhouse and began firing his own reloaded six-gun. "I ain't gonna make it, Mr. Tanner. Get outta here. I'll cover ya." Patch was smiling as he said the words.

George mounted the now-crazed horse and reached down to grab Patch under his arms. Using every bit of his strength, he held onto the young cowboy as he rode out of the ranch yard, Patch's legs dragging on the ground, his boot toes digging two small trenches in the mud. A bullet skinned the already-spooked horse and sent him racing away. Brock continued his covering fire for several more minutes then suddenly quit. The fire from the syndicate men slowly stopped. A quiet disturbed only by the falling rain followed.

McKiernan opened the door slowly and peered out. The yard looked empty. A hazy mist of gun smoke hung over the ground; the smell of burned gunpowder was everywhere. The rain was falling heavier trying to wash it away. McKiernan turned to Evans. "Get some men up to the main house and check it out. The rest of you men saddle up and get after them," he said.

Sid, a tall, thin cowboy, stepped outside first. Brock's bullet took him in the chest and sent his body crashing back into the bunkhouse. He bumped into Evans and fell dead at his feet.

Brock had taken his time to reload both his weapons and now fired another barrage into the bullet-pocked building. Aiming at the window and door as George had done, he sent the men inside back to the floor.

George pulled up the galloping horse deep in the woods Patch had recently traveled as a shortcut. He let Patch's body down gently and dismounted. The youngster he hadn't had much use for was dead. George knelt beside him and held his head. His calloused hands were tender. The owner of the Box T didn't move. For several minutes, he just looked around. The woods were silent; the leaves on the ground were damp from the recent rains; the trees above were dark green. A curious owl looked on from a low branch.

"My daddy always said you can't tell about a man 'til you need to. I'm sorry I thought about you the way I did, boy." George was talking with a croak in his voice, but stopped suddenly at the sound of a horse coming. It wasn't Brock; the horse was coming from the wrong direction. It was Roy returning from the Langer farm.

"Roy, over here," George called out in a harsh whisper.

Roy rode up to his brother, a look of anxiety on his face. A large black raincoat and a hat covered his body. "George, what's going on? I thought I heard gunfire a while ago."

"You did, and now your friends from back East have control of my ranch."

The look on his brother's face told Roy how much he was hated right now. "George, I never meant for this to happen," he whined.

"Shut up, Roy. Don't say anything else."

The sound of Brock's horse quieted both men. "It's me, George—Brock—I'm comin' in—don't shoot." Brock rode up slowly. When he saw Patch's body, he stepped down off his horse and removed his hat. He bowed his head for a moment then looked at his new boss. "Damn, George, that boy sure had plenty of man in him."

George was still kneeling by Patch's body. "He did that, that's for sure. Help me get him on your horse. We ain't leaving him here."

They put Patch's body across the saddle and covered it with the ground cover sheet they found tied on the horse's back. George spoke to Brock and his brother for a few minutes, and then Brock and George rode toward town. Roy headed for the ranch.

♣

Matt decided to stay in Emily's barn for the night. On the way out to the farm from town, he watched a lone rider leaving the property and heading toward the Box T. Matt couldn't tell who it was, but he assumed it was a Box T rider. *The men from the East wouldn't know the area well enough to be out riding alone,* he thought. He looked after Raven and then made a bed of hay for himself, reminding him of when he had first met Emily. He busied himself the rest of the afternoon by bringing in firewood and hay for his men and their mounts when they arrived.

♣

Roy rode into the muddy Box T yard slowly and cautiously, his hands in plain sight. The rain had stopped. "McKiernan, it's me, Roy. Don't shoot." A bullet whizzed past his head, and then he heard the crack of a rifle shot. Roy slid out of the saddle and hunkered down by the corral where Brock had been firing from earlier. Ejected bullet shells were planted in the mud in every possible angle. Roy called out. "McKiernan, don't shoot. We have to talk. I got words from my brother George for you."

McKiernan and Evans were sitting on the floor in a back corner of the room. They had decided to be very cautious after Brock shot the last man. They planned to wait for nightfall and send some men out in the dark to secure the area. The rest of the gang was scattered to every corner of the bunkhouse—squatting down away from the door and window. Evans' face had been cut by a chunk of wood sent flying by one of Brock's bullets. He held a bandanna to his right cheek. The flow of blood had stopped, and an angry red welt replaced some of his three-day-old beard.

McKiernan crawled to the window. Sweat from his brow highlighted his pasty skin and dripped onto the floor. He told the men to hold their fire. Peering out of the gouged, smoldering hole that used to be a window, he shouted. "Show yourself, Roy, and keep your hands in sight."

Roy's hands slowly appeared above the top corral bar, and, eventually, his upper body followed. Evans joined McKiernan at the window and shouted, "Keep your hands up and come into the bunkhouse. Your next trick is your last." Roy started moving forward on weak, shaky legs.

An angry McKiernan confronted Roy at the bunkhouse door. "Take his damn gun." He hissed his order to Evans who was standing next to him. Evans shoved Roy roughly against the wall and pulled his pistol from its holster.

"What the hell's goin' on here, Roy? What's your brother up to?" McKiernan's face was red now; his upper lip was quivering.

Roy knew McKiernan was tough back East, but out here on the plains there weren't a lot of dark alleys where a man could hide for the purpose of waylaying someone. And, out here, most men were tough and would fight back hard when threatened. McKiernan was scared. He'd grown up in New York, the son of a Tammany Hall thug, and he was used to people fearing him as such. Very few fought back. Out West, things were different, and he was learning.

Roy spoke quickly as he looked around the room. "George said he thinks you went crazy shooting at his man for no reason. Him and Brock are heading to town now with the man's body over his saddle. He'll stay in town 'til his wife comes back from Denver. Meanwhile, let's get back to business and look for that gold tomorrow. If we start out early enough with all your men, we can locate all the spots that gold shows up in by nightfall. Then we can go set on the girl's land and claim that it's abandoned." McKiernan and Evans shared a conspiratorial glance at each other.

♣

Doc Mason had just finished changing the bandage on Alley's hand when a commotion in the street caught his attention. "Hold still a while, Alley, while I see what the hoo-hah is all about," Doc instructed his young patient.

The boy was looking much better, and even seemed to have filled out some. Alley sat on his bed, examining his newly bandaged hand. Doc was walking to his front door when he saw George Tanner leading a horse with a bundle draped over it, boots hanging down. George passed Doc's large window slowly and turned in to the hitching rail outside Doc's office. *George looked older and slightly bent over.* Doc stepped outside into the sodden street. Several people were gathered around George. "What happened, George? Who's that?" Doc asked.

Tanner tossed the reins over the rail and tied them. George looked at Doc. His eyes were sunken and dark, maybe a little red.

"It's one of Lucky's men, a feller named Patch. Do you know him?"

Doc nodded his head slightly. "Yeah, I met him when he came to ask about Lucky. And he was at Lucky's funeral. Are you sure he's dead?"

"Yeah." George sounded dour.

Doc stepped forward and removed the cover. The horse shied and moved against George. "Whoa, hold still, boy." George steadied the still-frightened horse.

Doc felt for a pulse and looked for any sign of life. There was none to be found. Looking at the Box T owner, Doc spoke almost inaudibly, but angrily, "Help me get him inside. I'll get Jesse to set up another burial. Each death seems to start the trouble all over again," he said.

George untied the rope that held Patch on the horse. "I'll stand responsible for the funeral, Doc, and for Lucky's too."

Doc looked at George; his eyes narrowed and he wondered if the man knew how true his words were.

Brock was standing nearby and came forward. "I'll get him, George," he said, as he reached for the body.

"No, take the horses to the stable and see if Dewey has something for that gunshot burn on the kid's horse. I'll meet you in the Three Eights later."

George reached up and pulled Patch's body over his shoulder.

"Open the door, Doc, please. I'll bring him in."

25 Truce

Porter was keeping a tight rein on the Box T wranglers. Most of them sat around the saloon talking and playing cards without any whiskey in front of them. Porter sat at a corner table in the back talking to Howard Rohls. He and Rohls had been friends for many years, and now they were telling each other what they knew of the current goings on. The bottle on their table was missing only two drinks and had stood unused for the last hour.

Porter's hat sat back on his head; bushy brown hair rolled down over his furrowed brow. His sun-stained, coarse fingers tapped on the table in front of him. "Most of this is news to me and the boys, I can tell you that for sure, Howard. I knew something shady was going on since Roy got here, but I didn't know what it was. George kept us pretty busy with all the cattle he's been buying. We got 'em spread out all over his range. Too many, if you ask me," Porter complained.

Rohls stood up and pushed his chair in. It scraped against the rough wooden floor and brought several pairs of eyes up to look at him. The Box T men were anxious and waiting for orders from Porter. Rohls unfurled his shirtsleeves, which had been rolled up over beefy forearms. He reached behind him and pulled his coat from the back of his chair and put it on. Howard Rohls then leaned in toward his old friend to shake his hand. He spoke softly, "Porter, from what you tell me and from what I know, there seems to be three sides to this fight now. And, if you say George didn't want no part in killing Emily Langer, I believe you. Let's try to put a powwow together with George and this fella Matt. Maybe we can at least put a stop to you and your men fighting with other honest men. I'll get started on my end right now. Good luck."

Porter stood up with Rohls' hand still in his. "I'll speak to George about it as soon as I see him. I'm sure he'll be agreeable. Thanks, Howard."

Rohls left the Three Eights and headed to the livery to see Dewey, figuring he would know where Matt was and how to get in touch with him. The rain had stopped a few minutes earlier, and a warm sun had finally broken through the murky sky. A humid mist crept up out of the wet ground. When he reached the livery, Rohls entered through the side door. Brock was unsaddling a worn-out brown horse. Dewey was walking up from the back, a can of salve in his hand. Brock turned quickly as the door opened. His right hand flashed, and his gun appeared in it.

"Hold up there, Brock! You got no cause to pull a gun on Howard." Dewey looked Brock in the eye and motioned with his free hand for Brock to lower his gun. A tense stillness filled the stable. The brown horse whinnied and stepped nervously toward Howard. The ex sheriff holstered his pistol.

"Sorry, Howard. I had a run-in with some tough hombres earlier today, and I'm still on edge. Didn't mean to scare ya none."

Rohls had been caught off guard by Brock's move, but now was staring hard at him. He realized how close he'd just come to being killed by this crooked lawman. But he was a strong man himself and quickly regained his composure. From what Porter had told him, he figured Brock was working for George Tanner now.

Acting as if he was unimpressed with Brock's gun handling, Rohls asked him, "You know where George Tanner is, Brock? It's important he speaks with Porter right away."

Brock looked at Rohls; curiosity shaped his face. "He's up to the doc's. We brought that young feller, rode with Lucky, in. He was killed by that bunch from back East—gave them hell first though."

Rohls looked at Brock; his disgust with the man wasn't hidden. "Well, Porter's in the saloon," he said. "You need to get George to go see him right away before you get more people killed."

Brock knew what the people in town thought of him, and he wasn't surprised at Rohls' comment. All he wanted now was to get George back on his ranch and send the troublemakers from back East packing. Then he'd collect the stake George had promised him and head west to start a new life.

"Go ahead, sher… I mean Brock. I'll tend the horses, see this wound gets taken care of, and feed and water 'em both. You get

George and Porter together." Dewey spoke out as he put the can of salve down and took hold of the halter of the brown horse.

Brock put the saddle on the floor near the first stall. "All right, Dewey. Do the best you can for the kid's horse, will ya?"

Brock brushed past Howard Rohls and left through the side door. Rohls' eyes followed him with a scathing look.

Dewey watched Brock move through the door and close it. He took Patch's horse over to the back wall and tied him to a metal ring that hung from an upright beam, then walked back and picked up the salve. "Howard, what's going on? Why do you want George to meet with Porter?"

Rohls walked over and put his hands on the back of the brown horse near the sore-looking wound caused by one of Patch's killers. "I been talking to Porter. Me and him pushed cows together for a few outfits when I first came out West from Ohio. He's always been a good man and a straight shooter. He says George didn't intend for Emily to get hurt, but he admits he let Roy talk him into chasing her from her property. He says he regrets it now. Anyway, that's done now, but I think a new, bigger problem might be them fellas from back East."

Dewey was spreading salve on the wounded horse. He looked over at Howard. "What's Porter gonna tell George, do you know?"

"That's why I came here, Dewey. Do you know where Matt is now? I think him and George should talk. It might be there's no need for them to fight each other anymore. George is going to have his hands full with them eastern fellas. They're sitting on his property right now."

Dewey put the cap on the tin of salve and placed it on a shelf. His face registered the shocking news. Pulling slowly on the rope, he unloosed the wounded horse and led him to a stall. The news that George Tanner had been moved off his ranch was startling. Dewey thought about it as he scratched his ear. "Matt headed out to Emily's place earlier today. Probably going to stay there overnight. Figures to keep an eye on it 'til his men get here. Expects them soon, he said. If you think it's that important, Howard, I'll ride out there now and tell him what you said."

"I think it is, Dewey. We may be able to stop some of this bloodshed amongst decent people. I'll send my helper Frank down here to look after your shop."

"Thanks, Howard. I'll be ready to leave in ten minutes."

"Good. I'd go myself, but, it's been so long since I've been out there, I'd spend the rest of the afternoon looking for her house. Thanks, and be careful. We can't know what them fools from back East are thinking."

♣

McKiernan and Evans had been at Roy for over an hour asking him question after question since he arrived back at the ranch. An edgy restlessness permeated the room. Though not seen, it was there—like a smell. The bunkhouse was quiet; most of the men sat on the floor or lay in bunks waiting for orders. McKiernan surveyed the room and then looked at Evans and pointed at the door. "Come outside with me," he said, then stopped short. "Wait a minute!" He showed a scornful look at Roy. "You, Roy, go out first and stand by that corral."

Doing what he was told, Roy opened the door and stepped out. Grateful to be leaving the bunkhouse, he blew out a silent breath. Water dripped from the soaking roof. Evans and McKiernan followed him. Roy looked back at them and then walked over to the corral and leaned on a top rail, which was chewed up from some of the bullets that had missed Patch.

McKiernan pulled on Evans' shirtsleeve and guided him away from the open window. "Listen, I don't trust Roy at all ever since I seen this layout. His brother obviously owns this ranch by himself, and he just tolerates Roy 'cause he's his brother. I want you to send some of your men with Roy, and I want them to go and squat on that woman's farm. I'll tell Roy to lead them to the farm and then come back here. I want him nearby in case his brother comes back looking for trouble. In the morning we'll go look at the places he says there's gold at, but I'm leaving some men here. If his brother does come back, he'll have to burn that bunkhouse down to get them outta there."

Evans was staring at Roy. He was listening to McKiernan's words, but his mind was focused on different thoughts. During the gunfight, McKiernan hadn't been leading the men as he should have. Instead, he'd been in the corner watching out for his own hide. Evans decided that he was the stronger of the two, and it was time for him to exert himself. He turned to look at McKiernan and put his right palm up to him. "Hold on a minute, McKiernan. I can find that farm by myself. I'll get Roy to give me directions, and I'll take the men there myself. I'll take some food and what-all with me for a few days. I don't think that brother of his is looking to take on our bunch. He lit outta here like a scared rabbit. In the morning, why don't you take the rest of the men and gather up as much of that gold, as fast as you can. That way, if they do get the cavalry to help them, we'll have something to light outta here with."

McKiernan studied hard on what Evans had just said. His eyes squinted, and his lips were pinched together. McKiernan wondered if George really could get the army to help him. He knew the political crooks he worked for didn't want a run-in with the U.S. Cavalry. Roy had said it was unlikely. He thought George would just wait until they left. McKiernan didn't like giving in to Evans, but he had to admit his idea made sense. "Maybe you're right this time, Evans. Pick the men you want and get started. There won't be much daylight left by the time you get there. I'll tell Roy to give you directions while you saddle up."

Evans went back into the bunkhouse and started calling out names. McKiernan walked over to speak to Roy.

It was late in the day when Matt took two buckets and a towel down to the creek. He walked down the path behind the house. With the rock wall on his left and the dark forest on his other side, Matt felt at ease. The water was still running fast from all the recent rains. Matt undressed and plunged into the cold stream for a quick bath. The rushing water was noisy as it splashed over the boulders and smaller rocks that were strewn in random order throughout the streambed, framed sometimes by the red- and purple-colored bushes that flourished in the creek. The surrounding scenery was soothing, with the green moss running up and down the dark brown banks and shadowy tree limbs hanging down into the water—all of it highlighted by the last of the day's sunlight streaming through the trees overhead. Matt walked out of the creek and dried off in the warm afternoon air. He walked bare-chested back to the barn, carrying a bucket of water for Raven in each hand.

As Matt stepped through the back door to the barn, he was grabbed by two men and wrestled to the floor. The water buckets spilled and wet all three men as they grappled on the floor. Matt managed to free his right arm and swing a heavy punch at one of his attackers, knocking him out. Struggling to his feet, Matt spun the second man around and threw him against the wall. Someone punched him in the back, pushing the air out of his lungs, while another kicked his legs out from under him, sending him to the floor again. More men jumped into the fray, and Matt was restrained and dragged to his feet. The barn was dark with shadows, and faces were difficult to see. Matt hadn't planned on lighting any lamps in the event late-night intruders might show.

"Bring him outside. Let's see what we caught." Evans growled his command as he grabbed Matt's left arm and bent it back. Two other men grabbed Matt and pushed him through the large front door. Evans pushed Matt into a circle of his men. They dragged him away from the barn toward the creek where some afternoon light was still available.

"Ho, boys, look who we got here. It's the joker we met on the trail earlier," Evans said.

Matt and Evans had recognized each other as soon as Evans spun Matt around and pushed him into his men. Matt was looking around trying to think of an escape plan. He looked past the stone wall into the woods. A pair of eyes was watching the scene from the tree line beyond the wall. Evans stepped up to Matt. "What are you doin' here, planning on claiming this farm for yourself, are ya?" Evans and McKiernan had never been told about Matt's involvement in protecting Emily's farm. Roy didn't want to alarm the bosses back in New York. He was hoping to find enough gold to pay off his loan before they sent someone out to investigate the situation.

Two men held Matt while Evans slapped him hard across the face. Water flew from Matt's still-wet hair; his face reddened from the slap.

"What are you doin' here? You got a hand in this business, mister?"

One of the men poked Matt's breastbone with a large sharp knife. A small flow of blood ran down his chest. A punch to his stomach sent Matt to his knees. Several men pulled him to his feet, and Evans hit him in the jaw with a balled fist. Matt rolled with the punch as King Bill had taught him to, and the blow had little effect. But the next blow landed on Matt's ear, stinging it like a pack of biting hornets. The rage building in Matt from all the recent events surged through his body. He used it to break free of the men holding him. He hauled off and punched Evans. The punch, thrown too quickly, hit the outlaw only a glancing blow, but knocked him down anyway. Matt ran for the barn where his guns were.

"Shoot him—shoot him!" Evans screamed, even as he was drawing his own gun, which wasn't easy, as he was sitting on the ground. Bullets zinged past Matt's head as he ran, in a crouched position, toward the barn door. One of the eyes that were watching from the woods closed, and the other turned red as a rifle cracked. A man who was steadying his aim at Matt felt a bullet go through his left arm and into his heart. He died on the way to the ground.

A roar filled the yard as bullets flew at Matt. The rifle in the woods continued to bark, causing some shooters to change their target. Another outlaw fell to the ground, screaming he was gut shot. Matt reached the barn and grabbed his rifle. Most of Evans' men were firing at the woods when he stepped back outside.

Holding the rifle on his hip, Matt cranked the lever and fired in the rapid-fire move he had practiced so often while searching for the men who had killed his father. Two men were already down, and Matt's bullets sent two more to the ground.

"It's an ambush! Let's get outta here," a portly, stoop-shouldered man was yelling as he ran for the horses tied nearby.

One of the gunmen helped another who was on the ground. Matt took aim at his back, but didn't fire. He searched for Evans instead.

Evans had emptied his gun at Matt and was reloading when a bullet tore at his shirtsleeve. Fearing they no longer had the upper hand, and caught out in the open as they were, Evans drifted back to his horse as he fired at the rifleman in the woods. Evans was already riding away when he heard one of his men shout the advice to the others to leave. Matt saw Evans crossing the creek and fired at him. His bullet skipped off the water and thudded into the mud just in front of Evans' horse. Five other men were now racing behind him. Matt's rifle clicked on an empty chamber. He wiped his damp face with his hand and looked around. Three of the gunmen lay dead in Emily's yard.

Matt turned toward the woods. A slip of white smoke was clinging to the leaves before rising to the sky near the spot where he'd seen the eyes looking at him. Matt called out. "Hello!"

Nobody came forward, so he called again. "Hello! Thanks for saving my life. Who are you?"

Silence followed as Matt's words seeped into the woods and vanished. Fear strained Matt's voice. "Are you all right?" he called out and began running over to the woods.

Maybe he's been shot, Matt worried as he ran to find the rifleman who had helped him. The trees were still, and the leafy earth around them showed no sign of the person who had saved Matt's life. Only the spent cartridges lying on the ground kept Matt from thinking he had imagined his rescuer. He called out again, "Hello! Hello!" Again no answer came back.

Darkness already owned the woods and was now finishing the deal over the rest of the farm. Galloping hoof-beats caught Matt's attention, and he ran to the barn for more ammunition.

Dewey had heard the shooting from almost a mile away and urged his mount to a risky hoof-pounding dash toward Emily's farm in the dim light of late day. As he reached the creek, he stopped and listened. Only the breathing of his horse and the pounding of his heart could be heard. The rest of the world was silent—not even the evening crickets were chattering. His horse whinnied to break the spell. Dewey patted the animal's neck and silenced him with gentle words. He tied the reins to a branch and slowly crossed the swollen creek. Rifle in hand, Dewey moved across the front yard toward the barn. In the dusky light, he tripped over a body and fell to the ground. The gun, with a round ready in the chamber, went off. The bullet thunked into the open barn door.

Matt was watching the shadow moving in from the creek. He saw it drop to the ground and fire at him. He fired back through the small window. The bullet splattered the earth in front of Dewey and hurtled shattered stone and mud at his face. A shard of rock dug into his skin just above his right eye. Blood flowed down into that eye, blurring its vision. Confused, Dewey rolled over and over on the damp ground until he bumped into a tree stump. Gathering himself behind the stump, he wiped his bloody brow with a muddy sleeve. Someone was shooting at him from the barn. *Where is Matt?* he wondered. He plucked a bloody piece of stone from his forehead and tossed it away. Dewey wanted to know what was going on. He sighted down the barrel of his rifle at the barn window and called out. "Who's in the barn? Why are you shooting at me?"

"Dewey, is that you?" Matt called back to the voice in the yard; it sounded familiar.

"Yes, Matt, don't shoot. It's me, Dewey." Dewey stood up slowly, hunched over, rifle still pointing at the barn. Matt recognized the shape as Dewey.

"Come on in, Dewey. I can see you." Matt met Dewey at the large barn door and guided him in to the spot where he had set up for the night. "Are you all right?"

"Yeah, just a scratch. I'm okay."

"Sorry, Dewey. I just had a battle with a bunch of that gang from back East."

Dewey rubbed at his sore eye. "That's why I rode out here, Matt. George Tanner's in town and Howard Rohls thinks it's important you two talk to each other. And, after hearing what Howard had to say, I agree with him."

The two men spoke for a few more minutes, telling each other their latest news. Finally, knowing Dewey would have called out from the woods if he had been the mystery rifleman, Matt told him about the rifleman who saved his life.

"Maybe it was Burge Muller, Matt. He doesn't live far from here, and I hear he's a crack shot," Dewey said.

"I thought of that myself, but why wouldn't he answer me when I called out to him?"

"Well, let's take that trail back by the creek that leads to his farm. It's not a horse-friendly trail, but it is shorter. We'll just have to be more careful. Then we can ride that small lane from there. It'll take us to the edge of town by the train depot."

"Do you know the trails well enough to follow them in the dark?"

"I know them pretty well, but we'll need lanterns to be sure."

"All right. There are some here in the barn. I hate to leave the farm unguarded, but, if they come back again with more men, I won't be able to hold them off by myself anyway. First, let's drag those bodies in here so the animals can't get to 'em. We'll cover them with canvas for now and bury them proper tomorrow."

Dewey helped Matt carry the bodies into the barn and cover them, then Matt saddled Raven, and the two men rode off toward the Muller farm. The trail they rode soon joined the one Matt and Emily had taken to the Muller's farm when they left her possessions there several days ago.

"It don't make sense for Burge not to call out if he was the one firing from the woods," Matt said again to Dewey.

The going was slow in the dark, but soon the golden glow of a lamp near a side window showed them the Mullers' cabin.

Evans stormed into the bunkhouse. Roy was sitting at a table playing cards with McKiernan and two other men. Evans grabbed a fistful of Roy's shirt and hauled him to his feet. McKiernan started to get off his chair, but he fell back against the far wall. Evans' face was beet red as he confronted Roy. "You set us up!

You knew they was waitin' for us… you got three of my men killed," he screamed. Spit rained on Roy's face with every word Evans managed to get out of his anger-twisted mouth. Evans held his face inches from Roy's face, then he threw Roy against the wall.

Finally, McKiernan regained his footing and rushed to put himself between Roy and Evans. He put a hand on each man's chest and pushed them apart. "Hold up a minute, Evans. What are you talking about?" McKiernan asked.

The rest of the men, who had been sleeping and lying about, were all on their feet now, most holding a rifle or pistol in hand.

Evans angrily pushed McKiernan's hand off his chest. "Keep your hands off me, McKiernan. I told you when me and my men signed up with you we'd fight for you and earn our pay, but you let this one send us into a trap." Evans reached out and grabbed Roy again. "His brother and some of his men musta been waitin' on us at the girl's farm. We grabbed one of them in the barn and took him outside to talk to him. Then the rest of them started shootin' at us from the woods. Killed Bert, Frank, and Willis— three good men."

McKiernan's mind was churning. He couldn't let Evans get too big for his britches, but, if they had run into a trap, Roy must have known something about it. He turned to Roy and pushed him back against the wall. "You'd better speak up fast and explain this, Roy. Evans seems to have a good case against you. And if you double crossed us… well… I already told you what I'd do."

Roy's eyes were darting back and forth between the two men. He smelled his own fear. "No, listen to me! You got it wrong. It wasn't my brother—he's in town. It was probably this nosey cowboy who's been butting in over there lately." Roy rubbed at his neck, coughed several times, then looked back and forth between McKiernan and Evans. He was buying time. "I ain't said nothin' about him," he continued, "'cause I planned to kill him myself before he became a problem. But he keeps hiding from me. He's got a few friends in town. Musta been some of them took over the place. There can't be more'n two or three of them. And now that we know they're there, we can flush 'em out easy enough. I wouldn't double cross you, McKiernan. And, when you see that gold in the morning, you'll know it." Truth be told, Roy had no intention of being nearby come morning. He'd find a way to get clear by then, he was sure.

McKiernan, however, believed that Roy was telling the truth—at least he believed that some of what he said was true. But he knew Evans was boiling sore and had to be soothed if he was going to keep control of him and his men. He looked slyly at Evans and nodded his head. "See if he's telling the truth," McKiernan said.

Evans smiled.

The gang of men took Roy outside and tore his shirt open. Two men led the way with lanterns, and another carried a rope. They dragged Roy into the corral and tied him to a post. Evans was the first to start hitting him. When his hand got sore, two other men took his place. The beating was fierce; with each punch, Roy was challenged to stay conscious. Some hits were to the body causing Roy to grunt and cry out in pain. Other punches were to his head and face. He knew he was being killed. No one had asked him any questions.

When he finally fell unconscious, someone threw water on him, and another man picked him up. Evans slapped him. He was convinced that he and his men had been ambushed and that Roy knew all about it. "You can start telling the truth whenever you like, Roy," Evans taunted. "What's going on around here we don't know about? Why were them fellas laying for us?"

Roy's face was covered in blood. His teeth were broken, and his mouth was a ragged wound. He tried to spit at Evans, but couldn't. He slobbered a crimson drool instead. Evans stood back rubbing his swollen right hand. He turned and looked at the men gathered around until he saw the one he wanted. "Colby, your turn." He spoke to the man who had jabbed Matt with his knife earlier.

Colby, a tall, slim cowboy with a pocked face, stepped forward and drew a large knife from his belt. Without saying a word, he began to cut thin, shallow lines down Roy's body. Most of the men returned to the bunkhouse. Colby came in ten minutes later wiping his knife on part of Roy's shirt and announced to Evans, "You can leave him out there tonight. He'll be ready to bury in the morning."

Evans grinned at him. "I have a better idea," he said.

McKiernan looked at Evans and shook his head. He didn't want Roy killed yet, but he knew it was too late. He'd have to change his plans.

Matt and Dewey approached the Muller house cautiously calling out as they rode into the yard. "Hello the house! It's Matt Benton and Dewey from the town livery."

Both men stopped and waited. The gold in the window turned black. Several minutes went by and then a door opened slowly. Burge Muller appeared in the doorway, rifle in one hand, lantern in the other, his eyes squinting into the dark. "Come on in, Matt, Dewey. Ma'll be putting tea on for you; it'll be ready in a minute."

The window turned gold again. Muller held the door open for them. "What's got you fellers traipsing around this time o' night?"

The two men dismounted, tied their horses to the hitching rail by the Muller's porch, and walked inside as Burge Muller directed them to.

"Don't mean to bother you, Burge," explained Matt, "but I was wondering if you were up by Emily's place recently. I was just involved in a shootout there, and someone took my part from the woods—but whoever it was left before I could thank 'em."

"No, wasn't me, Matt. I would have if I'd known, but I haven't been up that way since yesterday morning. I go up there every other day or so just to check on the place. There's a lot of deer around her farm lately—turkeys too. But I don't like to leave the missus alone too long—she's been suffering the dizzies the last few weeks."

Mrs. Muller had placed four cups on the table and then had busied herself with kettle and teapot by the cook stove. When the tea was ready, she brought it over to the table. "Sit down, men, I'll put some bread and preserves out in a second." She poured the tea and then set out a tray with bread and a jar of blueberry preserves. The men sat down and ate the snack while Matt told the Mullers about his run-in with the gunmen from back East. Mrs. Muller sat next to her husband, worriedly listening to Matt's tale. When he was finished, he thanked them for the food and urged them to be careful. Then Matt and Dewey left for town.

After an uneventful journey, they slipped in quietly through the back end of town, passed the darkened train depot, and headed for the livery. Several horses were in the corral; some walked up to the fence as the riders approached. Dewey stopped his horse and stood up in the stirrups. He looked over the horses and knew they weren't his. He pointed toward the corral. "Look there, Matt, it looks like we got more company in town."

Matt signaled Dewey and they both stepped down and walked softly over to the stable. Near the door, they heard voices. Matt tugged on Dewey's shirt and whispered. "C'mon let's take a look." They tiptoed around the building and looked in the side window. Eight men were standing around, and Emily was talking to them.

Matt knocked on the door and called out. "Orville, it's me, Matt, I'm coming in." He opened the door slowly, a big grin on his face.

Matt's lanky segundo rushed over and shook Matt's hand and slapped him on the back. "Boy, I'm glad to see you, Matt. This young lady's just been telling us about this hornet's nest you stirred up."

"It sure seems that way—good to see you too, old friend."

Emily stepped over by them. "They arrived about an hour ago, Matt. I thought it best if they stayed out of sight for a while, being as the Box T men are all in the Three Eights. I asked Frank to tell Doc and Mr. Rohls that they're here and to bring some food for them. I'll cook it up when it gets here."

"Smart thinking, Emily, thanks," said Matt. "I guess you already met Orville and the boys."

Emily looked excited; her face was slightly flushed. She was happy that Matt had some more help. "I finally feel like I'm doing something to help, Matt," she said.

The small side door opened quickly, and Doc Mason stepped in. A half dozen pulled guns greeted him. "Whoa, boys," Matt hollered, raising his hands. "Hold on, this is my friend Doc Mason." Doc stood still in the doorway, a pistol in his own hand. No one in the livery had missed the speed of his draw.

"Doc, say hello to Orville Piker. And this big galoot is called Bronc." Matt started the introductions as all the men were putting away their hardware—including Doc, who was wearing a Navy Colt in an old cracked leather holster. Matt stood between Doc and Orville, a hand on each man's shoulder. Orville reached out first and took Doc's hand and shook it firmly. Then Bronc offered his hand. He was a large, beefy man who looked too big to sit a horse. Doc shook hands with the rest of Matt's men, nodding to each one in turn.

Doc was wearing a white shirt with smudges of dried blood on it. Matt stepped in close to him and pointed to the stains. "What's that, Doc, someone else been hurt?"

"Afraid so, Matt. That feller Patch's been killed. George Tanner brought him in across his saddle earlier today. Said those fellas from back East killed him. Seems they've taken over his ranch. George and his men are all up in the Three Eights now. I think he wants to talk to you, Matt. Might not be a bad idea."

"Yeah, maybe, Doc," said Matt. "Dewey told me that Howard Rohls and George's top hand Porter are good friends, and them two had a long talk about what's been going on. Howard thinks we should talk too."

A banging at the side door caught everyone's attention. "Open up—I got my arms full."

Dewey stepped to the door. "Must be Howard now," he said as he opened the door.

Howard and his helper Frank stepped in, each carrying a box of groceries in their arms. Orville and the large man named Bronc reached out and took the boxes from them. Orville turned to Emily and asked where the cook stove was. "Follow me, Orville," she said as she started walking to the back of the building where the kitchen was. Orville and Bronc followed after her.

Matt said hello to Howard and then reached out to shake Frank's hand. "I met you when I first came to town," he said to the store clerk.

"Sure thing, I remember," Frank answered back.

Howard looked around at the new men in town and nodded hello to each one. He had been told that Matt's men had finally arrived and that was who the food was for. He looked back at Matt. "Well, I guess Dewey's filled you in about George. What do you think, Matt?"

"I guess we got to listen to what he has to say, Howard. If you'll set it up, I'll meet with him."

Matt, Doc, and Howard stood together for several more minutes discussing the situation as it was and considering what it could become. The three generally agreed that a reckoning was about to occur in the Red Wall community.

Doc walked over, put his foot up on a bench by the door, and looked out the small window. His fingers scratched at his forehead in thought. "Why don't you set the meeting up in my office? It'll give you a quiet place to meet, and, if you come in by the side door, you won't attract much attention."

Matt looked to the back of the livery and then turned back to Doc. "That sounds like a good idea, Doc. Howard, will you arrange it? And let me know when he wants to meet."

Howard looked at Doc then Matt. "I'll go see him right now. I'll get his answer to you as soon as I can."

Doc headed for the door. "I'll go put my front lights out and close up for the day," Doc said.

Matt spoke to Howard as he started to the back of the livery where Orville and his men were waiting. "Howard, give me a half hour to talk to my men and bring them up to date on the situation."

"Okay, Matt." Howard waved his hand at Matt as he and his helper followed Doc out the door.

Dewey's private quarters were crowded with Matt's men when he went back there. The ones who couldn't find chairs were sitting on the floor. Some were already eating steak and beans, and more cooked on the stove. Emily brushed back a wisp of hair from her forehead. The steam from the sizzling steaks was settling on her face. Her eyes were happier than he'd ever seen them. As Matt watched her, he thought, *A man couldn't do any better.*

Emily spoke, bringing Matt out of his personal thoughts. "Matt, will you meet with Tanner like Doc and Howard suggested? Do you think you can trust him?" Emily's questions quieted the room of noisy cowboys.

Matt blinked his eyes and smiled at her. "Yes, in a little while, Emily, after I talk to my men."

Matt looked around at the men in the room. He had ridden with all of them and knew them to be good, tough men who could always be counted on. Orville was sitting on a short stool with his knees up by his chin. He was sopping up the last of the gravy on his tin plate with a piece of bread. He swallowed and said, "Go ahead, Matt, tell us what you need done here. This young, beautiful, good-cooking gal has told us quite a bit already. But we got a whole bunch of nasty broncs back home need to be saddle broke by next spring. I say we get to it and get it done."

The other men in the room grunted approval.

Dewey had been outside looking after the stock. He stepped into the room and walked to the stove and stood next to Emily. "Coffee, Matt?" he asked as he poured hot coffee into a cup.

"Yes, thanks, Dewey." Matt reached out for the steaming cup. He sipped at the coffee and looked around the room. "Boys, if you asked me yesterday what my plan was, I could have told you in a minute. But, just recently, I've learned some news that I don't fully understand yet. So I'm going to ask you to hold tight for a spell, 'til I meet with this feller, Tanner. Meanwhile, I'll tell you as much as I know." Matt continued talking for some time going over the events that had transpired since he'd left them at Fort Wilson.

George Tanner sat at a back table hunched over a glass of whiskey. Porter sat across from him. The rest of the Box T men were scattered about in the saloon, some leaning on the bar, others sitting at tables. It was unusually quiet in the room. Brock was across the street sitting at a window table in Helmer's restaurant watching the town.

George lifted his head and looked at his longtime friend. Porter looked back at the man who had never seemed so unsure of himself. George's face had aged; his eyes had a weakness in them Porter had never seen before. Porter spoke to his boss. "George, your plan sounds all right to me, and you know me and the boys will stick with you all the way through this mess 'til we're back punchin' cows on the Box T again."

George favored Porter with a grim smile. "I know I can count on you and the boys. I just want to do the most I can to see none of ya get hurt. I've made enough bad decisions lately. Now I got to try to set some of them right."

Porter pulled out a silver timepiece and looked at it. "Reckon it's time for your meeting with that fella Benton. You sure you don't want me to go along?"

"No, I trust Howard, same as you do. If he says it'll be a friendly meeting, that's good enough for me. I'll catch up to you when it's over. Why don't you and the men get some grub over at Helmer's."

A warm breeze stirred the smell of the damp earth up to Matt's face as he walked down the alley and stopped at Doc's side door. The glow from the window light cast a yellow sheen over the still-muddy alley. He turned the knob and entered the office. Doc was talking to a man Matt figured to be George

Tanner. Tanner turned to the door, and the two men looked at each other up close for the first time. Matt didn't try to disguise his feelings toward Tanner. "You the hero has his men shoot at a lone woman?"

Matt stood in the doorway, the dark alleyway at his back. His body cast a black shadow on the yellow alley floor. Once Matt saw George face to face, he couldn't hold back the venom that spat out of his mouth. George swallowed hard, his jaw tightened, and his eyes stayed on Matt. He knew he had it coming and half expected it. Doc stepped quickly between them, stunned that George hadn't drawn his gun. He put his hands up facing Matt. "Hold on, men, both of you stand still. Matt," Doc said the name with stern reprimand to it. "Ralph and I promised George a peaceful meeting, and you agreed to it. I expect you to live up to that and hold your tongue."

Doc turned to George and was surprised at how calm he looked. The ranch owner looked past Doc and focused on Matt. He said it slow and deliberately. "I had it coming, Doc. It's all right." George was actually relieved that Matt had put it out in front of them. The young cowboy reminded him of himself some thirty years earlier. "You're what I expected, Mr. Benton... full of fight and righteousness. I've done some things that were wrong, and, as soon as I straighten out the problem I have on my ranch, I intend to do what I can to make them right—as much as is possible now." George unbuckled his gun belt and hung it over the back of a tall-back wooden chair by the entrance to Doc's private office.

George's words took Matt by surprise. He didn't know what to make of the man he'd learned to hate; he'd expected a harsh, unbending man. He thought of how he had felt about Lucky before he'd got to know him. The man in front him had the look of someone who'd asked no quarter from anyone and bought everything he owned with hard work and kept it with whatever else it took. Matt took his own gun belt off and hung it on the chair next to George's. Matt reached back and closed the outside door. He looked at Doc, who was still unsure of Matt's next move. "Sorry, Doc. Didn't plan on saying that." He looked at George, but didn't extend the apology.

Doc took a breath and walked to his office door and opened it. "Come on in and sit down. Let's try to figure out where we stand and how you two can stop fighting each other. Fair enough? Matt? George?" Doc looked at each man and led the way into his office. George put his hand out in a gesture to have Matt enter first. He had thought of offering it for Matt to shake, but thought better of it. Doc walked behind his desk and sat down. George and Matt sat down in chairs facing him.

Doc leaned forward, looked at Matt, and started the meeting. "Matt, I was talking to George for a little while before you got here, and, before that, I spoke to Howard about the situation involving George's ranch. George and I also talked about what's happened to Emily. You and I feel the same way about that, and he knows it. But I think, for now, you two have to agree to a truce so George can concentrate on getting his ranch back. I believe we all can agree that allowing those outlaws from back East to take it over isn't good for Emily or this town."

Doc looked from Matt to George; he was trying to think of something else to say that would help them decide to cooperate in a truce pact. The ticking of the large clock on the wall grew louder as the room grew quieter. Doc tapped a pencil on his desk signaling the end of his participation in the meeting. He looked at each man. "I think that sums up how we got here, so

I'll leave now and let you two talk it out." Doc stood up and left the room, closing the door behind him.

With the closing of the door, each man felt he was in an empty space. Both men sensed the awkwardness of the situation. George decided that, as the elder of the two, he should try to clear the air as much as he was going to be able to. He stood and offered his hand to Matt. Matt sat still, looking at him. George grinned sadly and put his hand down. "I want to congratulate you," he said quietly to Matt, "on being the man I once was—or thought I was. Fact is, I've become weak. Trying to take that land from my neighbor was just plain wrong. I let myself be talked into it, and that's to my shame. I'll answer for that when the time comes." George walked over to a back window and looked out into the night. His reflection wavered on the glass as the lamp wick flickered. He turned sideways and looked at Matt. "I understand some of your men arrived today to help you fight me. I don't have a fight with you or your men, and I don't want my men fighting two battles at once if I can help it. If you'll let us handle those Eastern yahoos who are on my ranch now, I'll own up to my wrongs against Miss Langer as soon as it's over. You have my word on that." He walked back over to Matt with his hand out.

Matt stood, took George's hand, and shook it. His face was firm as he looked at George. "All right, Tanner, but my men and I will be sitting on Emily's land as of early tomorrow morning. From what I understand, these men from back East are interested in gold they think is on her land. Tell your men to stay off Emily's land, and they won't have any trouble from us. Anyone else will."

George considered what Matt said and agreed. The two men talked for a few more minutes about possibilities that could arise, and then left to rejoin their men. Neither man felt a longer powwow was needed.

George crossed the street and entered Helmer's. The room was noisy with animated talk. He caught Porter's eye and signaled him to step outside. Porter had been listening to Earl, a rusty-haired cowboy, who had been telling him a story of a similar fight he'd been in some years earlier. Porter nodded to his boss and made his way through the crowded restaurant to the door. Outside, he walked down the street a bit with George and leaned on a post when George stopped walking. A cigarette was stuck between his lips. He drew on it, blew the smoke up to the evening sky, and asked, "How'd it go boss?"

The town had quieted down for the night; a few soft lantern lights dispelled the darkness near them. George hitched his thumbs in his gun belt and looked at his right-hand man. "'Bout like I figured. This hombre Benton's a man to reckon with, looks like. But he's agreed to back off until we run McKiernan and his gang off the Box T. Told him I'd put myself in front of him once we done that. That's about as good a deal as I'd hoped for."

Porter flipped his smoke into the night air and watched the red glow spin to the ground and spark. He looked at George and saw the age in his eyes that hadn't been there two weeks earlier. He knew that age would be the difference if he and Matt Benton ever met over smoking pistols. "First things first, George, but know this: I aim to stop you and him from drawing down on each other."

George put his hand out and patted Porter's arm. "First things first," he said.

26 Evans' Plan

McKiernan and Evans had moved over to the main house and searched all the rooms. McKiernan was on one knee in front of the open safe, some incidental documents in his hand. He threw them back into the safe and slammed the door. It bounced back open and hit his leg, making his sour mood even worse. He watched Evans, who was sitting with his feet up on George's desk pouring more whiskey into his glass. McKiernan's fury burst through his better judgment. He ran to the desk and grabbed Evans' boots and flung them off the desk.

"Damn you, Evans, you knew I needed Roy alive."

Evans reacted quickly and righted himself. His hand went to his gun.

"Go ahead, pull it." McKiernan's glare challenged him. He stood in front of Evans, right hand on his own holstered pistol, his face a livid red, his teeth bared.

Evans knew he was dead if he drew now. Even if he shot McKiernan, he was sure to get killed too. As mad as McKiernan was now, there was no way he would die quick. He'd be sure to get off one shot if not more, and, this close, he wouldn't miss.

Before going to the main house with Evans, McKiernan had stopped and checked on Roy. He had been seething ever since. Roy's body was hanging from the fence, small streams of blood dripping from his torn skin forming a pool near his boots. His face was a ghostly grey with red lines and blue blotches defining it. If he made it through the night, it would be a hard one. McKiernan had signaled two men and told them to put Roy in a bunk in the bunkhouse.

He'd told Evans earlier not to kill him—that he might be needed later to deal with his brother. What he hadn't told Evans was more important. If things went bad here, he planned to drag Roy back East to his bosses as a sacrifice to try and save his own life. It had been his personal recommendation that had gotten Roy the loan in the first place.

Evans eased up and slowly took hold of the whiskey bottle. He looked at McKiernan. "You need a drink, McKiernan." He pointed to a shelf where more glasses stood.

McKiernan backed off and reached slowly, left handed, to grab one. His right hand stayed on his pistol. His eyes stayed on Evans as he slid the glass across George's desk. "You need to know who's in charge of this outfit," he said. "Remember, Evans, you only got half your pay. You get the rest back East, when I say the job's done."

Evans' plan didn't include sharing the second half with his men.

Evans filled McKiernan's glass and then his own. He drank the whiskey in one gulp and set the glass down on George's desk and spun it slowly. He turned to McKiernan. His face was as serious as McKiernan had ever seen it. Here was a man who looked certain of what he was going to say. "Sure thing, McKiernan, but you gotta understand something. Out here you can't talk a man's wallet outa his pocket. You gotta grab it. If you give these folks time to consider things, they'll get their backs up and fight you something fierce. We gotta use my plan and hit them hard first thing tomorrow morning."

McKiernan looked at Evans and poured more of George's whiskey into his glass.

The wind that blew down Main Street was a cleansing one. It blew pieces of paper and other assorted trash over the railroad tracks and out across the prairie. Horse droppings and the more stubborn debris was picked up by Bub Fallow. Bub started his rounds every morning an hour before daybreak—with his barrel on wheels and a rake and a shovel. He was working in front of Rohls' general store when he heard the horse approach. Always a careful man, he slipped into the alley between the store and the hotel.

The dun-colored horse trotted into town and stopped in front of the Three Eights saloon. Its rider was bent over low in the saddle. Bub's old eyes weren't good enough to see the ropes that bound Roy Tanner to his horse. The two men who had led his horse to the edge of town had stayed back by the bridge, unseen in the darkness. They were waiting for the rest of their gang to catch up with them. McKiernan was leading them at a slow pace to keep the sound of the horses down and because some of them had proved to be very bad horsemen. The darkness didn't help.

Evans' goal was to catch George and his men out in the open street. The plan was for the men by the bridge to get the attention of some townspeople by firing some shots. Then, they'd let Roy's body draw a crowd. Evans figured everyone would be waking from a sound sleep and be groggy. Some might even forget to belt on their six-guns.

When Bub wasn't cleaning the streets, he was in the saloon or sleeping in a small room in back of the hotel. In the saloon the day before, he'd heard about the trouble George was having out at his ranch. He liked George. George had given him several chances to ride for him, but the bottle always brought him back to town. Bub hurried to the back of the hotel and up the back stairs. He knocked on the door of room 10—the one George always stayed in when he was in town—and called George's name.

The door opened quickly; George stood there, gun in hand. He was fully dressed, but his room was dark. Only the dim hall lamp illuminated Bub. "What's going on, Bub, you sound troubled? Come in here."

George turned and walked back into his room. Bub followed him. He rubbed his hands nervously on his pant legs. When he finally spoke, his voice was almost shrill. "Mr. Tanner, a lone horse with a hurtin' rider just rode into town and stopped in front of the Three Eights next door. My eyes ain't so good no more, but my hearin's still pretty fair. They's at least one or two more riders over to the bridge too, I'd say. I know you got some trouble out to your ranch, and I figger this might be part of it."

George put a hand up to quiet Bub and went to the window. He looked down into the street and to his right. He saw the horse and rider Bub was talking about. They were next door in front of the saloon. The bridge was only a little further down the street to his right but he couldn't see anything—only darkness. His focus returned to the man in the saddle. He squinted his eyes and shook his head sadly. He knew who the man in the saddle was.

George moved past Bub and went out into the hall, and banged on the door opposite his. Cal opened it. George explained what Bub had reported. Porter was already looking out the window. His room was also at the front of the hotel. He had the same view as George but closer to the bridge and he had younger eyes. He spoke to the window. "I think I see them, George. Looks like two riders over by the bridge."

Porter and the two other men sharing the room had heard the old man coming up the stairs and had heard everything he'd said to their boss in the quiet hotel. The rest of the Box T riders were scattered throughout the hotel—all sharing rooms. They were all awake and waiting on George's order to move out to take back his ranch. No lamps were lit in case McKiernan had a spy in town.

George took a coin from his pocket and handed it to Bub. "Thanks, Bub. Now stay here in my room 'til this is over."

Porter moved from the window and looked at George. His voice was as soft as anyone in the room had ever heard it. "George, you know who that rider is, don't you? It looks like Roy."

George moved to the window and looked down into the street. He saw the rider pick his head up and seem to look right at him. Then the head fell against the horse's neck and was still.

George turned back and looked at his men. "I know." He said it quietly, vengeance dripping with each word. He looked at the men with Porter. "Collect all our boys and tell them to meet Porter downstairs in five minutes. It looks like these polecats are going to try to surprise us. Make sure everyone's fully armed and ready."

Cal and the other man left as soon as George stopped talking. Porter pulled his pistol from its holster and loaded a sixth bullet in the barrel. Like most men who wore six-guns on the range, Porter always left an empty chamber for the hammer to rest on—less chance for an accidental firing while riding or doing other ranch work.

"George, where're you gonna be while I'm meetin' with the men?"

"I'm going to see who's over by the bridge. Maybe I can learn something from them."

"There's two of 'em, George; let me go with you."

"No, one man's quieter than two. I'll be back in a short while. Get the men in position and make up a system so we don't shoot at each other. It'll be light soon. It looks like they're going to attack just before daylight." George looked toward the window. His cheeks seemed to slide down his face. "I'll take care of Roy," he said. He drew in a breath, put his hand on Porter's shoulder, and nudged him out the door. George took the back stairs down to the rear alley where Bub had just come from.

The two men by the bridge were Evans' most experienced gunmen. They sat their horses quietly, waiting for McKiernan to show up and give the order to start shooting. Neither spoke a word as they watched the front of the hotel.

Joe Bryceland

George knew he was in a bind; he needed to walk slowly so as not to make any noise, but sunup was coming nearer each minute. He could see the men and their horses just off the bridge. Both men were staring at Roy's body. George wiped his sweaty brow and pulled his pistol as he crept closer to the gunmen.

As he neared the rider closest to him, a twig snapped under his boot. In the quiet night, it sounded like cannon fire. Both men turned toward him, guns coming out of their holsters. "Don't need to die, boys," George shouted at them.

But the rider furthest from him quick-fired a shot that nicked George's shoulder. George emptied his gun at the two men and ducked behind a tree. The closest horse screamed at the gunfire and reared up, tossing his dead rider to the ground. The gunman hit the ground with a thud as his horse ran wild-eyed down the street and past the saloon, at full gallop. He was the first man to die on that day. The other rider raced over the bridge and away from town. His horse's hooves clopped loudly on the wooden planks, a bloody trail following him.

George ran to Roy's horse and grabbed its reins just as the crazed animal was about to bolt after the horse fleeing down the street. George struggled for several seconds, pulling with strong hands on the reins and brought the horse under control. He led the frightened animal into the hotel alley. Porter and two other men—one of them Red, the lone survivor of Lucky's men—met him there.

The sun was getting an early start over the eastern horizon. The blackness that had filled the alley only minutes earlier when George left it was now tinged with a faint pink as the sunlight bounced off the red wall that guarded the town. It made an eerie color of the blood that covered Roy's body. Red opened his pocketknife and freed Roy's dying body from the rope that bound him to his horse. Then he helped George pull his brother off the horse. Porter kicked open the door to Bub's room. "Put him down on Bub's cot, George. I'll send for the doc."

George had insisted on carrying his brother into the hotel. He walked past Porter and laid Roy on Bub's unmade bed. Porter grabbed Red by the shoulder. "Go get the doc. Hurry!"

"No, wait, send Smith." George pointed a bloody hand at the man standing next to Red, a tall, thin cowboy with a Texas twang in his voice. Smith had ridden into the Box T Ranch yard looking for work three years earlier. When asked his name, he'd said simply, "Smith," and that's what he had been called ever since. No further words were needed; Smith backed out of the door and headed for Doc's office.

George wiped his stained hands on Bub's blanket. It was mostly Roy's blood, but some came from the ragged wound on his shoulder. He looked at Porter. "What signal did you come up with?"

"White cloth on our left arms. Me and Red were just going to get ours when we heard the shooting. Cal is ripping up a bed sheet and giving everyone a strip."

"Good. Red, you know what Benton looks like, don't you?" Red nodded his head to George. "Go down to the livery and tell him to get his men some white armbands on their left arms in case they get drawn into this scrap. Go by the back way, and— here—put this on."

George ripped a piece of Bub's sheet and handed it to Red. Porter tied it on for him and patted Red's shoulder. "Be careful," he said. Red took off running.

The wounded gunman stood on the trail waving his right arm at the approaching horsemen. His left arm was useless—one of George's bullets had shattered his elbow; another had lodged in his side. McKiernan and Evans had heard the gunfire and were racing to town. McKiernan thought Evans' men had got jumpy and started shooting too soon. Evans knew the men he'd sent were steady hands and wouldn't fire their guns without good cause. The wounded man fell from his horse not far from the bridge and couldn't remount it. Now he watched McKiernan's horse skidding toward him. McKiernan pulled frantically on the reins, but couldn't stop in time. He knocked the gunman to the ground.

Evans cursed McKiernan as he got down to help his man. "What happened, Burt? Who started the shootin'?"

Burt grimaced in pain and shot a look of contempt McKiernan's way as he answered Evans' question. "Someone tried to ambush us, but he was alone. I don't think they was waitin' for us. Nobody else fired a shot."

McKiernan shouted down from his horse, "Pull him to the side of the road. We'll come back for him later. We can still catch them unawares. For all that town knows, some drunk's finishing his night off with a little fireworks. Let's go, Evans!"

McKiernan had his pistol in his hand as he shouted his orders at Evans. Evans pulled Burt to the side of the road and leaned him against a tree. He whispered to the wounded man. "I'll be back for ya, don't worry, and we'll settle up with this McKiernan too."

Evans mounted his horse and they rode off.

♣

Doc woke with the gunshots just like most everyone else in town. He was reaching for the door handle when it started moving. Smith was banging on his side door with all his might. Doc flung the door open and stepped to the side. Smith rushed in, words spilling out of his mouth. "Doc, George Tanner needs ya bad. He's down at the hotel."

Doc stiffened at the news. "How bad is he hurt? Where is he shot?" He already had his medical bag in his hand; he wanted to know if he'd need anything else—like a stretcher.

Smith shook his head from side to side. "Ain't George, Doc, it's his brother Roy. Looks like someone skinned him. C'mon, Doc, we gotta hurry!"

Smith led the way back to the hotel by the same way he'd come.

♣

"Mr. Benton, George says ya gotta get your men to wear white rags on their left arms so's none of us mistakes each other in this fight. All our men are wearing 'em too." Red's chest was heaving, and his face was as red as his hair as he fought to catch his breath and speak George's message at the same time. He'd run all the way from the hotel and now was standing in front of Matt and his men. Like the Box T riders, Matt and his men had already been awake when the shooting started. They had planned an early start out to Emily's farm, but now Matt and Orville were just heading out to find the source of the shooting. Instead, Matt questioned Red and found out about the two riders by the bridge and Roy's condition. What troubled him most was George's suspicion that his trouble was coming to Red Wall looking for him. If that was the case, there was no way Matt and his men could stay out of the fight. Matt had taken a liking to the town and many of the people in it. *Besides*, he thought, *just like I told Emily when I first met her, when bullets start flying, people get hurt that aren't supposed to sometimes.* No one in town would be safe.

"Red, get back to George and tell him that me and my men will cover this part of town. But remind him not everyone in town knows to wear a white cloth. Lots of townspeople will come out shooting when their town's being attacked."

"I got ya, mister." Red answered Matt even as he was heading out the side door of Dewey's livery. He ducked his head involuntarily as the first rounds of a long volley of gunshots barked angrily at the other end of town. He raised mud in the alley as he headed back to his boss.

McKiernan led the way over the bridge, his gun blazing away at the hotel as he rode past it. His men followed close behind him. They were all shooting six-shooters, and, while they emptied their guns, there was no return fire from the hotel. Now as they stopped to re-load, a fusillade of shots rang out at them.

Porter was in charge of the men who were stationed upstairs, while George led the men stationed downstairs. They had planned this strategy earlier. George had fought many a battle in which he'd been out-gunned, and he'd learned several tricks to help even things out. Four of McKiernan's men fell dead or wounded into the street from that surprise volley. Others rode away with the bite of a bullet in them in less serious places.

McKiernan dismounted and ran into an alley across from the hotel. He felt comfortable there. He'd done his best dirty work in the alleys of New York. Evans and his men rode away from the withering rifle and pistol fire toward the railroad station and Dewey's livery. Some of the other Easterners dismounted or fell off their horses and raced to the safety of the alleyways. Some rode down the street with Evans and his men.

Jesse woke to the gunshots and put his pregnant wife under their bed. He overturned every piece of furniture he could lay his hands on and used them to barricade the bed. He threw on some clothes and strapped on his pistol. More shots rang out; Jesse looked out his window and saw two Easterners run into the alley next to his carpentry shop. One of the Easterners was the small man with a bowler hat. The other was heavyset with dirty, disheveled clothes. Jesse ran from their living quarters at the back of the shop to the shop itself as both men walked down the alley and stopped at his side door. The big man put his weight against the door and broke it open. Jesse saw the fat man fall through the door and hollered at him. "What the hell you think you're doing?"

The fat man answered with a gunshot that tore into the wall near Jesse's hand. Jesse drew his gun and shot the man. The big man tried to shoot again, but two more of Jesse's bullets tore into him, and he fell to the floor dying, his blood soaking the sawdust Jesse's wife was constantly cleaning up.

Another shot rang out from the doorway as the little man fired his gun and ran away. He ran past a dusty window as two bullets flew through it and knocked the bowler off his head. He wouldn't need it anymore. They don't bury people with their hats on. Jesse reloaded his gun and called toward the back room. "Everything's okay, Sarah. Stay where you are!" Jessie had promised his wife he'd stay clear of trouble, but, just like the other evening out by the Langer place, sometimes you just couldn't. He'd been in the woods looking for a turkey for dinner when he'd heard the commotion in the barn and saw the men drag Matt out into the yard.

♣

Matt and Orville started across the street to check on the women at the Loren home. With Matt and his men staying in the livery, Emily had decided to stay with the Loren sisters for the night. The second volley of shots had just quieted, but the sound of running horses brought both men's attention up the street. While Orville was looking for white armbands, Matt's gun jumped into his hand and flashed two shots at a gunman aiming at Orville. The man fell back on his horse and was bumped off into the street. Matt knew by the way some of the men were riding their mounts that they were part of the eastern crew. Gunfire erupted out of the crowd of horsemen. It was aimed at Matt and his second in command, Orville. Bullets zinged past them and plucked into the walls of the livery. Matt's six-gun answered with hot lead, and was joined by accurate fire from Orville's gun. Out in the open as they were, Matt knew bullets were bound to find them soon.

Thunder crashed in the air, and metal shot whizzed over Matt's head as Dewey's shotgun laced into the front riders. Too far away to kill the outlaws, the buckshot pellets stung several of them and knocked two men off their horses. The two outlaws ran into the alley next to the Lorens' home, unnoticed in the chaos surrounding them. Dewey's second blast distracted the rest and gave Matt and Orville a chance to retreat toward his barn. Cross River men poured out of the livery firing a volley of shots at the remaining horsemen, covering for Matt and Orville, who had both emptied their guns.

Matt pushed Orville through the side door and tumbled into the livery after him. The riders that could, turned their mounts and headed back up the street. Others lashed their ponies and raced across the tracks out on to the open plains. Minutes later, they were no more than thinning clouds of dust.

Bodies of horses and men littered the street outside. The sounds of the wounded men and horses wove through the air into the livery along with the strong smell of gunpowder and blood. Matt reloaded his gun and checked on his men. He walked from man to man. A few flesh wounds were all they had suffered. Thanks to Dewey's shotgun, the outlaws had been too busy ducking to fire accurately.

"Thanks again, Dewey." Matt waved a hand at the livery owner.

Dewey reloaded and nodded to Matt.

"We'd better get across the street and check on the women," Matt said.

Dewey snapped his shotgun closed. "Go ahead, Matt, me and your men will block off this end of town so they don't get this close again."

"Good idea. I'll take Orville with me. We'll collect the women and escort them back here. I think we can protect them better if we're all together."

"All right, Matt, but give us a few minutes to take care of the horses that are down and get the wounded in here."

Matt looked around at his men. "Follow his lead, boys. He's a good man, and I trust him," he said. Matt and Orville slipped out the side door.

A few random shots rang out from the other end of town as Matt and Orville stepped back into the street. The outlaws who were left had dismounted and found cover behind water troughs, wooden crates, and whatever else was available. The few who tried to enter the town's homes or businesses had been greeted with rifle and shotgun fire as Matt had figured. The men and women in these small western towns hadn't arrived in silk-lined carriages, he'd always said.

The Box T men had taken the better spots, while the outlaws were down by Dewey's stable. George heard the battle going on down there and knew that Matt and his men would send McKiernan's men scurrying back his way. Now both sides were aiming carefully, and fewer shots were fired. A stalemate was in progress with the Box T men in the best positions.

Sensing a lull in the action, George went to Bub's room to check on Roy. From the doorway, he watched Doc Mason pull the sheet over his brother's head. George closed his eyes for a moment and bowed his head; he continued on out the back door. With things quieted down, he went on the hunt for the man who'd killed Roy. George had seen McKiernan run into the alley across the street after their first exchange of fire. He took the same route he'd taken earlier, but this time he continued on under the bridge. He walked in the stream; the water was halfway up his boots. Just past the bridge, George crept cautiously out of the brush that lined the stream. He was behind the buildings McKiernan and his crew were using for cover. His eyes were as alert as he could ever remember them. His senses felt keen.

McKiernan had tried twice to enter a dwelling, and each time he had been turned back by gunfire. One bullet had smashed through a locked door inches from his face and sent tiny wooden spears into his face. The splinters went deep into his skin and were painful. He pulled some out and had to leave others where they were. His mood was foul. He'd deliberately separated from his own men. McKiernan knew that all he wanted to do now was escape, and that was best done alone. Stealth was his best tactic. He looked out from under a broken buggy in someone's backyard. His plan was to wait until things quieted down and then sneak out along the railroad tracks. He hoped to jump on an east-bound train. The brush behind him was filled with thorns that were impenetrable—they would rip his skin off. He thought of Roy, and decided he'd wait for nightfall if he had to.

"Doc, you seen George?" Porter was standing in the doorway his boss had occupied two minutes earlier. His question startled Lee Mason. Doc was sitting on a chair, deep in thought, arguing with himself about his role in the ongoing battle. One part of him wanted to join the fight and start sending these owl-hoots scampering out of the territory and away from his friends and neighbors. The other part of him remembered that he was a doctor, and healing rather than killing was his calling. He was reminded, too, that many already needed his doctoring skills, and, before the fight was over, many more would likely need him as well.

Doc swiped a hand across his brow and looked at Porter. "No... uhm... I haven't seen him since we talked when I first got here. Someone went out the back door a short while ago; it might have been George." He pointed to the bloody sheet on Bub's bed. "Roy's dead. There was nothing I could do."

Porter nodded. Doc stood up and rubbed the back of his hand across his mouth. It trembled slightly. The fight was still going on inside him. He shook his head. "I have to get back to my clinic. Lots of work to do there." Doc closed the back door behind him and left.

The street had quieted down considerably. Howard Rohls tied a white towel on a broomstick and began calling for a ceasefire. He was passing by Doc Mason's alley and saw movement. Brock, the former sheriff, was letting a wounded Box T man off his shoulder onto the ground by Doc's side door. Howard turned into the alley and called out, "No more shooting!"

Brock stood up, drew his gun, and fired. A man across the street, who had been pointing a rifle at the storekeeper, jumped backwards and crashed through Helmer's window. His lifeless body sprawled across a table covered in blood and glass fragments. Brock's bullet had taken his life before he could shoot Rohls in the back. Rohls threw down the broomstick and drew his own gun. "Why, you lowdown…" He aimed at Brock and fired, emptying his gun. Brock was hit three times and fell to alley floor dead. Howard would never know Brock had just saved his life.

George saw three men standing behind Helmer's. All had their guns out; none of them wore a white armband. The tallest of the three saw George at the same time and fired off a quick shot in his direction. George aimed and fired more accurately, and two of the men fell. The third man ran down the alley toward the street. Gunfire erupted briefly from that direction then quieted. McKiernan stepped out from behind the buggy and sighted on George's back.

Gunshots reverberated throughout the alley when Porter emerged from the stream in the same spot George had earlier. He guessed his boss had gone looking for McKiernan and knew the only way he could cross the road without being seen was to cross under the bridge. Porter followed the stream and found George's footprints coming out of the water. When he heard the shots, he hurried to follow the wet footprints. George was reloading his gun when McKiernan came out from behind a derelict wagon.

Porter fired an instant before McKiernan did, but he was firing on the run, and his normally flawless aim was off. He hit McKiernan in the left arm, barely nicking his skin—enough, though, to spoil McKiernan's shot. George took McKiernan's bullet in his left leg and fell to the ground. McKiernan's next shot poked a hole in a rain barrel just over George's head. Porter fired again and again until his pistol was empty. He kept McKiernan pinned behind the buggy he'd run back to for cover. Porter had no cover; he knelt down close to a building and started to reload.

With George down, McKiernan turned his gun on the meddling cowboy. He stepped out from behind the wagon and turned his shooter on Porter.

George's gun had fallen from his hand when he was hit, and it had landed several feet away from him. He was crawling to his gun when he saw McKiernan getting ready to kill his friend. Quickly, he called out, "Over here, McKiernan, I'm over here!" McKiernan spun quickly and shot George again—in the same leg, then he turned back to Porter who was closing his loaded cylinder. George had never stopped reaching for his gun; he grabbed it and fired, emptying his gun at McKiernan. McKiernan was slammed into the dilapidated buggy. He slid down to sit against a rear wheel. He had four bullets in him. The gangster said something no one heard, and then he died.

♣

Beth turned the knob slowly; she didn't want her sister to know she was going to sneak out to the barn to check on Lady— and to get her gun out of her saddlebags. She was surprised her horse hadn't been whinnying nervously with all the shooting going on. Alma and Emily were sitting on the floor in Alma's room, which was, Alma thought, the safest thing to do until the shooting was over. Beth told her sister she was going to get a pitcher of water for them from the bucket they kept full in the kitchen. Alma protested, but Beth insisted and went downstairs.

Beth was running over to the barn when the man jumped from behind a large tree and grabbed her. He clamped his dirty hand over her mouth and held her by the waist, lifting her off her feet. She tried to scream, but he squeezed his hand over her mouth harder. "Shut up or I'll kill ya." His breath stunk like a rotting animal. Beth thought she was going to be sick. She felt weak.

"Bring her inside, Colby, quick."

Another man she hadn't seen at first was pulling at her arm, dragging her back to the house. He opened the back door and stepped inside. He pointed his pistol around the room as he looked into the parlor. "Who else is here with you?"

Evans emphasized the question by squeezing her arm. Beth let out a yell of pain. She regretted it immediately. "Beth, is something wrong?" Alma called down from upstairs.

Evans slapped Beth hard and she fell to the floor. He picked her up by the hair. "Who's that? And who else is in the house?"

Evans grabbed the back of her neck and put her in front of him. Colby put his knife to her face. "The man asked you a question, missy. Speak up," he ordered.

Beth felt the blade pierce her skin.

"Beth what's going on?" Alma came downstairs and walked into the back room looking for her sister. Colby grabbed Alma and silenced her with his dirty hand too. Emily stood on the stairs wearing a long bathrobe. The relief that had showed on her face the night before was gone. "Is everything all right?" she called out, a familiar fear returned to her voice.

Evans pushed Beth in front of him; she looked as white as a ghost. He walked to the stairs and pointed his gun at Emily. "Get down here and be quick about it." Emily put her hands in her pockets and started down the stairs.

Alley had been sleeping in the Loren barn until the first gunshots woke him. Doc had been loosening the reins on the young man as his wounds seemed to be healing well. Alley heard the shooting and wanted to help, but knew he'd only be in the way. He remembered what Matt had said about having only your enemies in front of you when you're in a shootout—fewer people to worry about that way.

The boy stayed in the barn and comforted Lady when she started to panic. He was watching the Loren house through a crack in the barn doors when he saw Beth come out of the back door. Alley was glad to see her. Maybe that meant the trouble was past and he could get some breakfast. He was just about to call out to her when he saw the man rush from behind the tree and grab her. The man had holes in his shirt and red spots on his face. The face of other man who joined him was marked too. Dewey's shot had hit them hard and put burning pellets under their skin. Not serious wounds—just painful. Both men were looking to take revenge anywhere they could.

Alley's first thought was to run out and protect Beth. Then he remembered the gun she kept in her saddlebags. He poked around in the bags, throwing aside scarves and gloves and other spare paraphernalia Beth kept in there. He found the gun finally, but pulling it out was difficult. He'd forgotten how weak his hand still was. Doc said it would be as good as new in a few months, but it was still so weak he couldn't even pull a trigger. He stuck the gun in his belt and headed for the livery. He walked quietly along the side of the Loren home as he headed for Dewey's place.

The youngster was stunned when he reached the street. The sight of the men and horses writhing on the ground confused and frightened him. He'd heard all the shooting, but never imagined it could cause this much harm. Alley stopped in mid stride as Dewey's side door opened. Matt and his friend Orville stepped through the door. The boy waved his hands in the air above his head and got their attention. When they acknowledged him, he put his finger to his lips to signal them to be quiet and waved them over to him. Matt and Orville ran across the street to meet Alley.

"What's the matter, boy?" Matt reached Alley first and took hold of his arm. The boy's eyes were wide with fright. He pointed to the Loren house, only a few feet from where they were standing, and once again signaled with his finger to his lips. He whispered, "They got Beth in there. Two men with guns grabbed her a minute ago out back and took her inside." Matt felt as if he'd been hit in the belly by a punch he wasn't expecting. He realized immediately what must have happened. Two of the outlaws had been hiding, waiting to escape, and, when they'd seen Beth come out of her home, they had taken advantage of the situation. Now all three women were probably their prisoners—maybe even hostages. He had to get into that house.

Matt and Orville discussed a strategy that would cause the two outlaws to watch the front door while Matt slipped in the through the back door. "Orville, first take Alley over to the livery where he'll be safe. I'll need some time to look around. Then you can create a distraction at the front door." Matt spoke quietly and calmly, but Orville saw the fear in Matt's eyes. This was the worst outcome possible, and those three women Matt cared for so much were in terrible danger. These thugs would kill a woman as easily as a man.

The gunshot from the street startled the three of them. Matt and Orville had momentarily forgotten that the others were going to put the wounded animals down. Several men were in the street just up from the Loren home. Some were carrying the wounded into Dewey's barn while others shot the downed horses. "This might be just what we need," Matt said.

Matt pulled the white rag off his arm and put it on Alley, then he motioned for Orville and Alley to move into the street and mix in with the men there. Matt turned and moved quickly to the Loren backyard.

♣

Porter ripped McKiernan's shirt into strips and made bandages for George's leg wounds. Neither bullet had done serious harm. "Just chipped some flesh," George said.

The shooting had stopped. Most of McKiernan's gang were surrendering, throwing their guns into the street. Movement caught George's eye. A man was sneaking to the back of the Loren home. "Look, Porter, there's one of them now." George pointed toward the Loren house at the end of the row of buildings they were behind.

"Wait here, George, I'll git him."

Porter started off, but George grabbed his arm. "No, I gotta see this thing through to the end."

"All right, boss, but I'm going with ya, or I'll run on ahead of ya."

George looked at his longtime friend and saw no give in his eyes. "Let's go," he said.

Matt was staring in through the Loren back window. Only Beth and Emily and a man with a knife were in view. *Alma and the other man must be in the front room*, he figured, *looking at the commotion in the street*. In fact, Evans was watching the men in the street while his cohort kept the women in check with his knife to Beth's neck. Evans lowered the drapery he was hiding behind and turned back into the room. "Looks like they figure it's over. They're starting to clean up. If you ladies stay quiet and do what you're told 'til nightfall, might be we won't hurt ya. Right, Colby?"

Colby gave out a mean laugh. "Yeah, right… that's likely." He took the knife from Beth's neck and brushed her cheek with the back of his hand. Beth shivered.

Matt put his hand on the doorknob.

George and Porter had still been two houses away when they'd seen the man sneaking into the Loren home. "Stop, don't move!" Both men shouted as one. Both had their guns pointing at Matt. Matt turned quickly to the voices hollering at him. He had no choice but to move away from the door and confront the men who were running at him. They all recognized each other as soon as Matt turned.

Matt ran up to them, "Put your guns down and be quiet," he ordered. Matt motioned for them to follow him into an alley one house over from the Lorens' home.

"What's going on Benton, why're you sneaking into the Loren house?" George was out of breath as he asked the question. He leaned a weathered hand on the sidewall of the house and drew a deep breath.

Porter looked at his boss. He turned an empty barrel over. "George, sit here and rest that leg, 'fore you fall out."

Matt hadn't noticed George limping before, but now he saw the blood staining his pants. "You hit bad?" Matt pointed at George's leg.

"Naw, just skin-shot's all," he answered. He grimaced as he sat on the barrel.

Matt explained the situation in the Loren home, including a description of the men. Then he outlined the plan he and Orville had devised to distract the men inside.

"Won't work, Matt, it'd take a big deal to get both of them away from that back door—and I'm it. They know me, and one of the men in there would like nothing better than to put a bullet in my hide." George put a hand on the wall and pushed himself off the barrel. "From what you tell me, one of them men in there is a dog named Evans. He was in charge of the owl-hoots from out here that joined up with them Easterners."

"What's your idea then?" Matt looked at George and then down at his leg.

George pulled off his bandages and began explaining his plan. "… and they won't be looking to make any noise because of your men in the street." George finished telling Matt and Porter his plan and started walking out to the street. Porter joined him, and Matt headed to the Lorens' back door once more.

Porter met up with Dewey first, then both men began mingling with the rest of Matt's ranch hands explaining their part in the plan. George walked up to the Loren front door and began banging his fist on the wooden frame. "Miss Loren, help, please… I've been hit," he shouted.

Evans grabbed Alma as soon as he heard George's voice. He pushed her in front of him and went to the door. Through the curtain, he saw George's face—a face he'd come to hate.

"Why's he coming here?" Evans pushed his gun hard into Alma's side.

"We help the town doctor when he's busy; George must think he'll be treated here sooner than at the doctor's office, with all the wounded there must be by now. I'll send him away."

Evans pulled Alma with him and went to the window. "Shut up and don't move," he told her. He poked his gun harder into her ribs. Alma took a breath and looked at her sister. Evans peeked from behind the drapes again. The street outside was crowded with men, tying ropes to the dead horses, getting ready to haul them off.

George again pounded on the door. "Please, Miss Loren, don't hold a grudge... help me." The men in the street started looking at George.

"Damn him! Let him in and close that door in a hurry or I'll start shootin'." Evans shoved Alma over to the door.

Alma opened the door and George limped in. The terrified woman closed the door quickly. Evans moved from behind the chair that was hiding him, his gun pointed at George. "Don't move a muscle, Tanner, and keep your mouth shut."

George looked stunned. "How'd you get here?" he stuttered, his mouth seeming to tremble.

"Never mind; just shut up." Evans turned and called to the back room. "Hey, Colby, look who dropped in on us. Come on out here and say hello. Bring your new friends." He gave an evil chuckle.

With George under his gun, Evans was in a much better mood. "Not so damn tough now are you, George?" He reached over and pulled George's gun from its holster and put it in his own. "Meet Colby," he said. "He does real nice knife work, don't you think?"

George's jaw clenched and his eyes tightened at the sight of his brother's murderer. Evans continued to laugh as he pointed at the cold-blooded man who still held Beth in his grasp. Evans pointed at George's leg. "Hey, Colby, why don't you cut those trousers from George so we can see where it hurts. Maybe you can get that bullet outta there for him." Evans was enjoying himself. Colby pushed Beth away and started for George.

"Don't move!" Matt shouted the order. He'd slipped in the back door and was waiting for his chance. He'd wanted to come in shooting, but that would have put too many friends in danger. Now he had no choice. He stood in the doorway between the back room and the front parlor. Evans fired at him and ducked behind a chair. Matt shot through the chair, hitting Evans with all three shots. Evans fell back against the wall as his gun dropped from his hand. His life bled out on the Lorens' floor. Colby lunged for Alma, his knife at the ready. George stepped in front of him and grabbed the knife blade. It sliced through his hand to the bone, like cutting warm butter. Matt couldn't shoot; Beth and Alma stood between him and the two men. Colby drew back his knife to finish George. Emily was standing at Colby's back, Dewey's gun in her hand. She fired twice; Colby's body lurched forward and fell at Evans' feet.

George Tanner's right hand had almost been severed from his arm. Doc Mason couldn't help comparing the damage to what had been done to Alley's hand. *Ironic*, he thought. The leg wounds were minor. The most seriously wounded Box T hand was Red, the man Brock had carried to Doc Mason's door. Lucky's last man had been hit in the chest, and it seemed to Doc the bullet had nicked his lung.

"How's he doing, Doc, he got a chance?" George asked when Doc Mason finally came out of the treatment room.

George's wounds had been cared for by Alma and Beth after Doc looked at them. Doc Mason's smock was blood smeared; his face was drawn. Dark circles had formed under his eyes in the last few hours. "I'd say he has a good chance if there are no complications."

Doc looked at George. "You'll never pull a gun with that hand again. You'll be able to do a lot with it eventually, but no shooting."

George lifted his heavily bandaged hand and looked at it. "Suppose not, Doc, but thanks for giving me back that much."

Bub Fallow had set the gold story to rest. The traces found on the Langer farm were from mines that had been abandoned in the far-off mountains. The small pieces had been flushed out of the ground where the stream came above ground and stayed there because the rocks were jagged above ground and not worn smooth by the flow of rushing water beneath the soil. The gold traces had been caught in the rocks and accumulated in a small pool for many years before they were noticed. Five years of panning there might yield a few hundred dollars. Bub had been a miner, and, when the big mines petered out, he had followed the streams like the one on Emily's land until he realized he couldn't make a living at it.

Matt had ordered his men to regroup at the livery. The more seriously injured had been treated by Doc and Alma; the rest had been treated by Beth and Emily. Fortunately, his men and the Box T men had come through the battle without any loss of life. Red was hurt the worst, and Doc said he should make it.

Matt sat down hard on a bench and blew air out between his lips. Orville leaned on the front wall; he shuffled his feet and looked at his boss. "Matt, I'm going to take the boys up to the saloon for a while, then I'll go talk to the train master about getting us home. See you in a while. I guess you got some business here." He nodded his head toward the back room.

Matt looked around. Beth and Emily were cleaning up their nursing gear in Dewey's living quarters. Dewey was by the first stall caring for a wounded horse. He heard what Orville had said. "Matt, I'm going to ask Emily to have lunch with me, why don't you and Beth join us later?"

Matt looked up at Dewey, a small smile slipped across his face. "Thanks, friend," was all he said.

A few minutes later, Emily passed Matt on her way to lunch with Dewey. She looked at Matt, and they shared a warm smile. Emily's smile was a sisterly smile; she was wishing her good friend well.

As Beth finished up in Dewey's back room, Matt watched Emily and Dewey walk up to Helmer's restaurant. Some of the townsmen and cowboys had joined together and cleaned the place up as soon as the shooting had stopped. A large canvas tarp covered the front window. A loose corner waved in the slight breeze. Matt took a deep breath and walked to the back of the livery.

Beth was waiting for him. She knew what he was going to say, but let him say it anyway. *He has a lot of work to do back at his ranch. The cabin he lives in needs work, but he'll return in the spring for me if I want him to.* Beth whistled and smiled at Matt. "I'll wait one spring, Matt Benton." She hugged Matt and took hold of his arm. "Let's get some lunch." They joined the others at Helmer's.

♣

Matt said his good-byes the following morning. Some were cheery; others, sad. As he stood on the train steps, he saw Doc walking to the train depot with Alma and Alley. Doc carried a suitcase. Matt looked at him. "Where you going, Doc?" he asked.

Doc handed the case to Alley. "Not me, Matt—Alley. He needs to start his own life. I'm sure you can find a job for him. I'll vouch he's a good worker. Just let that hand heal a few more weeks, and he'll work circles around your best man." That was the first time Matt had seen Doc smile. Matt reached down and took hold of Alley's suitcase. "Come on, then. I'm sure Orville will find plenty for you to do to earn your keep."

George Tanner helped his wife off the train. Matt could see her point to his hand as George put his arm around her. The night before, Matt and George had sat for an hour in George's hotel room. George had promised to help Emily get her farm up and running; he'd send men over to help her whenever she needed it. He had already apologized to her many times.

George waved his bandaged hand at Matt. Matt waved back, turned, and walked into the train car. He put his hand on Alley's shoulder as he led him down the aisle and pointed to a seat. "Sit with your back to the front wall, and keep the window closed so's you don't get soot and cinders on you." He smiled at Alley and looked out the window. The train was moving. Beth stood on the platform, waving. Matt waved back at her and whistled.